TO     Mum.

Christmas 1991
Best wishes
Tanya and Nye
        X. X

*Atlantic*

# *Atlantic*

—

*A Novel by*

## LUKE JENNINGS

**HUTCHINSON**
London

This edition first published in 1995 by
Hutchinson

1 3 5 7 9 8 6 4 2

**Random House UK Ltd**
20 Vauxhall Bridge Road, London SW1V 2SA

**Random House Australia (Pty) Ltd**
20 Alfred Street, Milsons Point, Sydney, NSW 2061, Australia

**Random House New Zealand Ltd**
18 Poland Road, Glenfield, Auckland 10, New Zealand

**Random House South Africa (Pty) Ltd**
PO Box 337, Bergvlei, 2012, South Africa

A CiP catalogue record for this book
is available from the British Library

ISBN 0 09 178659 2

Papers used by Random House UK Limited are natural,
recyclable products made from wood grown in sustainable
forests. The manufacturing processes conform to the
environmental regulations of the country of origin.

'I've Got a Girl in Kalamazoo' reproduced by permission of
International Music Publications Ltd

Phototypeset in Ehrhardt 12/13 by Intype, London
Printed in Great Britain by Mackays of Chatham PLC

For M.J. and P.M.J.

# I

As they pulled out of Waterloo Station, Cato's father opened his dispatch case, removed *The Times* and a silver propelling pencil, smoothed the newspaper over his crossed legs with the back of his hand, and exhaled briskly through his nose. The train gathered speed, and he raised his eyes to confirm that all of the compartment's windows were closed against the steam. Reassured – theirs was a carriage without a corridor – he returned his attention to the back page of *The Times*, and a tiny arrhythmic hissing soon marked his absorption.

Through half-closed eyes, Cato watched him. At intervals the hissing – which Cato recognised with a prick of embarrassment as 'Paper Doll', which had been playing on the hotel wireless that morning – would stop, and the mouth beneath the scrubby moustache would silently essay the shapes of words. It had always touched Cato that his father, who occupied a senior position at the War Office, should move his lips as he thought.

The crossword, Cato knew from experience, would take some forty-five minutes to either complete or concede. After that, had the two of them been alone in the compartment, they might have talked. Crossword clues, for want of an easier subject, might have been shared. The presence of a third passenger, however, and Cato's eyes moved from his father's bone-pale brogues to the scuffed Oxfords planted in the far corner, made conversation unlikely.

After a week, Cato was not yet quite used to the sight

of his father in full civilian fig. Reginald Parkes had put away his uniform at some arbitrary point (probably, Cato guessed, as a result of an official memorandum) during the last school term, and although Cato would never have put it into words, even to himself, he appeared somehow diminished by the transformation. The flannel suit seemed to have been made for a larger man and had clearly, from the horizontal creases which obstinately remained in place at calf and thigh, spent the war years in a trunk. The sky-blue tie had something about it of the theatrical drawing room.

Untypically for him, Cato did not have a book to hand. He had decided, for reasons he would not easily have admitted to, to look out of the window for the journey's duration. Sitting as they were in the first carriage behind the engine, however, little beyond the windows was visible through the steam, and Cato began to regret consigning *The Case of the Gilded Fly* to his overnight case. The suitcase in question, he knew, was in the luggage rack above his head, but to ask his father to lift it down for him in front of the other passenger was not really a possibility. Instead, he stared into the whiteness of the steam, gradually allowing his eyes to lose their focus. With concentration, he was able to detect his own heart-beat, to separate it from the more insistent pulse of the train. Covertly, he examined himself for signs of excitement. These, when present, were apparent enough ('Distress, with visible facial cyanosis, particularly of lips, upon effort or excitement . . .'), and Cato found himself calm.

When you *really* looked forward to something, he thought, it had a curious way of staying ahead of you, of dancing out of reach. And just as you thought you had the thing by the collar, it turned out that all that you had was more waiting. The end of term at Cleeve had been like that. Although he had deliberately not begun counting until the end of June, the last few weeks had surrendered themselves in a leaden, disengaged sort of way which somehow obliterated memory as it went. Of the dozen cricket matches at which he had been a spectator, for example, Cato found that he recalled only a single moment, a visiting fielder's spin-flickering return from the boundary. Of an entire fortnight of Higher Certificate exams he could summon only the persistent buzzing of a fly at a hot gymnasium window.

And in the same way, this journey. Now that the day of departure had arrived, it seemed, like one of the duller primitive organisms that he had studied, to be endlessly subdividing itself into its preparatory stages. The word 'boat-train' suggested an urgency entirely at odds with this leisurely suburban progress. One of the more frustrating elements of anticipation, Cato decided, was that because in your mind you were always one stage ahead of whatever you were doing, you never enjoyed things as they happened. A week ago he had thought of this journey as practically part of the voyage; now that it was actually taking place, it just seemed like a rather weary-making extension of packing.

Another thing, of course, was that greatly looked-forward-to moments, when achieved, had a way of turning out to have something of an oblique edge to them. There had been an occasion at Cleeve, on a still July afternoon shortly before the term's end, when he had walked out of the changing rooms and found the newly whitened plimsolls of the athletics team laid out on the lawn to dry. Something in the warmth of the day and the scent of whitener and mown grass had induced a sadness in Cato, a sudden knowledge of all that he would be leaving behind him. He missed, for a moment, the certainties that the future might otherwise have held. Even the certainty that late September would have brought about a return to school: a return that would have signalled, with utter finality, the present summer's end.

As the steam from the engine wavered and cleared to reveal rows of pink- and green-roofed suburban villas, Cato wondered what would be the end of his own summer. In his mind, he had a series of very particular images of life aboard the *Carmelia*. Like illustrations from *Picture Post* or from the *Illustrated London News*, many of these had titles printed beneath them: 'A Steward serves Breakfast', 'A Last Turn on the Deck before Dinner' and 'The Cocktail Hour' were three such. Other, less admissible, snapshots involved Riviera and Brazilian coastlines, the satin shoulder-straps of certain actresses, and illuminated liners viewed from beneath palm trees. While Cato knew these to be entirely inapplicable to the North Atlantic crossing, he permitted them, for the time being, to reside alongside their more plausible brethren. For in the question of the crossing, of course, lay the paradox of his present anticipation. Inseparable from the voyage as a whole was the end of the voyage. To look forward to the voyage was, in part, to look forward to its end. And at the end of the voyage waited the operation.

'Smoke?'

Cato and his father looked up at the same moment at the proffered Gold Flake packet, whose contents had been arranged, as if in an advertisement, like the pipes of an organ. Half-turning to the awkwardly poised figure, Cato's father delivered a small negative movement of the head. He did not speak, as Cato knew, because even the briefest of spoken refusals might have been interpreted as an invitation to further conversation. Cato also knew that his father would be experiencing a certain irritation that the exchange had effectively disbarred him, for the hour or so remaining of the journey, from smoking his own Senior Service. He watched as, tapping the base of a Gold Flake against the darkwood frame of the window, the man produced an American cigarette lighter from a small felt pouch. As brown smoke plumed across the compartment, Cato flickered a glance at the stained hat-band and the long marsupial features. Commercial traveller, he decided;

certainly hadn't fought. Blinking a little at the smoke, he raised his eyes to a framed and glassed view of Little-hampton.

Twenty minutes later the train slowed, the yellow-bleared glass of the window shuddered briefly, and there was silence. To the lingering orange-peel smell of the brakes, Cato yawned, loosened his sixth-form tie, and inclined his head against the white antimacassar. It proved an unrestful position, a collar-stud pressed at his neck, and the compartment, unventilated now that the train was still, was smokily, plushly close. From the seat opposite, his father watched with brief concern as Cato stood, reached for the broad leather strap, and pulled down the window. Warm clarity flooded the compartment, and disregarding the warning transfer above the door, Cato leant outwards over his folded arms. Searching the landscape, he could see no obvious reason for the halt. To his left, steam-blurred, stood the engine and coal tender, and to his right, diminishing in hard perspective, waited further carriages and the guard's van. There was a dazed and birdless silence. In the field beyond the railway embankment stood a grey-tarred tele-graph pole and a buttressed and flaking placard reading 'TUSSOID Lozenges'. The field climbed to a red-brick farmhouse, an empty clothes-line, and a stand of trees.

Gradually, to Cato, this montage, unreal in its very ordin-ariness, became charged with invitation. Touched by a dreamlike temptation, he imagined the heavy release of the door-handle, the silent crunch of cinders, the nettled and leather-soled scramble up the embankment to the fields beyond. He would occupy this sun-dazed landscape, be contained by it, and there would be new rules of being. His illness would never be mentioned, and in consequence, would cease to be. His mother ... Running a finger between neck and collar, he looked back through the side window at the indistinct figures of his father and the com-partment's third passenger. For as long as I watch them, he thought, they are frozen in time, their watches are stopped, they cannot move. And so it was. For as long as his head was turned, they were still.

Finally, beneath Cato's feet, the silence became vibration, a vibration which soon set up a clattering tremor in the lowered window on which he was leaning. As the engine began to make steam at the head of the train, a grey shadow climbed the field. Significance drained from the scene and Cato, aware of his father's attention, ducked back inside the compartment. Again, with the pistons' sigh, the smell, little more this time than a catch at the edge of awareness. For a moment he was at his tenth birthday tea, his mother dividing the prized orange, his teeth meeting through a white stalk of pith. He swatted the memory away with ease. Oranges had been back in the shops for more than two years.

As the train approached Southampton, rain began to flick at the windows. Through the blurred glass, Cato watched as the smaller stations – Twyford, Swaythling, others whose names he did not catch – raced past. There was evidence of a jettisoned bomb-load on the outskirts of one such village, but the craters were brambled and the rubble long claimed by coltsfoot and wild lupins. Reginald Parkes, glancing at his watch and noting, almost subconsciously, the train's punctuality, covertly watched his son. In profile, with his forehead pressed to the window's plate glass, Cato looked younger than his sixteen years ('Every reasonable hope, given his age, of a successful intervention . . .'). There were times, of course, when he looked older, and most particularly, thought Reginald, when he was receiving bad news. At those times his acceptance, the calm and almost practised way in which he allowed himself to be occupied by pain, was unbearably adult. It occurred to him, not for the first time, that both he and Cato had been eight years old at the outbreak of the wars which were to rob them of a parent.

In his own case, it had been his father. He remembered

his last sight of him: the high-buttoned khaki figure (amongst many, but the others invisible) leaning from the window of the departing train. He remembered his father's wink, his insouciant touch of swagger-stick to cap, and his visible impatience, now that the time had come, to be gone.

Thirty years later, though, and however hard he tried, Reginald Parkes could not remember his father's face, could summon up no portrait of the man that was more than the brief animation of one or other of the photographs. It seemed that, like all of the crowding dead of that earlier war, he had become a ghost, silvered and sepia-toned. Later, and with a soldier's knowledge, Reginald had been worried by this transubstantiation, but by then the ghost-pictures were all that remained. Even the processes of grief were beyond recall. There had been the days following the arrival of the telegram, of which he remembered nothing at all, and then a further, longer, time of which he remembered only the sound of church bells and that it had been summer. And somehow, by the time that he had returned to school, to the autumn winds pulling at the beech trees, the words of that March telegram had been translated into a more or less manageable sequence of streaming grasses, painless falling, and fading light. Even the name, Neuve Chapelle, had suggested a kind of consecration.

Reginald watched the small pulse at his son's temple, noted the thumb-smudge of shadow beneath the razored school haircut. What possible narrative, he wondered, had Cato contrived for his mother's death ('She didn't feel a thing'? 'She never even . . .'?). He remembered the fine hair at Claudia's temple, and then, unable to prevent himself viewing the entire slide-show, he remembered Claudia dead. There was a falling-away, against which Reginald invisibly braced himself and invisibly ordered his features, and gradually the image of Cato with his forehead against the compartment window – and that window unbroken – replaced the glass-starred, coagulate montage that was his final memory of his wife.

A sudden jarring bump caused Cato to lift his head sharply from the glass, and Reginald returned his eyes to the crossword. A final unsolved clue swam into incomprehensible focus. He reread it. A quote.

' . . . To *blank* with Amaryllis in the shade,' he suddenly and unexpectedly found himself reading out. 'Five letters, starts with S.'

Surprised, Cato looked across at him. 'Five letters?'

'Five letters,' repeated his father. 'Starting with S.'

The train slowed as it entered the outskirts of Southampton, and the tone of its passage deepened. Cato turned back to the window, and to the city's gapped and damaged terraces.

'They certainly took it down here,' he said, although it occurred to him as he spoke that the destruction now spoke at least as much of ventilation, of light admitted into darkness, as it did of suffering and loss.

His father nodded. Distant cranes, some of them in gentle motion, showed above the houses. Cato detected salt air.

'Smoke?' the man in the corner suddenly queried.

Identical of expression, both Cato and Reginald Parkes turned to him.

'The clue,' he offered apologetically. 'Five letters. Starts with S.'

Cato looked to his father, who remained unmoving for a moment before nodding and appearing to write. 'Good enough,' he said, and with an indeterminate smile, returned the propelling pencil to his dispatch case.

Slowing, the train emerged from between tall buildings, the tallest and grandest of them the South Western Hotel, into the blustery sunshine of a main road. Halted cars waited as the train crawled between a pair of – to Cato's eyes – unmistakably maritime offices, and on to a rain-slicked tarmacadam area marked out by telegraph poles, low brick buildings, and grey-painted cranes. Against the sky, blurred by rain, stood the dark, bomb-gutted shell of a warehouse. Closer at hand, the gently nodding funnels of tugs showed above the pier-sides where, with smaller craft, they rode at anchor. From the train Cato saw all of this, registered the entire cyclorama, but saw none of it. For at its centre, rising vast and black above the main pier and the Ocean Terminal, was the bow of the *Carmelia*.

Cato had seen many illustrations of the Royal Albion Line's flagship, in both her peacetime and her grey war livery. Some years earlier, as it happened, he had made a balsa-wood model of her, which he had painted with enamel paints, stabilised with lead stripped from the school roof, and launched, not without trepidation, into a Berkshire pond. None of this, however, no magazine or cigarette card, had prepared him for the bafflingly giant scale of the *Carmelia* herself.

The train drew closer, rounded the dock, and for a long moment, as they approached the canopied sheds of the terminal, passed alongside her. Abandoning all restraint, Cato pulled down the window and craned upwards. Above him, as he lifted his face into the drizzle, hung a vast, bellying, salt-streaked wall of steel. To a mansion block's height the *Carmelia* rose a rivet-studded black, and then the topmost crown of plating and superstructure climbed white against the sky.

The sheer, incomprehensible size of her drove all further thought from Cato's mind. She mystified him, but at the same time something in the broad flaring strakes of her hull and the gleaming whiteness of her upper parts corresponded to a deep sense within him of things as he wished them to be. He was briefly able to make out the top band of her forward funnel, floating high above the bridge in the rising steam, and then a low canopy shadowed the compartment, the ship slid from view, and they were surrounded by the clamour of the terminal.

Cato returned to his seat to discover his father's features touched with severe pleasure. Does he, wondered Cato possessively, understand? Does he see her as I do?

To the long dying scream of the brake, steam rose to surround the train windows. Reaching for the Gladstone bag at his side, the third passenger assumed a half-sitting, half-standing attitude, supported by one hand against the back of the seat. Cato watched his father. With what appeared to be intemperate patience, Reginald Parkes waited for the train's final lurch before standing to lift his own and his son's hand-luggage from the netted overhead rack. On the platform, passengers from other compartments, impelled by a sense of urgency which Cato shared, streamed past them. Reginald, however, as Cato had known he would, waited for the porter. Eventually, and with a brisk 'Southampton, gents!', the door opened. The third passenger could wait no longer. Raising his hat a centimetre, and with a brief 'Beg yours' as he barked Reginald's knee with the Gladstone bag, he ducked from the compartment.

'*Smoke* with Amaryllis in the shade,' Reginald dryly enunciated as he lifted both his own and Cato's canvas grips from the seat. 'Very good indeed.'

Cato laid his coat over his arm, patted his breast pocket and followed his father on to the platform.

'Which class, sir? Cabin? Follow me, sir.'

The baggage, the dock porter explained to Reginald, would be removed from the train and stacked alphabetically and by class for clearance through customs. Until that moment, when he found his father and himself purposefully conducted through the confusion of passengers, inspectors, and Cook's men to the shortest and most deferentially attended of the customs queues, it had not occurred to Cato that any social divisions might apply on board the *Carmelia*. The moment that he saw his fellow-passengers divided into their three shipboard classes, however, he understood the absolute necessity of such distinctions. Surrounding them in the Cabin Class waiting area were, broadly speaking, people like themselves. Not, Cato noted, obviously aristocratic people, not necessarily terribly smart people, just men and women who, without ever really thinking about it, did things in a certain way: the sort you might see at Cleeve on Sports Day. Several of the men, like his father, were obviously not long out of uniform, and their civilian clothes had the same slightly over-large appearance. Their wives, as Cato assumed them to be, tended to those mutedly unmemorable styles which, without drawing attention to themselves, unhesitatingly highlighted any incorrectness or vulgarity in others.

Alongside his fellow-countrymen, Cato identified a minority of Americans, readily distinguishable by a quality that he thought of as 'breeze', and a sprinkling of Europeans and Levantines of the Homburg-hatted, financially important variety. Amongst these obviously foreign elements, the men appeared to outnumber the women. Amongst British and non-British alike, there was a certain polite reserve in evidence: no one, at this stage, wished to be drawn into any indissoluble association. Uniting all of the Cabin Class passengers, however, was a good-humoured but clearly ironic attitude of subordination to bureaucracy. We will play the game, their stance suggested, but our patience is not without limit. We are who we are.

Some fifty yards away, beyond a waiting Pathé News crew and several low walls of trunks, waited the Tourist Class passengers. Seats had not been provided for them, and they waited in an orderly and obedient queue. The Tourists, thought Cato, were harder to characterise than the Cabins. The Gold Flake smoker from the train, for example, had clearly been born into Tourist Class, but there were many in the queue who, from a distance at least, were indistinguishable in dress and attitude from the Cabins. Cato was aware of a *frisson* of unease, of discomfiture narrowly averted, and was glad the subject had not occurred to him in advance. It would have been unthinkable to have asked his father in which class they were to travel, and the uncertainty, as the day of the voyage approached, might well have clouded his anticipation. For, as Cato reluctantly admitted to himself, he and his father would not have appeared utterly and ludicrously out of place amongst the Tourists. Or, at least, not to outsiders. The truth was, he supposed, that people had been reading shoulder flashes and insignia for so long that the finer distinctions of personal authority – of breeding, in fact – had all but disappeared.

Suddenly, obliquely, Cato caught sight of his father frowning at a pamphlet headed 'Information for Passengers', and the flow of his thoughts inverted itself. Perhaps, and the idea became icy certainty as it formed, his father had paid far more for their tickets than he, than they, could afford. Perhaps, in the knowledge that his son might not survive the approaching surgery, Reginald Parkes had wished to give him a last glimpse of 'the best'.

Cato thought of the newly bought dinner-jacket and the boxed dress-shirt in his cabin trunk, and, hot and cold with distressed love, stared blinking at the floor.

He looked up to the popping of magnesium photo-flashes and the hurried manoeuvrings of the newsreel team.

'Straighten your tie, old boy. We seem to be in the spotlight.'

Taking his father literally, Cato touched the knot of his Cleeve tie. He turned to see half a dozen porters – at least three more than seemed necessary – unloading the numbered and differently sized elements of a set of pigskin luggage. Around the resulting island of baggage, unseeing of their surroundings, moved several elegantly disordered young men and women. To Cato, their voices seemed slightly louder, their gestures slightly more extravagant, than their distance from each other warranted. He smelt Balkan cigarette smoke and, suddenly, a dizzying floral scent. To his side, the film-cameras whirred.

Addressed by none of the party, but clearly the reason for its existence, stood a thoughtful-looking woman dressed, with the exception of a black-banded hat, entirely in white. The slant of the hat prevented Cato seeing much more of her face than a pale jawline and a small, vermilion-painted mouth. To this mouth, as he watched, a white-gloved hand conveyed a lighted cigarette.

'Who is she?' he asked his father.

'No idea,' answered his father, affecting a tolerant non-interest.

'Actress, perhaps?'

'That's Ayrest MacLean,' volunteered an easily conversational voice behind them. 'Fashion model before the war. Walked out on Johnny Wendover for the newspaper fellow, Ballater. Recently left Ballater high and dry too, from what I hear.'

Father and son turned from the tableau before them to the conveyer of this information, a wild-haired, dark-featured man in his late twenties dressed in faded corduroys.

'Or what I read, I should say,' he amended, pushing back the springing, unruly hair. 'There's been a fair bit about her in Inchcape's column.'

'Society type, then,' said Reginald Parkes, non-committally.

'Absolutely. She is, that is, not me.' The wild-haired young man patted the breast pocket of his jacket and proffered a battered silver cigarette case. 'I'm Pierre Watson, by the way.'

For a long moment, as Reginald introduced them, Cato considered accepting a cigarette. He was rather impressed by Pierre's urbane bohemianism – by his air of simultaneously belonging to smart society and disdaining it – and he appreciated beyond all expressing the way the older man, even in Reginald's presence, addressed him as an equal. 'What did you say her name was?' he asked finally, shaking his head.

'MacLean,' Pierre said, snapping shut the case. 'Ayrest MacLean.' At the sound of her name, and despite the overall noise and Pierre's several yards' distance, the woman looked up. The eyes that she met, however, were not Pierre's but Cato's. She saw a tall, angular boy with a pale, intelligent gaze, attended by a man who was probably both his father and the previous owner of the suit which hung somewhat lifelessly from his shoulders. The other, the Fitzroy Tavern type, she decided, was unlikely to be of their party.

Cato, in his turn, found himself held by a pair of eyes whose soft eau-de-Nil reflected exactly the lacquered, virescent world he imagined their owner to occupy. Her features, fine but tired, were a powdered matte; the vermilion mouth expressed a thoughtful irony.

They regarded each other for several seconds, and then the woman's arm was taken by one of her brilliantined chorus, a matter of amusement reported, and the moment and her attention evaporated in soundless laughter.

A voice sounded at Cato's ear.

'I'm sorry?'

'Still quite a looker, isn't she?' remarked Pierre.

'Um . . . yes.' Cato nodded enthusiastically, flattered by this confidence. 'A looker. Absolutely.'

The queue had begun to move forward. At the barrier Reginald was handing a customs officer a list of the contents of their baggage. They were soon gestured through, and Cato followed his father into the sudden gull-screaming brightness of the quayside. Immediately ahead of them, occupying all of the space that their eyes commanded, was the ship. Close up, she was even huger than she had appeared from the train, and despite the movement of the water in the dock, absolutely and vastly still. To both sides of them, watched by white-uniformed stewards, cranes were hoisting netted baggage on to conveyors. A steady line of passengers and their visitors moved between the terminal and the steel and canvas tunnel of the Cabin Class gangway. Of the other passengers, the Tourists and the curiously designated Tourist Third Cabins, there was as yet no sign.

'So what do you think of the *Carmelia*?' asked Reginald, lowering their hand-luggage and rocking back on his heels proprietorially.

'She's . . . enormous. Extraordinary.' Cato shook his head. 'I can't quite get the measure of her.'

'Your mother and I once crossed the Atlantic on the *Mauretania*. The old *Mauretania*, that is, the four-stacker. Wonderful ship; broke her up in '34. Bugler played "The Last Post" as she passed Bembridge for the last time.' Reginald frowned, raising his chin, but whether his father was moved by the memory of the old Cunarder or by that of his wife, Cato was unable to tell.

Turning towards the ship's distant stern, he touched the grey flannel of Reginald's arm.

'Dad, while we've got the quay more or less to ourselves, do you mind if I . . .' He nodded seawards. 'Because once we're on board, we won't really be able to see her.'

Reginald tugged the brim of his hat downwards against the wind.

'Run along, then.' He caught himself. 'But don't actually . . .'

'It's Okay, Dad, I'll walk.'

The walk to the stern, which he paced at almost two hundred yards, took several long minutes, the wind increasing as he approached the open expanse of Southampton Water. Ahead of him, on the far shore, the steepled town of Hythe stood vague through the bright spindrift. Cato stared down for a moment at the black, unmoving basin of the *Carmelia*'s stern, and then, the wind roaring at his ears, turned back. Tiny between the quarter-mile of rail terminus and ship, the lead-soldier figure of his father stood to attention over the bags. As Cato walked back, trousers wind-flattened against his calves, he suddenly knew from the dragging in his chest – the stone behind his ribs – that he had set himself too demanding a distance. He stopped, and lowering his hands to his knees, closed his eyes. Breathing with deliberate slowness, he waited for the stone to lift, the clamping tightness to pass. Eventually, to the silent bursts of light that he knew both as a warning and a release, he straightened his back and reopened his eyes. The flaring subsided, and a proper focus returned to his gaze. A hundred and fifty yards away his father stood over the bags. Netted luggage and provisions were being swung into the ship's hold by crane. The wind had dropped.

After the morning daylight of the pier, the steel and canvas tunnel of the gangplank was dark. In the dim electric light at its head, just inside the ship's shell, a detachment of brass-buttoned bellboys stood to attention on either side of a long, bristled mat bearing the Royal Albion crest. Reginald and Cato passed between them into the ship's Embarkation Hall, an area of veneered columns and panelled walls where an impromptu cocktail party appeared to be in progress. Stewards and stewardesses laden with ribboned bouquets, trays of telegrams, 'Bon Voyage' fruit-baskets, valises, band-boxes and golf-bags threaded an urgent path through the passengers – most of whom had glasses in their hands – and their guests. The noise level was considerable, almost hysterical at times, its crescendos marked by the popping of champagne corks, bursts of laughter, and sudden outbreaks of applause. A prominent group, Cato noticed, was the party accompanying Mrs MacLean. Her, he could not see, until he realised that she was standing at his side, all but hidden by the bouquet that she absently cradled in one arm. Lowering his eyelids, he breathed a powdery hot-house scent.

'Champagne?'

Pierre Watson, a glass in each hand, stood in front of them. Cato was simultaneously touched by his thoughtfulness and aware that his action somehow related as much to Mrs MacLean as to his father and himself. He wondered whether the champagne was provided by the Royal Albion

Line or by one of the passengers. He took the glass and saw his father hesitate before smiling his own acceptance.

'Chap was just saying they had to replace every square inch of this floor,' said Pierre, looking about him and attempting to flatten his hair. 'Apparently all the soldiers' boots . . .'

Obediently, Cato and Reginald looked down at the tan flooring.

'They would've done,' said Reginald eventually, rocking on his heels.

'Worse, apparently,' persevered Pierre, 'in the boats like the *Queen Mary* where they had the American troops. Gum stuck to everything, he told me.'

Reginald nodded silently.

'Where was she in the war again, Dad?'

Although Cato knew the answer to this question very well, and knew that Reginald knew that he knew, he also knew that his father would be much more at ease once he had pronounced at length and with authority on some complex logistical subject.

'Started off in Sydney,' said Reginald, raising his chin thoughtfully. 'North Africa run of course . . . Suez . . .'

As his father spoke, Cato looked beyond him to where one of Mrs MacLean's crowd, an actorish figure with an oval cigarette in the side of his mouth, was waltzing with an imaginary partner. The dance ended, the man's mani-cured hands crept around his shoulders, and he mimed an embrace. This grew more passionate, the long fingers at the flannel shoulders taking their timing from the tiny rhythmic shudderings of the hips below. Somewhere a cork popped, and as if startled, the actor-figure sprang apart from his imaginary partner. To laughter and applause from his circle he pouted, frowned into an imaginary powder compact, and carefully replaced a soft felt hat.

Cato, who had never witnessed adult behaviour of this sort, stared. As the circle closed around the performer, Pierre and Reginald – who had brought to a close his expatiation on the *Carmelia*'s wartime exploits – turned to follow his gaze. In the exquisite's place, searching the crowd, stood a square, gingery hot-looking man. Catching Reginald's eye he marched towards them, and ignoring Pierre, held out his hand.

'Jerry Farrell. Major of that ilk. Seen the purser?'

'Reggie Parkes. Um . . . No.'

Not once in sixteen years of life had Cato heard his father so addressed. Reggie, he wondered, *Reggie*?

Farrell nodded furiously. Close up, Cato saw that he had, at some point, been wounded. His left eye appeared crimped, the surrounding skin shiny and peppered with bluish, subcutaneous fragments.

Cato realised that he had not touched his wine, and raised his glass. It was only the second time in his life that he had tasted champagne. Glamour, he thought, as, to the scent of freesias, the bubbles prickled at his mouth.

'Most important man on the ship,' continued Farrell. 'Square it with the purser, and all's right in heaven and earth. Put up a black, of course, not worth living. Senior?'

Reginald accepted the cigarette, and Farrell lit it with a hand which, Cato noticed, shook badly. *Reggie*, he wondered again.

'Thought I'd better report in,' continued Farrell. 'Introduce myself.' He was sweating. A shred of tobacco hung from his lip.

'Not sure that's strictly necessary, is it?' asked Reginald.

'Ounce of prevention, old boy,' said Farrell, his eyes searching the crowd suspiciously. 'Ounce of prevention.' He lifted a dry martini from the tray of a passing waiter, but his hand was shaking too badly for much of the drink to reach his mouth. 'First of the day,' he apologised with a barking laugh, wiping gin and vermouth down the front of his British Warm overcoat with the back of a large hand, 'Often the way. Now you'll excuse me, but I have to go to the lavatory.'

They watched him go in silence. Eventually Reginald looked down at his empty glass and then up at Pierre.

'Well, I think we might . . .' He looked around him for somewhere to stand his glass.

'Absolutely,' said Pierre, taking it.

Cato gulped down the last of his wine, but too fast. The champagne raced to his nostrils and he doubled over, coughing. Mrs MacLean's coterie were suddenly silent. Finding a handkerchief in his trouser pocket, Cato wiped his eyes, and discovered himself the object of their ironic concern.

'First of the day,' explained Pierre, slapping him hard between the shoulder blades.

'This', said Reginald, consulting his plan of the ship ten minutes later, 'ought to be it.'

A steward appeared behind them.

'What name, sir?'

'Parkes. Reginald Parkes. Colonel.'

The steward glanced at a plan of his own. 'That's right, sir, this is yourself and the young gentleman.' He indicated with the ghost of a bow that they precede him. 'Let me show you the cabin.'

In his mind, Cato had entertained a very specific picture of the berth which he and his father were to occupy. It would be higher than it was wide, with bunk beds. The walls would be of riveted steel-plate, painted white, and there would be a single, polished brass porthole. Although he had no idea what was meant by 'the smell of salt', he felt sure that there would be such a smell.

The low, darkish room (smelling, Cato immediately noticed, of first days of term, of new pyjamas and commercial furniture-polish) bore no relation to any of his imaginings. The cabin was carpeted in a heavy plum-coloured Wilton, while the walls and fittings were of veneered wood, silver-bronze metal, and etched peach glass. Alongside a mirrored dressing table on which were aligned a

Bible, a clothes-brush and an ashtray, a tiled fireplace surrounded a small electric grate. Between the two beds lay the Parkes' cabin trunks.

'The wardrobe, sir.' Cato saw that the trunks had already been unpacked, 'And the bathroom.' The door opened on to a tiny mauve-tiled chamber, and the smell of furniture-wax was briefly overlaid by that of lavender bath salts.

To Cato, the whole had a curious period feel, reminding him, not uncomfortably, of early childhood. It was a room through which his mother might have moved; a room in the sort of hotel to which one was taken out to tea, on Sundays, from Cleeve. The multiplicity of wood veneers somehow contributed strongly to this impression. And for a moment, in the dull unmoving light, Cato forgot that they were aboard ship. Only the low ceiling and the twin chintz-curtained portholes above the further of the two beds suggested the nautical.

'Why don't you take this one, old boy?' suggested Reginald, placing Cato's overnight case at the foot of the bed beneath the portholes. Slowly, Cato lowered himself to the ivory-quilted bedspread. It was cold beneath his hands. The steward, whose repertory-juvenile features exhibited signs of careful preservation, appeared to be examining his fingertips. As Reginald frowned at a wall-sconce containing long-stemmed roses, he looked up.

'My name is Herbert, sir. I am your cabin steward for the voyage. So if there's anything at all that you require . . .' He indicated, with minute irony, a small electric bell.

Reginald handed him a folded banknote which, thought Cato, he must have palmed some minutes ago.

'Thank you, sir. Colonel. Thank you, Mr Parkes.'

Realising too late that this last was directed at him, Cato directed a smile at the closing door.

'Well,' said Reginald eventually, 'here we are, anyway. Remember how to get here?'

'I think so,' said Cato, examining a curling-iron plug set into the wall at his bedside. 'This is "A" deck, isn't it?'

'That's right.'

They looked around them. Neither much wished to remain in the cabin. Through the dividing wall came the sounds of a party. 'Shall we . . .?' started Cato.

He was interrupted by the brassy crash of a gong and a sing-song cry from outside the cabin door: 'All ashore that's going ashore.'

The ritual repeated itself up the corridor, growing fainter with each delivery. For an almost conspiratorial moment, father and son looked at each other, and then Reginald turned to the dressing table, reared his chin, and straightened his tie.

'Up on deck, then?' he demanded of the mirror.

'How high can we go?' asked Cato.

'Let's see,' said Reginald. He consulted his plan. 'Well, we can go up to the Sports Deck, that's probably as high as it goes; it looks like a bit of a haul, though, so gently does it.'

'Okay.'

They retraced their steps. Despite the warning to visitors, which Cato could hear being repeated in some distant quarter, a number of cabin parties were still under way, and the area around the Entrance Hall seemed as crowded as ever.

'Reggie!'

Waving as if to flag down a fast-moving car, still wearing his heavy overcoat, Jerry Farrell forced his way towards them.

'Reggie, bit of a flap on. Have you seen the bloody deck-steward?'

''Fraid not, um . . . Jerry.'

'No matter. My pigeon. See him, though, could you . . .?' He mimed catching a man by the collar.

Reginald nodded.

'Thanks, old man.' He rubbed at the crimped and furious eye with a handkerchief. 'Spot while you're here?'

Reginald shook his head.

'We were just going up to the Sports Deck, actually. Watch the off.'

'Might join you. This your boy?'

'Yes, this is Cato.'

'Ah, a North Africa man. "*Delenda est Carthago*" and all that. Salt in the ruins. Jolly good.' His voice tailed off, he swayed, and the urgency departed him. A wiry, narrow-featured man appeared at his side, handed him a glass, and turned away.

'That's my man Docherty,' Farrell nodded at the retreating figure. 'And if this is Beefeater,' he sniffed moodily at the drink, 'then I'm the ruddy Mahatma Coat. Cheers.'

Cato turned up the collar of his jacket. They were standing at the port rail of the *Carmelia*'s topmost deck, sheltered from the wind by one of the vents to the boiler room. In front of them, sixty feet high, poppy-red and black top-banded, rose the forward of the three funnels. Its woven steel shrouds were secured to a deck-plate at Cato's side, and he could hear and feel their thrumming tension.

He peered forward between the lifeboat davits. A hundred feet below, between ship and pier, the water was a dark dizzying wrinkle. A steady line of visitors was leaving each of the three canvas-covered entrances to the ship, and tiny waving figures now crowded the quarter-mile length of Ocean Pier. Beyond them, a train was leaving the terminal. Cato followed it through the docks, past the South Western Hotel, and into the town, where, but for a trailing signature of steam, it disappeared. From how far inland, he wondered, could the ship's shining white superstructure and pillar-box funnels be seen. He looked beyond the depositories and suburbs of the port to sun-hazed fields.

'Farrell.' Reginald eventually broke the silence. 'What do you make of him?'

'He seems a little . . . odd,' replied Cato cautiously. His father's questions, he knew, were never completely without motive. A soundless vibration, emanating from far beneath them, gave the ship sudden and distracting life. Reginald cleared his throat and, as if to stay preparations in the engine-room, lifted his hands from the rail.

'He was an exceptionally brave man. There was a show in Crete that ... well, never mind, but he did very well, and later, after Normandy, picked up a D.S.O.. I read the citation at the W.O.. Recognised the name straight away. He returned his folded arms to the rail and frowned down at the crowds on the pier.

'Thing you have to understand is that a lot of people are still terribly messed up by what they went through. Probably always will be. So one must be ...'

He was interrupted, his words rendered negligible, by an ear-shattering blast from the *Carmelia*'s triple sirens. These were mounted on the funnels fore and aft of Reginald and Cato's position, and for a long incomprehending moment father and son were all but lifted from their feet by the bellow. It was only as the plangent ghost of the sound reached the distant fields that they knew its origin.

Below them, as the siren slowly died, visitors streamed from the exits to join the soundlessly waving crowds on the quay. On board the *Carmelia* the underfoot vibration grew deeper in tone, as, one by one, the baggage conveyors and the gangways were withdrawn and the shipside doors pulled to. To the port side, beneath them, the tugs took up their positions; to the starboard, the last moorings were cast off.

Looking around him, Cato saw that he and Reginald had been joined on the top deck by a number of other passengers, none of them speaking, none moving, their gazes aligned. Slightly apart from the rest, Ayrest MacLean stood with a white-gloved hand to her hat. Alone of them all, Cato noticed, she looked not to the land but out to sea.

Finally, and with a sudden freshness of wind, the tug-lines tautened, and berths 43 and 44 of Southampton's Ocean Dock began, slowly at first and then faster, to slip away.

Claudia, Cato's mother, had been dead for three years. A little more than three years, in fact, because in the field overlooking the road in which she had died there had stood a frozen grey block that had been a snowman. And the snowmen had all disappeared, that year, by the end of April.

The first Cato had known of it had been flames. Five in the afternoon, dark early, and flames showing over the hedge at the end of the drive. He had heard nothing, or at least remembered hearing nothing. Perhaps his father – who, tea-less, had been stabbing irritably at the logs in the fireplace for more than an hour – had heard something, had known the meaning of the flames beyond the hedge on that cold spring Saturday, when it was dark early and the flames made all else darker.

'Wait!' had been Reginald's only word. He had pulled on his overcoat, stared briefly at his wellington boots and scarf, and then, hatless, hurried through the porch-lit drizzle. Cato, standing there in his socks, hungry, heard the crunch of his father's footsteps on the drive and, soon afterwards, the beginning of a damped, distant shouting. That went on for a time, the flames burnt lower, and then a further vehicle arrived, lighting the area with yellow headlights. Expecting his father to return at any minute, Cato waited, as he had been told to wait. He had had no lunch, and having an idea that there was a pot of bloater paste in the larder, wondered about making some toast. The bread, though, he guessed was probably earmarked for some other purpose, and he was disinclined to leave the warmth of the sitting room for the chilly, washing-soda-smelling kitchen. Instead, he slumped in an armchair, his gaze trailing dully over the Jules Vernes and the G. A. Hentys between the kneeling elephant book-ends and continuing along the red-tiled mantelpiece to where, amongst spills and seed-packets and photographs, the ebony-pillared clock delivered itself of its measured and crepitant whirr. Drowsy, half-hypnotised by the warmth of the fire and the rain at the window and the clock's tiny progress, he turned on the wireless, and found the closing bars of a Mantovani concert.

Finally, coatless, skirting the Anderson shelter, he set off across the front garden. Its end wall, against which grew bushes of forsythia and japonica, black against the light, overlooked the road. From the field opposite, like a standing stone, rose the unthawed remains of the snowman.

In the shuddering rain-hatched headlights of a US army jeep, Cato saw that two cars had collided head-on. One had been an MG, open-roofed, the other he did not recognise. Fire had drawn all colour from the broken vehicles. Below him, on the grass verge, two negroes in American army uniform were carrying a blanketed stretcher towards the chugging exhaust of the jeep. As they did so, the wind dragged loose a triangle of blanket, flipping it back. Cato's first impression, against all logic, was that the men were transporting through the rain some kind of tribal fetish, some malevolent assembly of bone, hair and feather. The wind, however, carried towards him a clotted beefy stench, and where he thought that he had seen pitted ebony and cowrie-shells, Cato saw teeth, imploding flesh and a silent scream. Whatever lay in the blue Lan-Air-Cel blanket had been human.

Horror widened in Cato's chest, his knees weakened, and he retched. When he looked up again, wiping his eyes and mouth, the men and the stretcher had disappeared beyond the headlights, and his father was staring up at him, his face the dull frozen grey of the snowman.

At first Cato hadn't understood, had mistaken his father's expression for anger – anger at his disobedience. There were elements of the scene that his gaze had not yet taken in; the kneeling group, for example, around the smeared and glass-starred bundle in the road. A black corporal, carrying a rifle, had led him back to the house.

He learnt more from the inquest report in the local newspaper than he was ever told. His mother had been a passenger in the MG. The driver had been a US gunnery-instruction officer. The occupants of the second car, an Alvis, had been, respectively, a British sapper returning from leave and the Birmingham munitions-factory manager who had given him a lift. The inquest established that, at the moment of impact, the MG had been stationary, showing no lights, and that the Alvis had been travelling at approximately fifty miles per hour. All those involved had been killed. The occupants of the Alvis had been trapped as their petrol tank ignited; the American officer had died at the moment of impact, and Cato's mother, thrown into the road with her femoral artery severed by windscreen glass, had bled to death ten minutes later.

More than three years later he still dreamed her alive. That afternoon, as he slept on the bed beneath the portholes, he was back in the boat-train. His mother, this time, was there beside him, her long hands smoothing a pale cotton dress Cato knew to be one of her best. Outside, beyond the compartment windows, an emptiness, a place between places, nowhere.

Gradually, unhurriedly, the train came to a stop. Electric fans had been mounted in the compartment, and these slowed to silence and waited, felted with dust, behind their marcelled wire guards. For some minutes Cato and his mother sat in the silence, watching the sad suburban fields. Although it appeared to be morning, warmth and light were fading from the day, and when his mother, unsurprised by these changes, got to her feet, Cato knew that something unbearable was about to happen. She reached up to the luggage rack for her coat and, opening the carriage door, indicated that they leave the train. Paralysed by the emptiness and the endlessness without, Cato soundlessly begged her to stay, felt tears running down his cheeks. Readying herself, she bent to kiss him – a last scented touch – and stepped down to the side of the track. I have to, she gently explained, I have to go, and began to pick her careful way over the rough ground.

Responsive as he was, had always been, to the pull of the dull-skied terrain, Cato knew that he could not yet leave the compartment, that he had further to go.

Silently, the door swung shut and the train shuddered to a start. Through the streaked windows the pale figure became a juddering blur, was lost. The forward progress of the train became the *Carmelia*'s undulant roll; Cato, falling it seemed, felt the touch of curtains at his face.

He woke to electric light, half-light, and to the creaking of *boiserie*, the whispered and straining burr – as if the low laminate box of the cabin were deformed by every movement – of myrtle and ash veneer, of flitched sapele, zebrano, amboyna, peroba, betula and pear. In counterpoint, rising to the walls and headboard from deep beneath the korkoleum floor, was the deep, distant drum of the *Carmelia*'s heart, of the engines driving her four great propellers through the dark water below.

His father, crouched in front of the frameless dressing-table mirror with an ivory hairbrush palmed in each hand, half-turned and, as if aware of none of these sounds, spoke.

Confused as to the time of day, Cato turned, found the porthole and the dying light of the Channel. At the horizon, just discernible, the darker line of a breakwater. The ship was moving at a steady, restless speed, as if anxious for the scale and depth of ocean.

'We've just left Cherbourg,' continued Reginald, knees still bent. 'For open sea.'

Cato rubbed his eyes. He felt dazed, stale. It occurred to him that if his father were to tilt the mirror, he would not have to crouch so uncomfortably. 'How long have I been asleep?' he asked, retrieving *The Case of the Gilded Fly* from the carpet, where it had fallen.

'Good few hours,' said Reginald, carefully aligning the wings of his black tie. 'It's gone eight. Haven't covered much ground, though. Sea, I should say. Cherbourg's not more than seventy miles due south of um ... Southampton.' He stood upright, shot his cuffs, and braced his shoulders. 'Hungry?'

Cato realised that he was indeed hungry.

'Spruce up then, old boy, and we'll go to dinner. There's some sort of cocktail scrum on in the main lounge first, apparently, but I don't expect we'll be missed.'

In the bathroom, Cato immersed his head, eyes closed, in a basin of cold water. The beat of the engines was magnified, and his head cleared.

Cantaloup, read Cato. Terrine de Foie Gras. Grapefruit Maraschino. Caviare de Beluga. Sweet Gherkins à la Moutarde. Bordeaux Sardines. Filleted Anchovies in oil. Little Neck Clam Cocktails.

Of these, he had tasted only grapefruit and sardines (the former twice, the latter, on limp toast, more often than he cared to remember). What a cantaloup was, he simply had no idea; a small gamebird, perhaps? He envisioned a tiny greyish carcase pierced by a splintered beak.

He and Reginald were seated at a table for six in a vast dining room, a peach-lit and disconcertingly shadowless well, three decks deep, whose mirrored walls extended to perspective infinity. Where the room ended and its reflection began, it was impossible to say; by searching the mirrored crowd Cato eventually found himself a dim hundred yards ahead, and over his shoulder, equidistantly, found himself again.

The room was two-thirds full, and a steady descent continued from the galleries above. Conversation, fretted with the tick of glass on glass, silver-nickel on bone china, lifted and fell to the muted vamp of the band. Despite ventilation the air was close, heavy with scent, cigar, and expansive release.

Reginald and Cato had been placed on the starboard side of the room, beneath a rounded cinema-like balcony. Cato wondered if he would ever find the table again, and attempted, by a rough process of triangulation, to fix his position. To his right was one of a dozen pillars, neither round nor square, around which sheets of pale wood had been bound by chromium strips. Inset into each of these pillars was an electric clock, the nearest, unhelpfully, showing the time in Recife. Some eight or nine tables to his left, in the centre of the hall and surrounded by dwarf palms, leapt a decorative fountain of luna-blue and white tubular glass, a feature which, to Cato's eye, exactly resembled frozen water jetting through an iceberg-impacted hull. And on a shallow dais some thirty yards forward of this creation, and beneath a large grouping in burnished phosphor-bronze depicting 'Progress' or 'The Marriage of Science and Art' or some such, stood the Captain's table. The majority of the places there were unfilled, Cato observed, most notably the Captain's.

At a pre-planned moment the band, which had trailed from its cornet and snare-drum vamping to a wavering sostenuto, struck up 'God Bless Charley, the Man who Invented Beer'. On cue, dispensing a wintery and general smile as he came, the Captain descended the main staircase.

In his wake came a small crowd of those who had remained at the cocktail party until its end. One couple, who introduced themselves as Max and Loelia Amber, were directed to the table beneath the balcony. As hands were shaken, Cato covertly examined the pair. Max Amber was a pale, aquiline figure of some thirty summers. His manner was one of concentrated if slightly absent courtesy, and the shadowed umber of his eyes seemed expressive of some private and mildly sinister amusement. He looked curiously familiar, until Cato realised that he resembled the porcelain figure of Punchinello that stood, dustily of late, on the landing windowsill at home.

Loelia Amber was – Cato guessed – older than her husband, and darker of complexion. Beneath the hennaed shingle, however, her face had the shadowed waxiness of one kept from the sun. There was a night-feeding quality about her, a jet and mordant glitter to her gaze. Her eyes held Cato's for a moment, unsmiling, and slid blackly away. Looking up, he was glad to see Pierre Watson picking his way towards them through the tables.

'Any chance of a spare place?' asked Pierre.

'There seems to be,' said Cato. 'Why don't you . . .?'

'I think I will,' said Pierre. 'Thanks.'

'How was the Captain's cocktail party?' Cato asked, when introductions had been made.

'Grimmish, really,' answered Pierre, glancing at the menu. 'We hung on too long and got corralled into the reception line to shake the old boy's hand. There were photographers to record the moment, but – when it came to my turn, at least – the good Commodore looked as if his mind was elsewhere.'

'Probably in Cheltenham,' said Loelia Amber. 'He told me that he and his wife had a flat there. They grow geraniums. I thought he was a pussy-cat, didn't I, darling?'

'I expect so,' said her husband shortly, polishing his spectacles on a foulard handkerchief. A filigree-work sapphire ring, Cato noticed, circled the slender index finger of his right hand.

'No, darling, didn't I say to you . . .? My husband is frightfully disagreeable,' she confided to Cato, with a sideways glance at Pierre. 'He neglects me dreadfully.' She squinted at Max through the lipsticked martini glass. 'Don't you darling?'

'Dreadfully' he agreed, with an umber smile.

A wine waiter appeared with champagne. The band segued into 'Cruising down the River', the wine waiter retired, they raised their glasses, but somehow, at the moment that a toast might have been proposed, no one spoke. As if the object of their silence, Ayrest MacLean walked past them towards the Captain's table. In black, pale of shoulder, scintillant with diamonds, she left a further silence in her wake. Loelia Amber was the first of them to speak.

36

'That's the kind of dress I meant, Max, if you can just take your eyes off its contents for a moment. I think it's a Worth.'

'Who is that woman?' asked Max. 'I'm sure I recognise her from somewhere. Isn't she a film star or something.'

'I'm surprised you don't recognise her', said Loelia archly, 'from your pre-me days. Ayrest MacLean, her name is. She was a débutante, one of that wild Scottish lot, and then for years a fashion model and had men shooting themselves for love of her all over the Riviera. Endless stories. Endless husbands. You *must* have heard of her.'

'I do recognise her face,' admitted Max.

Loelia turned to Pierre. 'Well I recognise good diamonds when I see them.' She laughed and shook her head. 'All I can say is that I'm glad *some* husbands are still prepared to look after their wives properly. Max can be frightfully Jewish at times.'

'I'm Jewish pretty much all of the time,' said Max, mildly.

'Don't split hairs, darling, it's perfectly obvious that you *are* Jewish; it's just that from time to time you can *be* awfully Jewish.'

There was a long moment's silence. The band struck up Arthur Askey's 'Bee Song'. Conscious that he was holding his second glass of champagne of the day, Cato sought to avoid his father's eye. Having slept in the afternoon it no longer felt as if it was the same day that he had drunk the first – it seemed a month since they had left Waterloo – but this was not a position that he felt inclined to defend in public.

A waiter appeared at the head of the table, smiled, and bowed. They reached for their menus. Cato, who had made his decisions earlier, ordered Beluga caviare, turtle soup, Poularde Demidoff with asparagus, and a beetroot salad.

Could he manage all that? he wondered. Unlikely. But it was certainly an improvement on Woolton pie or Baby's

Leg. With the waiter's departure, there was a moment's silence.

'So,' began Pierre Watson and Max Amber at the same moment. They smiled and exchanged you-first gestures, which Pierre finally conceded. 'What takes you to New York?' he asked.

Max Amber, it transpired, was a zoologist, a snake-man. His family were Jews – originally from Baghdad – who to avoid persecution had settled three generations earlier in Calcutta, where they had established themselves as jute shippers and traders. With Indian independence, however, and the nationalisation of the jute-trading industry, there was no longer a place for Calcutta's Jewry. The Ambers, like many others of their community, had taken what money and possessions they had been able from India, and had bought residences abroad. Max, who had spent the war years in London, where he had met and married Loelia, was now rejoining his family in New York.

Loelia, throughout this confessional, remained silent, staring at her hands as they slowly revolved the stem of her champagne glass. This may be the truth, the small jet eyes seemed to say, but it is not all of the truth. As Max fell silent, she smiled at him with dutiful if brief complicity, and turned, head interrogatively inclined, to Pierre. No one appeared to expect her story.

Pierre, they heard, the son of a Hampshire landowner, had left Oxford at the outbreak of war and 'found his way' to the Ministry of Information. There, he had worked in the film unit, initially as an assistant on documentary portraits of the home front and the Blitz, and later, as a writer, on a number of fictional wartime stories. The popular success of the last of these ('Meet Miss Dalby' and 'The Trees were Green') had led to an invitation to work in Hollywood, where a number of 'English' pictures had been planned.

The word 'Hollywood', despite Pierre's almost apologetic hurrying past it, had its inevitable effect. The men's eyebrows rose, Loelia's lips pursed, and Cato said 'Gosh!'

Pierre gave a self-deprecatory shrug. 'It's not exactly what I wanted to do. Writers are considered pretty low on the evolutionary scale in filmland, but . . .'

'Well, I think it's perfectly marvellous,' said Loelia. 'I mean, *Hollywood*, Max.' She licked a fingertip and traced one eyebrow. 'Just imagine.'

A decade of explaining his condition and of hearing it explained had not armoured Cato against moments such as he knew were approaching. He was certain that it would be to him that all eyes would turn from Pierre, and so it proved. He looked to his father, but his father's gaze was neutral. Get it over with, had always been Reginald's advice in all things unpleasant. Get it out of the way. Be truthful.

'I'm . . . well, we, my father and I, live in Berkshire, near Pangbourne, and I'm going for an operation in New York. It's called a closed mitral valvotomy. We'll be putting up at a hotel.'

There didn't seem much point in saying anything else. What else could he say? My mother was killed in an accident; I've never been allowed to play games; I like reading and going to the cinema; I do not intend to marry, and if I survive this operation I would like to work in Military Intelligence?

In the ensuing silence they looked at him with the frozen, distanced concern which characterised most reactions to his condition.

'I suppose that you could say', said Max, turning the dead-leaf pools of his eyes on to the boy, 'that it's an adventure of a kind, an operation like that.'

'Oh, for Heaven's sake,' said Loelia. She turned to Cato. 'I think you should put the whole thing from your mind and have the time of your life. What you need right now – what we all need – is more champagne. Max, call the waiter over!'

An hour later, Cato removed the last of the *petits fours* from its crimped paper cup. The food had been better than he had known possible, almost embarrassing in its volume and richness. Seeing his son so frankly wide-eyed, Reginald felt guilt. He wondered if he could perhaps have provided for him better over the long dark years. His rank and his principles had always precluded any involvement in black-market trading, and he had never quite moved in either the landowning or the yeoman circles in which such commodities as gamebirds and salmon were routinely exchanged. There was some decent fishing and rough shooting around Pangbourne, but for eight years now Reginald's Army and Navy twelve-bore and Hardy split-bamboo fly-rod had gathered dust in a cupboard. For six of those years, of course, it would have been inappropriate to have taken them out, would have trivialised the deadlier pursuits and surveillances of his fellows. He had cleaned the gun though, to start with, and had oiled the reel and the braided silk lines.

And then the war was over and Claudia was dead and Reginald had known that he and Cato would never, as he had dreamed, walk the hedgerows for a rabbit or the water-meadows for a summer trout. The cupboard would remain locked now, for he understood that the war had not ended but changed, and that the fighting of it would outlast his sight and his skill and his knowledge and would never, as long as he lived, end.

'Reggie, old man. What d'you think of the grub? Beats beagle balls, eh?'

Cato saw his father look up with a start from the statue-like reverie into which he had sunk. Jerry Farrell, cigar and drink in fist, stood at his elbow.

'Some of the chaps are talking about cards,' Farrell continued, allowing his flushed attention to linger, briefly, on Loelia Amber. 'Why don't you bring a brandy up to the smoking room.'

Sensing his father torn between paternal concern and a desire to smoke cigars and drink spirits in exclusively military company, Cato ventured that he was thinking of taking a turn on deck.

'Walking off the Spotted Dick?' ruminated Farrell, liberally expelling the smoke from his *Romeo y Julieta.* 'Sensible feller. Join us for a rubber or two later.'

With a grateful and cautionary glance at Cato and a brief nod to his fellow-diners, Reginald rose to his feet.

'Who was that quite extraordinary man?' asked Loelia, when they had departed earshot.

'His name's Jerry Farrell,' said Cato. 'D.S.O.; Crete and Normandy.'

'Your father's still serving, then?' asked Max.

'Sort of,' said Cato. 'War Office. He's been very busy.'

The room was beginning to empty. A group from the Captain's table, amongst whom Cato recognised Mrs MacLean, passed them, laughing.

'Feel like that stroll on deck?' Pierre asked Cato.

'Why not?' Cato answered.

Loelia Amber reached for her stole. 'Let's go up too, darling. It's such a heavenly evening. You boys don't mind if we join you, do you?'

For a long while, high above the rushing whiteness at the hull, the four of them stood in silence. It was the softest and palest of nights. Along the rail, Cato's fingers traced an intaglio of carved initials and dates. It would have been men on their way to death who had left these schoolboy memorials, he thought, and their NCOs would not have stopped them. Before leaving the *Carmelia* he would carve his initials amongst theirs.

'Max, darling, isn't that the Pole-Harcourts?' asked Loelia suddenly and quite loudly.

'No idea,' said her husband. 'Who are the Pole-Vaulters.'

'Harcourts, darling, and I'm certain it is. I saw their names on the passenger list and promised myself, *swore* in fact, I'd telephone Celia from the cabin. She's jealous-makingly beautiful and he's brilliant, so do try not to be *too* much of a bore.' She slipped her arm through Max's and turned to Cato and Pierre. 'Don't move, boys. Back in a tick. I'll send a steward over. Come on darling, quick march.' She steered him towards an animated throng two lifeboats away.

'This is really pretty good, isn't it,' said Pierre, offering Cato the battered cigarette case. Cato, searching the horizon for the joining of sea and sky, nodded.

'Yes, it is.' He took a cigarette. 'I'll remember it. It's like a film.' He smiled self-consciously, remembering Pierre's profession.

'No, you're right,' said Pierre. 'It is like a film. Can you put into words why?'

'Something to do', said Cato, 'with there being no back-ground, no horizon. Only light.'

Pierre nodded. 'Ever written anything?' he asked, cupping a flaring match.

Cato bowed to the flame. 'Oh . . . school stuff. Bits and pieces.' He exhaled. 'Nothing any good.'

'Do you know that Roy Cadwaladr poem called "Night-walk"?' Cato shook his head.

Pierre lit his own cigarette, examined it thoughtfully, and flicked the curling match over the rail. 'I can only remember the one verse:

> 'Walk, silent, walk the cold sand road
> of dazed and day's-end summers long gone by,
> the almond ether playground where the children
>    all fell down,
> the endless ratting wind
> the wired sky . . .'

Ruminatively, he pressed at his hair, as if it were a hat about to fly off, and frowned at his cigarette. 'I suppose it was those "dazed and day's-end summers" of his that made me think of it.'

'Did you . . .?'

'Roy? Yes. Quite well. We had a kind of . . . pub friendship, I suppose you'd call it. He was one of those people who could be blind drunk and frightfully austere at the same time, and he was completely uncompromising about poetry. He used to say that if you hadn't fought, hadn't killed and seen your friends killed, pretty much, then you bloody well had no business writing it.' He paused. 'We disagreed about that.'

'And did you – do you – write poetry as well as films?'

'Did, yes. Bits and pieces, anyway, and a few of them were published. *Scrutiny*, *Poetry London*, and so on.' Leaning forward he dropped his cigarette, watched its tiny sparking ricochets along the hull. 'I don't mean any disrespect to Roy and the rest of them by saying that it was a good deal easier to get your stuff into print if you *were* in the services . . .'

'And do you still?' asked Cato. 'Write poetry, I mean.'

'A very good question,' said Pierre. 'In more pompous vein I might say that I'd fallen silent.' He swung round, turning his back on the sea, and extended his arms along the rail. 'I thought, naïvely I suppose, that the war had released something in me, that I would mark my life with poetry, and that the poetry would get better and better.' He nodded at an elderly couple, waited for them to pass. 'The fact is that the war ended and the pubs emptied and I was left standing at the bar with an empty glass and nothing to say.'

'I'm sure it'll . . . come back,' said Cato, uncertainly.

'There are no subjects left,' said Pierre, turning restlessly back to the sea. 'Of the immediate past, nothing remains unsaid. Of the present and the future all that can be accurately described is the useless passing of time. And I'm frankly not quite Parisian enough to want to do that. All that remains these days is to dot the "i"s and cross the "t"s of stuff I've already started.'

'What will you write about in Hollywood?' asked Cato, after a short silence.

'England, I suppose,' said Pierre. He half-turned to Cato. 'She looked pretty wonderful tonight, didn't you think?'

Cato immediately knew to whom he referred.

'Yes, she did. She glittered. What do you make of these two? The Ambers.'

'They're rather Grand Guignol, aren't they? She especially, with that sort of gorged . . .'

Catching sight of the returning Ambers, mess-jacketed steward in tow, Cato meaningfully cleared his throat. Pierre fell silent and Loelia, approaching, turned to Max.

' . . . do you know, darling, that's quite the most sensible thing you've said all evening,' she announced, clasping her hands. 'Man*hattans*. A heavenly idea. Boys?'

Cato was flattered by his inclusion in this male trinity but uncertain of exactly what was being offered. He turned, smiling interrogatively, to Pierre, who folded his arms fatalistically.

'Why not?'

Smiling brightly, Cato nodded at Loelia. 'Why not?'

'That makes four Why Nots, steward. Stiffish, please.'

'Certainly, madam. Right away.'

'That's all right, is it, Cato?' asked Max, his eyes suddenly fluid with concern. 'I mean, you're not . . .?'

'For Heaven's *sake*, Max,' interjected Loelia, 'He's perfectly capable of making his own mind up. Let's eat, drink, and be merry, for God's sake, for tomorrow . . .'

The ensuing silence was edged by the distant rush of the sea and the papery syncopations of a dance tune from the Tourist Class promenade below.

'I'm a little worried', began Max, turning to Loelia and lowering his voice, 'about the *Naja*. She might be upset.'

'The *Naja* will be just fine, darling. What more can we . . .?' She hesitated, and turned to Pierre. 'I'm sorry.

We're speaking in tongues. You must think us quite, quite mad.'

'No.' Pierre shook his head as if to disclaim any such idea. 'But what exactly is the . . .?'

She and Max exchanged glances. '*Naja Hannah*, the hamadryad or King Cobra. My husband – and, I suppose, I – are transporting a particularly large and venomous specimen, presently crated in the hold, to the Chicago Zoo.'

'There's a King Cobra on the ship?' breathed Cato, rapt.

'There is indeed,' said Max. 'Queen, in this case, as it happens. Approximately twelve feet of her. Are you interested in snakes?'

'Well, yes,' said Cato. 'I mean, I don't really know that much about them, but I've always been keen on the idea of them. Could we . . . I . . . see her?'

Loelia flicked long enamelled fingernails at the rail. 'You have just', she said, turning on to Cato the marcasite glitter of her smile, 'made my husband the happiest man in the world.'

As one, they turned to Pierre, who raised both hands imploringly and took a step backwards. 'I'm sorry,' he said, patting the pockets of his dinner-jacket, 'Fains. Afraid I've an *absolute horror* of snakes.'

'Please,' said Max. 'Forget it.'

Unsteadily, Pierre lit a cigarette.

'I'm forever saying . . .' began Loelia. 'For Heaven's sake, Max, the poor boy's the colour of *chartreuse*.'

Behind them, the Geraldo dance tune was briefly amplified as the steward, carrying a tray, returned through the stairway door.

'Down the hatch,' said Loelia, palming a glass. 'Pretty much literally, on this occasion.'

'What do you mean by that?' asked Max.

'Never mind. Here's health!'

Following her example, Cato threw back a third or so of the straw-coloured drink. Its taste was innocuous (raffia, *ratafia? Recife?*) and Cato was aware of a faint, suggestive scent. Lowering the glass, he noticed that although it was not yet dark, the stars were visible, pinpricks in the pale sky.

'And the moon, as well,' he heard himself saying.

Pierre raised his eyebrows interrogatively.

' . . . touches the spot.' This from Loelia.

'What were you saying, Cato?'

'Oh, just that . . .' As Cato turned to answer him, Max, or Max's upper half, appeared to shimmy behind an unseeing Loelia. Cato turned his head the other way to find Max looking past him, straightening his bow-tie to sea and sky as if to a mirror.

'It doesn't matter.' Cato's voice trailed off, and he took another, slower mouthful of the drink. It tasted, he decided, decidedly . . . subtle. An acquired taste. A taste he had acquired. He was aware of a perceptive shift, a sliding aside, at once logical and disordering. Pierre was speaking, a smile in his voice, a smile on his face, but the voice no longer correspondent to the face. The soundless and falling arc to the sea of Loelia's glass was followed, simultaneously it seemed, by her laugh and cry, thrown after the glass, ' . . . the *Atlantic*!'

Snapping back his head and the last of the Manhattan, Cato echoed Loelia's shout – the word already meaningless – and threw his glass after hers. As the stemmed triangle hung for a moment over the sea, inverted, necklaced by its centrifugal comet of drips, Cato experienced a blinding cortical flash. The deck fell sliding away, his knees buckled, and his hands reached out. They found the rail, and his eyes closed tight against a dark drumming in his chest.

How long this lasted, Cato was uncertain – somewhere between seconds and minutes. Gradually, and with minor and irregular starring, the dark receded. Cato's eyes opened, and he discovered himself standing at the rail, the deck level, and Pierre's concerned grip at his upper arm.

' . . . whatso*ever* to go all the way down there *now*,' came Loelia's voice. ' . . . I mean *is* there, darling? Really?'

Questioningly, Pierre released Cato's arm.

Cato nodded his silent thanks. The confusion flew from him like water from a dog. He felt fine, clear as day. 'If you're going to see the hamadryad,' he said to Max, blinking, 'may I come too?'

'Of course,' said Max hesitantly, staring at him closely. 'Most welcome.'

'Well, count me out,' said Loelia. 'I'm quite happy where I am.'

'Me too, I'm afraid,' said Pierre.

'Oh, you mustn't be afraid,' smiled Loelia Amber.


Cato followed Max down the stairway. They descended four muffled layers of music and silence to the stairs' end and found themselves in a corridor of cabins.

'This should be "B" deck,' said Max. 'What we want is . . . here. Excellent. The lift.'

He pressed the bell, a greased whirring was followed by a hydraulic gulp, and a bellboy swung open the gilt doors.

'Down, please.'

A second bellboy selected a button on a lighted panel, and the lift shuddered briefly downwards.

' "C" deck, sir.'

'Ah . . . Okay.'

'Where exactly was you looking for, sir?' asked the button-pressing youth.

'The, um . . . forward cargo hold.'

'Forward hold. Right.' He looked thoughtfully at his wristwatch. 'Tudor here'll take you, sir.' He turned to his younger and liberally acned colleague. 'Down to "D" this end of Alamein, near the fore Pig, and take the greasers' rail. Which deck, sir?'

' "G" deck. Just forward of number-two hatch, if that's of any help.'

'Certainly is, sir. Couldn't be plainer. Thank you, sir.' He looked away, rubbed his nose with a white-gloved finger, and rocked on his heels. Max, comprehending, felt in his pockets for change.

'Thank you, sir. Know where you're going then, Tudor?'

The acned bellboy, who was approximately Cato's age, nodded. Max and Cato followed him around a corner into an empty, utilitarian looking area with slatted wooden seating.

'Tudor,' began Max, 'perhaps you could tell us where we are as we go. Then, with a bit of luck, we should be able to find our own way down in future. What do you say?'

'Yes, sir. Well . . . ' He hesitated, and looked around him. 'This is the Third Class entrance – Third dining saloon's through those doors there, as you can probably hear – and we're on "C" deck.' He led them down a further flight. 'This is "D" now, and this here', he swung open a steel door at the foot of the stairs, releasing a rolling waft of cabbage-smelling steam and the sound of booted feet on steel flooring, 'is what the brass calls the working alleyway and we calls El Alamein.'

'Why's that?' asked Cato, following Max through the door into a girdered bulb-lit corridor, 'Why El Alamein?'

'Very hot, sir. And we all works like niggers is, I s'pose, the origin of it. Every ship's got one. The *Mary*'s's called the Burma Road, her being a Cunarder. On the Albions, long as I been here, it's always been Alamein.'

It was hot, thought Cato. It had been getting hotter with every deck. As they walked past a series of low, plated doors, the bellboy removed his braided cap and ran a comb through his hair. 'These here', he said, indicating the doors with the comb, 'are the glory-holes. Crew's quarters.'

Several men in soiled vests and aprons hurried towards them, shouting incomprehensibly, and then, as they saw Max and Cato, fell silent. Nodding self-conscious acknowledgement, the men ducked into a low entrance to one side.

'Fore Pig, sir. Crew's bar.'

Before reaching this entrance, Max and Cato were led through a different doorway and into a narrow steel corridor, dimly lit, in which the vibrations of the engine were suddenly more insistent. Cato felt sweat at his back. His hearing seemed abnormally acute, but he was not sure that he was understanding all that he heard.

'Here we are, sir. Greasers' rail. Three flights to go.'

The staircase, which spiralled narrow and oil-smelling around a lanterned shaft, clanged dully beneath their shoes. At intervals, where bulbs had failed, there was no light at all.

'It's hot,' said Cato.

'Number-one boiler-room right below us, sir. There's a switch here somewhere. Should have brought a torch. Ah.'

They were in a long, low-ceilinged area in which was stacked row upon row of trunks, suitcases, motorcycles and other cargo. The vibration, curiously, seemed to have retreated, and as they moved away from the staircase the heat became less oppressive.

'Forward of the hatch, was it, sir?'

'That's right.'

'Should be somewhere around here, then. What was it exactly, sir. Trunk?'

But Max had found what he was looking for. The hamadryad's cage, secured by steel cables to rings in the decking, stood in the exact centre of the hold. Its top and three of its sides were covered by a tarpaulin, leaving exposed a padlocked wire door. Inside the cage, and concealing most of its sand-covered floor, a canvas shade had been rigged. There was no sign of the snake. Followed by the bellboy, Cato approached the cage and warily genuflected before its padlocked door.

'What's in there?' asked Tudor, curious.

'Listen,' said Max. 'Watch.' He tapped softly at the cage.

There was nothing, and then, over the engine's drum, a susurration, a parting of sand, faint and regular as breath in sleep. Slowly, inexorably, a great blood-black cable streamed from the darkness. Electric light touched a dark lentil eye, and the hamadryad rose silent and interrogative before them.

'Here she is,' whispered Max possessively. '*Naja Hannah*. The hamadryad. Greatest of the Elapidae.'

Fascinated, Cato examined the formal spread of her hood, the amber-yellow bars at her throat.

'Is she yours, sir?' Tudor turned to ask Max.

'For now,' said Max, quietly, 'yes.'

'Poisonous?' asked Cato.

Max nodded. 'Very. Nerve poison. Paralyses the respiratory system.'

Level with her eyes, Cato watched the hamadryad's gently swaying head, from which intermittently flickered a long black tongue. She had absolute poise, he thought, absolute dignity. The knowledge of her deadliness, of her concealed neurotoxic fangs, was inseparable in Cato's mind from the admission of her beauty. It *was* her beauty.

Max Amber watched his gaze with a small triumphant smile.

As Cato followed Max and Tudor up the spiral staircase, the flashing started again; erratic and silent bursts of light at the edge of his vision.

'Sorry,' he began 'could we slow . . .?'

'God, yes,' said Max, ahead of him. 'I'm sorry. I wasn't thinking.'

At the top of the staircase, Cato rested with both hands on the rail, his eyes closed. Tudor glanced at Max.

'He's been unwell,' said Max. 'Perhaps you could give him a hand.'

Tudor placed an arm across Cato's narrow back. Slowly, they proceeded along El Alamein's steel flooring. As before, groups of crew-members fell silent at their passing, some of them raising a mute eyebrow at the sight of Tudor supporting the pale, dinner-jacketed figure of Cato.

'One more flight, sir, then the lift.'

They had paused in the Third Class entrance. Cato, supported by Tudor and with one hand on the banister, was standing with head bowed. The coils were tightening at his chest, there was a prickling in his left arm, and the flashing, now continuous, alternated between the dark amber of the hamadryad's throat and a sulphurous yellow. In the distance was the sound of laughter. As he waited, the doors to the dining saloon burst open, and through the dim linseed stain of his vision, Cato perceived a girl in a cotton dress and pullover. The girl was younger than he, but her eyes, slaty and critical, were older. For a moment, as if uncertain as to the precise nature of the tableau she had disturbed, she regarded the three of them with an open-mouthed frown.

'What's wrong with him?' she asked eventually, nodding at Cato.

'He's quite all right,' said Max. 'Please don't worry.'

'Oh, I'm not worried,' said the girl, scratching her bottom through the cotton dress.

Cato raised his eyes. She had flat brown hair held in a slide, and looked, he thought fleetingly, like the 'before' girl in the Drene shampoo advertisement. 'I'm just . . .' he began.

He wanted to say that he was just catching his breath, but the tightening serpentine coils at his chest cut off the words.

'His mouth's gone blue,' said the girl, peering at him.

Max looked concernedly at Tudor. Cato, closing his eyes, raised his hands to indicate that he was all right. Two minutes rest, he thought, and I'll be fine. Two minutes. He clung to the idea. Like his lips, the tips of his fingers had taken on a bluish tinge.

'Weren't you on your way somewhere?' Max asked the girl, his voice harder-edged.

'America,' said the girl, without looking away. 'What's his name, then?'

'That's really not your concern,' said Max. 'Please leave us alone.'

'He's more like suffocated,' she continued. 'I saw them carried up blue at Bethnal Green Station. Black and white and blue all over . . .' She smiled, yawned, and fluttered her fingers before Cato's eyes. 'Ta-ta, then.'

Max watched her go.

'Thirds, sir,' said Tudor. 'I wouldn't take no notice. Let's get the gentleman upstairs.'

For Cato, the half-hour that followed was one of confusion, unreality, and desperate fatigue. The day seemed to have had not one beginning but many, all crowded, all of them long ago. He was conscious of the solicitude of Tudor and Max, of a dark brown room with a fireplace, tumblers and flushed faces, and of Jerry Farrell's hearty 'Steady the Buffs!' as his father's arm went around his shoulders. After that, nothing.

# 2

'Cabin steward, Mr Parkes!'

Cato opened the door to the pink, dapper figure of the previous afternoon, who sidestepped into the cabin carrying a large covered tray.

'Breakfast, sir. Feeling a little better this morning?'

'Yes, thank you, er . . .'

'Herbert, sir. Was it the motion, sir?'

'I . . . um, expect so. Something like that.'

'I've brought you . . . let's see.' He peered beneath the tray's chafing-dishes, 'Prunes, Bonny Boy, and kippers. How's that?'

'Perfect,' said Cato, who felt like none of them, and was marvelling at the speed with which the news of his indisposition had travelled.

'Your father said to choose for you, sir,' said Herbert, deftly arranging the meal on one of the dressing tables.

'Ah.'

'Word of advice, sir. If the motion sickness returns, avoid jam.'

'I will. Did my father say . . .?'

'Said he'd be right back, sir. Will that be all?'

As the door closed, Cato drew a chair up to the dressing table and, without enthusiasm, addressed the meal.

It wasn't his stomach. Bar a small pounding at the temples, complemented by the vibration of the engines and the creaking and straining of the marquetry, he had woken feeling surprisingly well. Sunlight was streaming through the portholes, illuminating and expanding the cabin, and for quarter of an hour he had lain watching the sea's reflected play on the ceiling. That his father was already up and pacing the deck came as no surprise. As if reimposing some stern but evasive moral order, Reginald invariably followed a late night with an early morning.

Cato drew a bath, threw in one of the lavender cubes, and wondered a little self-consciously whether to shave. The Manhattan, he thought, as he lay in the scented and steaming salt water, had been a mistake. So, for that matter, had been going all that way down to the hold knowing that he had to slog all the way back up again. Stupid. What on *earth* could the others have . . .? Cringing mentally, he remembered hurling his glass over the side of the ship. Of what followed the Manhattan he remembered the cobra, the drumming heat, and – vaguely – the girl. What, for Heaven's sake, had he . . .? He shrugged, and allowed his head to slide beneath the water.

Five minutes later, full-bladdered, and with a trickle of lavendered salt water snaking between his shoulder blades, he stood on the gently shifting floor over the lavatory.

It was the smell which alerted him, a balsamic and broadly intimate piss-odour, soupy and opaque. Something to do with last night's drink, he thought initially, some dark morning-after secret revealed only to drinkers of the Manhattan cocktail. He shook himself, and looked down. His urine, swaying gently in the lavatory bowl, was dark, blood-clouded.

Fear, heavy and immediate, stamped at his heart. Had something collapsed, ruptured? Was he dying? His mind racing, he prodded experimentally at his spleen and appendix. Nothing obvious, anyway; must be something . . . some flooding of the . . .

He strained hopelessly for his Schools Certificate biology. A stone, perhaps, like Robespierre? (Was it Robespierre with a stone, or was it just that Robespierre, too, was marked for death?)

His knowledge was horribly gappy. The heart, of course he could manage, could pretty much pin out and name the parts. He was good on the heart. But the other stuff . . .

He bent, and as the thick ferrous smell rose to meet him, peered more closely into the bowl. Think. Think.

The liver. Remember Dr Webb's notes. Take the book (dark green, yes, the cloth of the spine faded to grey, a thread or two trailing) from the desk. Concentrate on the yellowed page, the pencilled-over engraving.

The Liver (he read, although the words had been altered by some green-black schoolboy nib to *The Lover*) secretes bile and – what was that phrase – *purifies venous blood* . . .

Nothing else? Eyes closed, turn the page. The Kidney. There were two, he saw, when the engraving swam into focus. A pair. Of course. Kidneys, plural, as in breakfast at the Llangammarch Lake Hotel. And somewhere beneath the numbered engraving, the words *effete nitrogenous matter*, to which, in knowing innocence, he had added several exclamation marks . . .

*It was his liver* they said about chronic drinkers. So could that brown and terrifying smell be of *unpurified* venous blood? And if so, what on earth did that have to do with the mitral valve of his heart? Tentatively he lifted his *membrum virile* (as it was referred to on a certain grimly thumbed page of Collinson's School Cert. Biology). For a longish moment he didn't look down, and then he did look down.

It was tiny with fear. At its tip trembled a single ruby drop. Cato laid his blanched cheek against the streaming mirror.

Reginald Parkes blew his nose, lowered his heavy Inverness cape to the bed, and glanced at his son.

'Cut yourself shaving, old boy, never make Sweeney Todd out of you. How was breakfast?'

'Fine, thanks.' Cato looked away. 'How was it on deck?'

'Marvellous. You should come up. Blow the cobwebs

away. How d'you feel? Rather tied one on last night, what?'
He lifted his ivory-backed brushes from the dressing table
and, bending his knees and narrowing his eyes before the
frameless oval mirror, flattened the steely hair back from
his forehead.

'I'm afraid I probably had a glass too many at dinner,'
Cato explained dully. 'Sorry.'

'Happens to us all sooner or later,' said Reginald, turning
his head patiently and without vanity to one side and then
to the other. 'How d'you feel now? Bit dusty?'

'Well . . .'

'Breath of fresh air, you'll be right as . . .' Lumping their
bristles together, he replaced the hairbrushes beneath the
oval mirror. Blowing his nose again, he cast around as if
for somewhere to sit. 'Look, I've been to see the ship's
doctor, feller by the name of Montmorency, and he's got
all Wheeler's notes. He asked if you could pop down for
five minutes, say hello and so on. It occurred to me that
you might ask him what you should and shouldn't drink.
I know Wheeler's always saying there's nothing better for
the system than claret, but you might just get a second
opinion on that.'

'When do I see him?' asked Cato miserably.

'Well, if you buck up, you should be able to catch him
now. Apparently he's got some sort of cabin round – sea-
sickness and so on – but he'll be down there for a bit. Oh
and', Reginald smiled faintly, 'you'll recognise him.'

'Recognise him?' asked Cato, incredulous at his father's
levity, 'Where on earth from?'

'Oh, you'll see.' Reginald rubbed his hands together. 'I'll
show you down.'

Buttoning his jacket, his face pale but expressionless,
Cato followed his father from the cabin.

The War Office
25 March 1947

Dear Reginald,

I have just had a lengthy telephone call from Jack McLeish and feel I should pass on his comments a.s.a.p. There's a letter on its way from him to me setting the whole thing out in black and white, but the gist of it, as I feared, is that he confirms Martineau's diagnosis and recommends immediate surgery.

The name of the condition is mitral stenosis. In layman's terms, this means that the valve in the heart which allows the passage of oxygenated blood to the lungs has become contracted, resulting in inadequate supply (hence the symptoms of fatigue, breathlessness, tightness of chest, cyanosis, et cetera). The condition is almost certainly a result of the rheumatic fever he suffered at Newton Priors (r.f. causes contraction of the mitral valve), and the fact that the bout was a mild one does not diminish this probability. Both Martineau's and McLeish's prognoses are of progressive deterioration and, I'm afraid, early death.

The condition, however, is treatable. Success rates for closed mitral valvotomy in this country have been poor, but McLeish informs me that a New York surgeon named Lawrence Tod has pushed his patients' chances of survival in these cases to something like fifty per cent. This might seem like an unencouraging statistic, but it is not one which can be bettered elsewhere, and the chest pains that Cato describes are an indication that rapid intervention is necessary.

On my telephoned instructions McLeish has written to Tod in New York with Cato's notes. As soon as he can give us a date (and I'm confident that pressure can be applied by this department) I suggest that you investigate crossings. If nothing else is available we can put you both on the *Queen Mary* with the G.I. brides, but Jean (something of an expert in these matters, I discover!) reports that Royal Albion should be fully decommissioned and restarting crossings within the month.

I realise that this New York business is all something of a *fait accompli*, but be assured that whatever you may hear to the contrary there is no realistic hope of successful treatment in this country. Your and your son's best hopes unquestionably lie in America and with Tod. If there's any question of financial difficulty, it goes without saying, let me know and I'll see what I can sort out with the fourth floor.

Reginald, accept my apologies for the bleak tone of this letter, but the last years have left me, as I would imagine they have left you, impatient with pretence. It is my hope that by giving you the worst first, all that follows may be positive. As regards Cato himself, he is far too intelligent not to guess at the gravity of the situation, but it is essential for his morale that no idea of the actual statistical risk be conveyed. The most powerful of his and your defences is hope.
Sincerely,
*John Rutherford*

Reginald had promised himself that he would throw Rutherford's letter away without rereading it. He wished he had got rid of it earlier – burnt it, perhaps – but over the last six weeks he had drawn a certain reassurance from its measured imperatives. Now that he and Cato were sharing a cabin, however, he felt that he should dispose of it once and for all. He knew his son, knew him as one from whom things were hard to conceal. If the letter remained in the cabin, he feared, it would somehow or other announce its presence. And while he recoiled at the idea of Cato going through his pockets or his wallet or his briefcase, he knew inside himself that Cato would flinch at none of these activities.

'Bouillon, sir?'

Reginald folded the letter and looked up. A steward stood between him and the sun, holding a tray of steaming mugs.

'Thank you, er . . .'

'Dusty, sir, Dusty Hay. Deck steward.' He inclined towards Reginald. Squinting, capping his eyes with one hand, Reginald reached for the bouillon.

'Another rug, perhaps, sir?'

'No, no. One's quite enough.' He pocketed the letter. 'Listen, Hay, are you the chap who allocates the chairs?'

'Yes, sir.'

'Then do you happen to have any idea who . . .?' He nodded to right and left.

'Yes, sir, of course. I've placed Mr Farrell on your right, sir, that was at his suggestion, and you have Mr Cato on your left.'

'Thank you, Hay.' He rubbed his eyes. It really was a beautiful day. 'Were you a soldier?'

'Navy, sir. Commandos.'

'Royals, eh? Good show. Dieppe?'

'Yes, sir. And Sicily.'

'How do you find all this after all that?'

'Very happy, sir. I was on the *Milly* for ten years before.'

'The *Milly*?'

'*Carmelia*, sir. Below decks she's always been the *Milly*.'

'I see. Well, she seems very . . . comfortable. Stable, and so forth.'

'Lord yes, sir. Sweet as a duck, that's the *Milly*. Always has been. Not like the *Mary*. The *Mary* was always a little tender, in my opinion. Roll the tea from your cup if there was a sea on. But the *Milly*, sir, no. She's sweet. Sweet as a duck. Bouillon all right, sir?'

'Yes, very good.'

'Some gentlemen prefer it with a dash of sherry and peppers. Perhaps you'd care to . . .?'

'Tomorrow, perhaps. Tell me, Hay. Are there many of
you left from before?'

'One or two, sir, one or two. Of the ones I joined up
with though, no. They're all gone. St Nazaire.'

'I'm very sorry.'

'They was good lads, sir. Singing as they died. Was there
anything else, sir?'

'No thanks, Hay. That's all.'

'Thank you, sir. Oh, and it's Dusty, sir. Everyone calls
me Dusty.'

'A thick smell, you say. And a dark brownish colour.' Pale
eyes thoughtful in his long face, Montmorency leant forward towards Cato over the white-painted steel table which
did service as his consulting desk.

'Well, to tell you the truth, old son, so was mine.' He
smiled briefly. 'And so probably was everybody's who had
the asparagus and the beetroot last night. They do rather
have that effect on the old Jimmy Riddle. Set your mind
at ease?'

Cato's relief was so overpowering that he felt faint. His
chest thumped, there was a champagne prickling at the
edge of his vision, and for a moment he had to reach for
the table's edge to prevent himself from falling. Montmorency, whose attention had been diverted to a search of the
pockets of his white coat, appeared not to notice. Cato
steadied himself, and blinking in the suddenly brilliant-
seeming light from the porthole, looked around the surgery.
It was a considerably smaller room than the cabin that he
shared with his father, and in the place of panelling and
decoration were plain steel bulkheads and a glass and metal
cabinet on whose shelves, to the engine's vibration, the
instruments minutely buzzed and danced. Behind
Montmorency's desk and hardwood chair hung a portrait
of the Royal Family and several framed photographs of
budgerigars to which rosettes had been pinned. The doctor,

as Cato had immediately recognised, was the man from the train, the third passenger.

Leaning back in his chair, his search finally successful, Montmorency lit one of his Gold Flakes and rested it on the edge of an enamel kidney-bowl. As an afterthought to this action he offered the packet to Cato, who hesitantly removed one of the cork-tipped cigarettes. Patiently, the doctor stared down at his shoes as the boy, his hands still unsteady, wielded the heavy desk lighter.

'The other thing, the operation. Worried about that at all?'

Smoke curled upwards from Montmorency's narrow mouth, and was drawn into his nostrils. Like a film, thought Cato, his earlier lightheadedness augmented by tobacco. Like a film of a waterfall in reverse.

'It's difficult', he began, 'to know exactly which bit to worry about, really. I've read a bit about heart operations. I know . . . I do know they can fail.'

Montmorency nodded, and blew a smoke ring. 'The Yanks are pretty good,' he said. 'Better than us in this field. They won't fail. It's a pretty routine procedure for them.'

'How do you do that?' asked Cato. 'Blow smoke rings, I mean?'

Montmorency smiled. 'It's a bit like a snake striking. You have to retract your lower jaw and then click it forwards. The smoke's pushed out round your tongue, like a doughnut.'

Cato tried several times. On the third attempt he succeeded in launching a tremulous circle across the desk. Montmorency, weighing the silver desk lighter in his hands, nodded.

'There's a snake,' said Cato, pleased with himself, 'talking of snakes, in the hold. A King Cobra, twelve feet long. A beauty.'

'Is there, by God?' Montmorency looked up. 'And who's

in charge of that, then? I'll need serum lodged with me for the duration of the crossing. Whose is it?'

'A chap called Max Amber,' said Cato. 'A zoologist. He's taking it to Chicago. Shall I tell him you want to see him?'

'You might,' said Montmorency, glancing at his watch and crushing the cigarette into the enamel bowl. 'Know about snakes, then?' he asked.

'Not really,' admitted Cato. He stared, unseeing, at the shelved trays of instruments. 'Can I ask you something?'

Montmorency nodded.

'When they operate on the heart, how exactly do they . . . get at it. I mean from underneath, or through the sternum, or how?'

The long marsupial features watched him, expressionless. 'Has this been . . . worrying you?'

'Well, I have been wondering a bit. Out of curiosity and so on. As one does.'

Montmorency, hesitating, steepled his fingers. 'The answer, old son, is that I'm not sure. If I find out for you, will you promise to put the whole thing from your mind?'

'Okay.'

'Promise?'

'Promise.'

'Good. In the meantime, and I promised your Dad I'd say this, go easy on the drink. No more than a glass or two at dinner – wine, not spirits – don't over-exert yourself, use the lifts rather than the stairs, et cetera, et cetera, et cetera. I expect', he glanced at the notes in front of him, 'Dr Wheeler's told you all this already?'

'Pretty much,' agreed Cato.

Montmorency nodded to himself, and then leaned back in the chair. 'Let me ask you something. At school, when everyone else was playing soccer and cricket and so on, what did you do?'

'I . . .' Cato shrugged his narrow shoulders. 'Oh, I just shuffled around on the touchline.'

Montmorency regarded him in silence for several

moments, nodded, and handed him a card. 'Right, then. You can telephone me at any time, either here or in my cabin. And whatever you do, don't *worry*. Remember,' he smiled palely, marsupially, 'worse things happen at sea.'

The sun was overhead and the sea like slate, silvered and burred. There was wind at Cato's face as he stood at the Boat Deck rail, but only the wind of their twenty-knot progress. There was no land, no cloud, no feature, only the ship's drumming heart-beat and her forward, singing swathe. I longed for this, thought Cato – the singing at his ears – and it is no less than I longed for.

Perhaps, he thought, there is always a certain unsweetened pleasure to be found in forward movement, no matter how fearful the destination. Those named and nameless riflemen scoring their passing presences into the ship's rail, knowing as they did so to what every nautical mile drew them closer, must have fought that same pleasure, fought the joy of their progress through sea and sky. And some, surely, must have allowed themselves to be subdued by it. We race to death, thought Cato, or at the very least we like a cracking pace. The horizon dissolved to a history-book illustration of Charles I, surrounded by clergymen and halberdiers, marching briskly to the scaffold through autumn leaves, and then suddenly and ludicrously Cato was in the headmaster's study at Newton Priors, bending over the chintzed arm of a chair with his shorts around his ankles, waiting to be caned for talking after lights-out. The problem was that the headmaster, a pedagogue of integrity if some austerity, had been unable to open the tallboy drawer which contained the cane. Finally he had had to require that Cato take one scrolled handle and he the other, and between them they had finally eased open the drawer. None of his own efforts, Cato remembered, had been less than enthusiastic. He could no more have further jammed the drawer than poor King Charles, he supposed, could have *dawdled* . . .

'Mr Cato, is it, sir? I'm sorry, Mr Cato, didn't mean to startle you. Dusty, sir, Dusty Hay. Deck steward. There's a chair reserved for you on the port side, forward. Can I . . .?'

Cato looked round into a pair of dark, concerned eyes set in a creased and brilliantined cannonball of a head. Dusty Hay was a little shorter than Cato, but easily twice as broad.

'Ummm . . . yes. Of course. Thank you very much.'

'I've placed you next to Mrs MacLean, sir. It was the lady's own suggestion.'

Cato was amazed. What possible interest could he hold for the glamorous Ayrest MacLean? Perhaps, he thought, she was simply looking for some peace and quiet, someone who wouldn't pester her. Gratification spread warmly through him. She would having nothing to fear. He would be the soul of . . .

'This way, sir. I told your father as soon as I saw you I'd bring you over.'

Cato followed Dusty's broad figure in its sparkling whites into the sudden darkness at the head of the interior stairs. They crossed the carpeted interior and exited on the port side.

'The sea seems very . . . calm,' said Cato, squinting.

'It seems so, sir. This your first crossing?'

'Yes.'

'Not your father's though, I'd guess.'

'What makes you say that?' asked Cato.

'Asked for a chair on the port side, sir. More sun that side, and less weather. The weather comes from the north in the Atlantic, by and large.'

'They went on the *Mauretania* once, I know that . . .'

Dusty nodded. They continued forward past an almost continuous line of rug-covered, immobile figures. Some of these were reading, some smoking, some conversing. Most however, were simply lying there, torpid, beneath a splintering midday sun.

Reginald and Jerry Farrell looked up, shading their eyes.
Farrell was telling a story, illustrating his points with stabs
of a small foul-smelling pipe. He looked a little more subdued than the day before, in so far as his furiously crimped
eye allowed him to look subdued at all.

'Here you are, sir,' said Dusty.

'Safe and sound from the sawbones, eh?' said Farrell to
Cato. 'Never trust a medicine man. Heap big trouble. Arse
swing low in shit-storm.' He barked mirthlessly. 'How's
the head?'

'On the mend, I think,' said Cato, trying to enter into
the spirit of things. 'Sorry about last night.'

'Never apologise, never explain. Ain't that right, Reggie?'

'Within reason, I suppose,' said Reginald.

'Will you be needing another rug, sir?' asked the steward.

'I'll be fine, Dusty,' said Cato. 'Thanks very much.'

He lowered himself experimentally to the cushioned
deckchair and drew up the rug. It was extremely comfortable, so comfortable that for a moment he felt almost guilty.
Experimentally again, conscious of the presence of the two
men, he closed his eyes. The sun was bright against his
eyelids, and a carnelian translucency swam before him. He
was aware, pleasurably, of the minute rise and fall of the
ship.

'As I said,' he heard Farrell resume, 'we're waiting up
in a wadi line above the bay, Docherty on the three-incher
and other bods variously disposed – hot as stink – when
the planes and gliders start coming in and before you can
say Cobham's Circus the sky's full of confetti. The day's
like today – May, of course, not June, but gin-clear, dark
blue sky – and as each parachute snapped open you could
see this little puff of French chalk drifting away.
*Fallschirmjäger*, you see; packed 'em themselves. And the
parachutes all different colours – blue, pink, green, yellow
– really frightfully jolly, and all you had to do was draw a
bead on the man with a .303 – boys, of course, most of
'em, as it turned out – drop a yard, and wallop, coconut.

Bit like shooting low hens, of course, but then no one invited the buggers round in the first place. Anyway, there's yours truly, bollocks-to-dust, ammo low, and – I remember this particularly – some Greek bloody cactus working its way stealthily up my arse, when a call comes over the net from Roddy at Brigade HQ. "Jerry, old man," he said, "if you haven't got anything special on, I wonder if you'd drop by . . ." '

'And what did you say to that?' Cato heard his father enquire, as if at some distance.

'Well, I told him not thwacking likely, that he may not have noticed but that up here we had the best part of a ruddy airborne division dropping by.'

'And how did he take that?'

'Oh, pretty high in the chest, but you know these desk-pilots. Anyway, at this point yours truly has a brain-wave. As well as the PIATs, we've got these Holophane lamps, six-volt battery jobbies, and . . .'

Cato slid from half-attention to sleep.

He opened his eyes to silence. At his side, his father, his features all but concealed by a broad-checked steamer cap, appeared to be asleep. Whether he actually was asleep, Cato was unsure; there was something in the exactly symmetrical disposition of his tweeded limbs that suggested at least partial consciousness.

Beyond Reginald, Farrell was certainly asleep. His jaw had fallen to his collar, and white mucous webs flexed at the corners of his open mouth. At the foot of Farrell's chair, leaning on the rail with the air of a man accustomed to long periods of semi-vigilance, was the narrow-featured figure of Docherty. Docherty was in shirt-sleeve order, his forearms as brown as his face and blued by ancient tattoos. A clip secured his nondescript tie, and a broad leather belt his demobilisation trousers. At intervals, as he stared expressionlessly out to sea, he raised to his lips a small crystal glass of some darkish spirit.

There was something odd about the glass, Cato noticed: its faceted stem tapered to a point. It appeared to have no base.

Turning to reach for his book, he saw that the chair next to him had been occupied while he was asleep. With a start of apprehensive pleasure, he recognised the recumbent figure as that of Mrs MacLean. A feathered hat slanted from the pale roll of her hair, shadowing her features, and her eyes were closed. Lifting and opening *The Case of the Gilded Fly* at random in front of him, he covertly examined her.

The feathers, he saw, were pheasant tail-feathers, long and glossed, their tips indicating both their wearer's breathing and the faint vibration of the ship. Beneath them, against the pale profile, lay the severe parallels of brows, lashes, shaded cheekbones and minutely parted mouth. A grey tailored jacket, whose gentle rise and fall Cato considered at some length, disappeared at the level of her waist beneath the Royal Albion rug. Despite her twice-married status her hands were free of rings, and lay lightly freckled and loosely clasped in her lap. Slowly Cato turned his head. No one moved. His father retained his attitude of medieval repose, and Farrell's breathing was silent. Docherty, at the rail with his baseless glass, was a figurehead, carved.

Cato's eyes, over the top of his book, returned to Mrs MacLean. Without knowing why especially, he wanted to identify signs of the oblique in her, of the vulnerable. He found, frowning into the light, the all but imperceptible slipping of the tortoiseshell comb from the shadowed honey-roll of her hair. An hour, perhaps, and the comb would fall, would clatter soundlessly to the deck. He found the drawn line of the pencil in the long eyebrows, and on the lowered eyelids, the finger-touch of created shadow. And then, to his wanting eyes, the rest – the vanished smiles, the tiny gathers of care, the whole powdered fretwork of the past – revealed itself, and he longed to lift the small boned and freckled hands (he knew exactly how they would feel: hard, soft, a little cold) and press them to his lips.

At that moment she opened her eyes, and discovered his speculative gaze. It was too late to pretend that he had been reading his book – that he hadn't been frankly staring at her – but the grey-green eyes held curiosity rather than affront, and passive, he allowed himself to be submerged in their cool regard. It was a situation, he thought vaguely, happily, of extraordinary intimacy; it was as if they had just woken in a double bed together.

'You're not very well, are you?' she asked, finally.

'I didn't feel so good last night,' said Cato hesitantly. 'I'm Okay now, though.'

'You know what I mean.' Her eyes were thoughtful, void of indulgence.

'Yes,' he said eventually. 'No. I'm not.'

She nodded, and looking to the horizon, drew the velvet collar of her coat to her chin.

'How do you come to know about me?' asked Cato.

There was a long silence, a silence which drew to itself all sound and within which he felt himself suspended.

'Oh, I like to know who's who,' she answered eventually. 'And that film man was talking about you. Pierre. He said it was a damn shame about your . . . illness.'

'When did he say this, exactly?' asked Cato.

'Last night, on deck.'

'Ah.'

So she and Pierre had met and talked, he thought. He and Max must have been in the hold at the time.

'Did you know', he asked, 'that there's a King Cobra on the ship, being taken to the Chicago Zoo?'

'Yes, the Captain told me at dinner. A truly horrible thought.'

'There was a doctor once', said Cato, 'who wanted to give me a course of treatments using cobra venom.'

'How fascinating.'

'The doctor was German. He was interned in the north

of England somewhere. The whole thing became impossible.'

'Might it have worked?'

'There were successes, apparently. Especially in the treatment of what they call "intractable pain".'

'Intractable pain,' she murmured, smiling. 'Yes.'

Her gaze left him, released him to the breeze, the salt and slanting light, the distant rush of the sea.

With the noon whistle, she rose to leave. At the rail Docherty drained his baseless glass and slipped it, stem first, into a trouser pocket. Moments later, Dusty passed them with a tray, and an elderly woman on the chair next to Farrell called the steward over, revealing amongst her furs a small Pekinese dog.

'This', she explained to Dusty, blinking querulous exophthalmic eyes, 'is Snorkly-Porkly.' She pulled a stiff little handkerchief from her cuff, wiped the dog's nose, and raked its fur with fond, rheumatic fingers. 'The cabin steward said that you might very kindly see to his business . . .'

'Of course, Mrs Klampmayer,' said Dusty. 'I'll send a bellboy. How far does he usually . . .?'

'Oh . . . From Clarges Street to the Ritz, perhaps. It always seems like miles, but I don't suppose it can be so terribly many.'

'I'll have a word with one of the bellboys, madam.'

'Thank you, that's *most* kind.'

With Dusty's departure, Farrell, Reginald, Docherty and Cato began to make their way towards the stairs. As they did so, they were approached by an improbable young man in tennis whites and a silk dressing gown.

'Morning, Corker,' said Jerry Farrell.

'Good morning to you, Jeremiah. Great day. Have you . . .? Ah,' he raised a hand to Reginald, 'there he is. And the lad. Looking somewhat jollier, I might say, than at our last meeting!' He winked at Cato, contorted his features as if to suggest strabismic Irishry, and tugged an imaginary forelock. ''Twas the drink, yer honour . . .' He laughed, twitched grotesquely, and then, intercepting Docherty's pale gaze, swiftly realigned his features. Turning to Reginald, he held out an envelope. 'Your winnings, Reggie. Have to allow us another rubber or two, of course. Win it all back.'

Reginald looked bemused. He looked from the improbable young man to Farrell and back again.

'I had no idea', he began, 'that we were playing for money . . .'

'One for one, old boy,' said the young man. 'House rules.' He placed the envelope in the pocket of Reginald's Norfolk jacket. 'Just as well I'm an honest chap, eh? Chump more like. Fool to myself. Still, time and tide, eh?' He sauntered off, leaving Reginald staring after him.

'Nice fellow, Corker,' said Farrell eventually. 'Rotten bridge-player, though, by all accounts.'

They dispersed to their cabins.

'I was turned down by the Medical Board twice,' said Max, carefully aligning his knife and fork on his empty plate. 'The second time, after I left Cambridge, I went along without my glasses. I managed to get my trousers down and deliver the traditional cough, but then I trod on an RAMC sergeant's boots, and he got rather shirty. I apologised to the weighing machine, and that was it. *Hors de combat.*'

Pierre laughed, and Loelia regarded her husband sourly.

'Must you sound so pleased about it?' she asked, touching her mouth with her napkin and darting a glance at Pierre. 'It's hardly a matter for self-congratulation.'

'Well, I *was* pleased, if I'm honest,' said Max, twisting the sapphire ring around his index finger. 'I would have made a perfectly rotten soldier. As it was, I was able to perform a genuinely useful function.'

'At the zoo,' said Loelia, quietly, drawing a cigarette from the packet in front of her. 'Vital work indeed.'

'As it happens, yes,' said Max evenly. 'It was vital in its way. Do you know where we got the meat for the animals from, Pierre?'

'No,' said Pierre.

'Battersea Dogs Home,' said Max. 'For some reason there were more strays than anyone could remember. I'd drive a vanful up to Regent's Park every day.'

Somehow, Cato found it impossible to imagine the fastidious-seeming Max at the wheel of a van, let alone hefting dog carcases.

'Why is it', asked Loelia, exhaling smoke, 'that you always insist on telling that story when people are eating.'

'Everybody's finished,' said Max. 'Unless you intend a return match with that chop.'

'Don't be disgusting,' said Loelia.

Conversationally, the table had divided. Jerry Farrell had joined them, abandoning his previous table, and had attached himself to Reginald. (Docherty, it seemed, despite the dispensation permitting him to attend Farrell on the Promenade Deck, took his meals in the Tourist Class dining room.) Although Farrell had so far ignored both Pierre and Max, from time to time he directed cannonfire stares at Loelia, to which she responded with a studied lowering of the eyes. If her husband noticed these exchanges, he did not show it.

'The worst things, of course,' Max continued, 'were the KBOs.'

'The . . .?' Pierre raised his eyebrows.

'Killed By Orders,' explained Max. 'As a snake man I was particularly badly hit. The day war was declared orders came down to kill every venomous snake in the place; cobras, kraits, vipers, tiger snakes, mambas . . . everything. I think someone at the Home Office had an idea of bombs falling on the Reptile House and Puff Adders escaping into Regent's Park. If I'd been more senior at the time I might have been able to do something; there was no question, for example, of killing the big cats.'

'Did any animals escape?' asked Pierre.

'A Capuchin monkey', said Max, 'spent an afternoon in an oak tree. There was an incident in Parkway with a zebra. And we lost an echidna and a pair of llamas to shrapnel. Other than that, I'm afraid, we did the rest in ourselves. I remember the day they killed poor old Jumbo. This awful phoney white-hunter type came over from one of the Mayfair gunmakers with a sort of flat canvas suitcase. None of us could bear to watch. We all sat in one of the keepers' lodges with our tea getting colder and colder, waiting for the bang. In the end there were four bangs. And if you can imagine ten middle-aged men in peaked caps sitting on a bench, smoking, tears streaming down their faces . . .'

'Oh, for God's *sake*!' said Loelia, snatching her cigarettes, and getting abruptly to her feet. 'If you can't be amusing, at least . . .'

With a shiver of cutlery, her back-flung chair struck the table behind her. Startled, its occupants looked round, but Loelia was half-way to the staircase. There was a moment's silence. Max spread his hands in helpless if ironic apology, and Farrell, half-rising, peered after her departing figure.

'Must have been something you said,' he called to Max, who made no response. 'I said . . . Oh, never mind.' He blotted his bad eye with his napkin as he sat down. 'Bitch pack,' he murmured to Reginald. 'Can't be too careful.'

There was a further silence. Cato applied himself to plum fool and custard.

'Any plans for the afternoon?' Max asked Pierre casually, reaching for a tangerine.

'There's . . . um, some work I've been meaning to get down to in the cabin,' Pierre replied. 'Couple of things that need tinkering with.'

'Poems?' asked Cato.

Pierre nodded.

'You write poetry as well as films?' asked Max.

'Oh, I've been trying to put a collection together for years now. A little late in the day, as I was saying to Cato last night, the Muse having rather taken French leave, but . . .' He shrugged. 'Let's just say that if I can hammer out another quatrain or two I can sell my soul to the Devil with a clear conscience.'

'I'm impressed,' said Max.

'Don't be,' replied Pierre. 'Pure self-indulgence.'

Max removed the skin of the tangerine with slender, careful fingers. 'From the sublime to the ridiculous,' he said to Cato, 'I thought I might give the deck games a try.'

Cato looked up, surprised.

'Purely in the role of spectator, of course,' said Max. He consulted his schedule, 'It says here that they are to be played on the aft Main Deck from fifteen to sixteen hundred hours.'

'Sounds like fun,' said Cato, without enthusiasm. He felt he had done enough spectating for one lifetime.

With an hour to go before the games, he was once more supine on the Boat Deck. His father was attending to some paperwork in their cabin, and of their earlier group, only Snorkly-Porkly and his fur-swathed owner remained, the latter's face concealed behind the *Tatler*. The sun, Cato noticed, had moved several degrees towards the ship's bow.

Unable to sleep, Cato decided to accompany Tudor and Snorkly-Porkly on their walk. Their progress, he thought, was unlikely to be exhausting, and so it proved. For every yard forward, the Pekinese scuttled in several tight circles around their feet.

'I'm afraid I can't remember much about last night,' said Cato, raising his eyes to the bulk of a suspended lifeboat, 'except for the snake.'

'I've seen some things on this ship,' said Tudor, ruminatively pinching his nose and sniffing, 'but I never seen a . . . what was it?'

'King Cobra.'

73

'Eat dogs, do they, King Cobras?'

''Spect so.'

'Hear that, Porkfat?' Tudor drew the dog towards him over the bleached decking. 'Any more, an' you're for the bleedin' snake.' Snorkly-Porkly's response was to revolve, nodding and panting enthusiastically, on his anus.

'You should come down the Pig some evening,' said Tudor, leaning on the rail and thoughtfully watching the turning Pekinese. 'Show you things there'd . . .'

'That girl,' said Cato. 'What was all that?'

'Girl?' asked Tudor.

'That . . . down in the Third Class.'

'Oh, *that*. Well, just a . . . You don't want to bother with them bloods in Third.'

'What did she say?'

'She was wondering what was wrong with you, is all. Your mate told her to sling it.'

'Ah.'

'They like to get a look-in, see how the other half live. Cabin and that.'

At their feet, Snorkly-Porkly delivered himself of a small ochraceous nut of excrement. Unfortunately, he appeared at some point to have swallowed a length of parcel twine and the turdlet bobbed along behind the dog like a conker. The two sixteen-year-olds peered down interestedly.

'I ought to call a Tabby.'

'Tabby?'

'Stewardess,' said Tudor. 'They have scissors.'

'I've got some paper,' said Cato. 'Maybe you could just . . . pull.' They looked at each other.

'Give us it, then.'

Cato handed over his copy of the afternoon's schedule. 'You're going to have to help me,' said Tudor. 'Hold 'im down.' Cato placed one hand on Snorkly-Porkly's jewelled collar, and the other in the thick fur at his back. The dog looked up at them with glossy, suspicious eyes.

'Okay,' said Tudor. 'Hold tight.' He lowered the folded sheet towards the animal's hindquarters.

The scream which followed was of extraordinary pitch and volume. Strolling passengers stopped dead in their tracks, and Dusty came running.

'What you doin' to that animal, Tudor. Begging your pardon, sir.' Cato stood back as Tudor indicated the remaining problem.

'String, eh? Get one of the butchers to grease 'im up.'

'Yes, Mr Hay.'

'Sharpish, lad.'

Gathering up Snorkly-Porkly with distasteful care, Tudor retreated into the ship.

'Man for every problem,' Dusty told Cato. 'Were you going for the games, sir?'

'It's probably rather more fun to do', said Max, 'than to watch.' He, Cato and Loelia were standing, with a number of others, on the companionway traversing the aft Main Deck. The Ambers' lunchtime spat appeared to have been forgotten.

Below them, watched by several hundred spectators, the 'Needle and Cigarette Race' was under way. Six men and six women, all of them, Cato guessed, drawn from the Tourist Third Cabins, were hunched in concentration. The men, apparently, were attempting to thread a needle with soft wool, the women to light a single match (and thus a cigarette) without the use of a matchbox. Both endeavours were rendered considerably more difficult by a stiffish breeze.

For more than five minutes, nothing happened. Cato looked away. On the grey sea behind them, the broad road of their passing, furrowed pale green by the twin screws, disappeared to the horizon.

There was a smattering of applause from below, and Cato looked round to see a woman – a girl, really – holding up a smoking cigarette.

'Oh, you *clever* little thing,' said Loelia, refastening the knot of her scarf, which was printed with a design of Airedale dogs. 'Did you see, darling? She lit it on her teeth.'

It was the girl of the night before, Cato saw. Even from a distance he recognised her flat, plain features. Success and the occasion, however, had bestowed on her a certain larky distinctiveness. She seemed a popular winner, and as the purser stepped forwards with her prize, she dropped into a mock curtsy. 'She'll remember this moment', said Loelia, without obvious irony, 'all her life.'

For fifteen seconds the girl held smiling and self-conscious sway, and then 'Whoops McGiffin' was announced.

For this event, a gymnasium beam was erected, and pairs of male passengers competed to unseat each other with pillows. Few of the contests lasted for more than half a minute; either a competitor slipped off-balance or his pillow split, leaving him defenceless as feathers whirled over the stern. Amongst the grimmer of the competitors was Docherty. Compact, seemingly impossible to dislodge, he had a way of blinding opponents with a whirlwind of blows to the face and then suddenly sideswiping them to the ground. A number of opponents were dispatched in this way, until, tiring, Docherty found himself opposite a bald and unsmiling tub of a man in vest and braces. Shouts arose for both competitors, the crowd edged forward, and Cato saw money passing hands. 'Too thrilling,' murmured Loelia.

But Docherty had shot his bolt. His opponent, squat, canny, and with a low centre of gravity, proved unbeatable. He had seen Docherty's moves, was ready for them all, and five minutes later was receiving a bottle of South African sherry from the purser. Cato was all the more surprised, therefore, to see a fatigued-looking Docherty waiting amongst the competitors for 'Are You There, Mike?'

This game involved the blindfolding, gagging and hood-ing of the competitors – again, all male – who were then required to squirm on their bellies attempting to land blows to the upper bodies of their opponents with rubber truncheons.

'British working man,' said Jerry Farrell's voice at Cato's shoulder. 'Bloody marvellous, eh? Must admit, though, my money was on that Lancastrian coal-heaver in the last. Knew the old bog-jockey didn't have the wind for a long 'un. Sent him straight back in to bat, though, and this time he may surprise us. Stealth, you see. Docherty's long suit.'

Farrell was right. In order to win a round, competitors had to land ten blows fair and square. Docherty, ears to the ground, lay unmoving, certain in the knowledge that his confused opponent would find his way to him. Finally, hearing breathing, he would rear like a snake, his truncheon a blur.

'Softly, softly, catchee monkey,' said Farrell, as the field thinned. 'Good lad.'

Faced with his final opponent, Docherty took advantage of the crowd's murmur to retreat to the furthest corner of the chalked arena. There, truncheon raised, he waited. His opponent, having witnessed the earlier success of this tactic, did likewise. For fifteen minutes the crowd stood in silence as the two men lay gagged, hooded and unmoving in opposite corners. Finally Docherty's opponent, gasping, rolled on his back, and was disqualified.

'Cramp,' explained Farrell. 'Sniper's doom. That's me a pony the richer. Tea?'

'This is definitely my favourite place on the ship,' said Farrell. 'I could *live* in this jolly old *fumoir*.'

'Jolly' would not have been Cato's choice of adjective. To his eye neither the parchment-shaded wall-lights nor the shadowless wash from the skylight quite succeeded in dispelling the smoking room's oaken and refectorial gloom. Despite the room's considerable volume, only a handful of their fellow-passengers were present. These, pipe-smokers for the most part, occupied their heavy leatherette chairs in silence. Farrell led Cato to an alcove to one side of the manorial fireplace in which a number of tables were set for cards and chess. Beating at his pockets, he assembled briar, spills and pouch, and disposed himself in the same expansive attitude as the friar in the coaching-inn scene above his head.

'You see, old boy, we're basically a *backs-to-the-wall* kind of a people. I mean, look at Dunkirk, look at Docherty, look at *all this*, for God's sake. I was saying the same thing to your father and although he plays his cards damn close to his chest, I'm certain he agrees. Certain of it.'

A tail-coated waiter materialised at the door. Farrell placed one hand over the other in a T-shape and followed it with two fingers. The waiter nodded and withdrew.

'So what do you think?'

Cato was unsure on what subject his opinion was being sought.

'I think when it comes down to it,' he began cautiously, 'most people would go along with your . . .'

'Of *course* they would,' nodded Farrell, sucking energetically at his pipe-dottle. 'Of course they would.'

A second waiter entered, tiptoed over to the chimney, knelt, and reached behind the dog grate. Pale electric light illuminated the brickwork fireplace. The waiter touched a second switch, and the bulbs looped beneath the baronial shields at the cornice glowed red.

Farrell rubbed his hands together energetically. 'Makes you wish it was winter, eh? Wassail and so on.'

To Cato, no illusion could have given a more exact impression of that dour season. He reached out and touched the greave of one of the carved armigerous figures above the table. It had a cold, dull bloom. Farrell, staring pensively at the oval shaft of light from the roof, wiped his tongue on a handkerchief.

'North Atlantic, of course,' he observed. 'Always a sort of winter.'

As if compelled by their surroundings, they sat in silence until the arrival of the tea. Despite the room's function as a male chummery, its darkwood fittings and cold light seemed to Cato to propose an unbending temperance. He thought of the girl, of her pitiless curiosity. He thought of her triumph, of her waving arms and self-conscious laughter. You were only yourself, he supposed vaguely, with your own people.

'Okay,' said Farrell, pocketing his pipe, pouch and matches as the waiter withdrew, 'House jaw.' Slowly, with the tongs, he dropped five lumps of sugar into his tea, crunching them as they dissolved with the back of an apostle spoon. Cato, embarrassed, stared up at the cornice, where amongst the carving he identified several playing-card figures, the Mad Hatter, and the entwined roses of York and Lancaster.

'When you *really* have your back to the wall,' said Farrell, 'Gatling jammed and captain dead, that sort of thing . . .' He rubbed absently at his eye, and opened his hands to Cato. 'Look, let me tell you a story, not all of it untrue.' He raised his cup. 'We – that is, elements of Ida Brigade – were in a re-entrant outside . . . well, never mind where, but in the White Mountains. Bad place, bugger-all cover, sun above. Platoon under sustained fire, source: twenty-millimetre light anti-aircraft gun sited on axis of advance plus multifarious other small arms. Long story short, J. Farrell Esquire pinned down, nose in rockface, finger up fundament. Two choices. Wait for it or go for it. Decided to go for it.

'Now what I'm about to tell you lasted, what, a fraction of a second, if that long, so bear with me. But as I got up, whacked in a new magazine, I had what I can only call – and this sounds damn silly, I know – a vision.

'Greek hillside, twenty-millimetre gun, sheepshit, whole shooting match disappears, and I'm back in England, in a village I've never actually been to, but – if you get my drift – always known. It's spring, there's a duckpond with weeping willows and a boy and a dog and a pub, and I know from the churchbells that it's Sunday morning, opening time, and that if I go into the pub there'll be some . . . good fellows there, friends I've lost, and they'll smile and they'll nod and they'll say, "Well, Jerry," they'll say, "*you*'ve taken your time, old lad . . ." '

He stared down at his tea and rubbed his nose. 'And the thing that I understand at that moment, bright as day, is why I'm there on that hill, what the hell I'm fighting for.' He dabbed at the crimped eye with his handkerchief. 'Damned sawbones. Still got half Normandy in there.'

'What happened?' asked Cato, after an interval of silence.

'Oh . . . took the position. Shot my way through. Meindl's glider-boys, most of them. Still had the sick on their smocks. Brave enough, though.'

Cato, at a loss for words, nodded.

'Your father had a word with me,' continued Farrell. 'Your seeing the medicine men, and so on. Said I'd have a word. He wouldn't hear of it, at first, typical Ops. Int., but I talked him round. Been under the ether once or twice myself, I told him, know the S.O.Ps.' He drained the tea, and spooned the undissolved sugar into his mouth. 'So there you have it, anyway. Jaw over.'

'Thank you,' said Cato.

'Don't mention it, old boy. Don't mention it. Glad we've had the chance to . . .' He lowered the cup and reached for his smoking paraphernalia. 'Isn't this a marvellous place, though?' He indicated a primitive arrangement of chain and steel teeth suspended from the wall. 'What d'you suppose *that*'s for, then?'

'Trap of some kind, perhaps?' ventured Cato.

''Spect so. Docherty'll know. Probably carries a couple round in his trousers. Coiled spring, you see. Wonder if there's a chance of some more hot water?'

It was with something like disbelief that Cato discovered, on deck, a clear late summer's afternoon. Making his way forward along the port side, he discovered the fur-swathed woman studying the passenger list with Snorkly-Porkly in her lap, Mrs MacLean in an elegant trance-like state, and, reclining in his own chair, Pierre Watson.

'Listen to this,' said Pierre.

Cato, seeing that Pierre had no intention of surrendering his seat, sat in his father's place.

It was a beautiful day: I was finished.
They said, of course, as they do, that I was still there,
that it was a beautiful day, but I had nothing left,
and saying nothing much, made safe,
let in the rushing calm,
and closed off time.

In the black tank of silence,
(the wind, much later, rain, against the tank)
Open-eyed, submerged, the rise and fall with breathing,
   open-eyed,
the lick of tears, but dark, and unborn years from
   hearing or from sight,
I knew the lies we tell,
I saw our rebirth into night.

He held the book like an actor, single-handed, and read with an actor's delivery. Cato wondered if Ayrest MacLean was asleep, as he could not help but feel that this recitation had been intended principally for her ears.

'What do you think of that?' asked Pierre.

'Yours?' asked Cato.

'Sadly, no,' said Pierre. 'Roy Cadwaladr again. He wrote it in the spring of '44. Dead by the summer's end. I think personally that he knew he wasn't going to make it, that he'd made a kind of peace with himself.'

'It doesn't sound', said Cato hesitantly, 'as if he liked what he saw coming . . . after.'

'None of us did,' said Pierre, and Cato was certain that

whether or not Ayrest MacLean was listening, Pierre was addressing her.

'Do you think he wanted to die, though?'

'I think that . . . he saw the ending of one thing as the beginning of another. It's easy enough to talk, as what's-his-name did in *Horizon*, of a stone lifted in Central Europe. What Roy used to say, when he was drunk enough, is that when you finally looked beneath the stone all that you saw was a mirror. Which sounds sententious in the cold light of day, but at the time . . . You have to imagine quite a short bloke, shorter than me anyway, but broad, solid as a rock, and when he was drinking he'd square up to you, swaying, reeking of beer, like a prizefighter, every word a punch . . .'

'Did you know many of that set?' asked Cato.

'You *saw* everyone, sooner or later . . .' Pierre looked towards the rail and the sea. 'It was Roy's height, you know, or lack of it, that killed him. Jumped out of the landing craft into six feet of water with a radio on his back. Never came up. They always gave him the radio, he once told me, because it was heavy and he was clever.' He shook his head, and smiled. 'He would have approved of the name, though. "Sword Beach," he'd have said, "now *there's* a place to die, boy . . ." '

'Things must be better,' said Cato, when the resonance of this last observation had faded. 'I mean, here we are. We can get on with things. Here this all is.'

'True,' said Pierre. 'I almost a hundred per cent agree. I more than ninety-nine per cent agree. I less than one per cent disagree. And that fraction of one per cent I would give anything to ignore. Do you know the story of the princess and the pea?'

'Yes,' said Cato, squinting at the almost imperceptible rise and fall of the *Carmelia*'s bow against the horizon. He suddenly very much wanted a glass of whisky and a cigarette. (At Cleeve they had collected dog-ends in tins. The resultant tobacco-mix, known in sixth-form code as

'Turban', gave a pungent smoke that kicked at the lungs like a mule, especially when rolled in a page of *The Anglican Hymnal*.)

Beyond Pierre, he saw Ayrest MacLean climb to her feet, reach to her hat with both hands, flutter her gloved fingers at Snorkly-Porkly, and depart.

There was silence. Pierre yawned, without covering his mouth, and stretched.

'I saw her once. In town.'

Cato raised his eyebrows.

'Come on, let's . . .' He climbed to his feet, pushed his hands into his pockets, and head bowed, began to walk. Below them seamen moved purposefully around the foremast and cable decks. 'It was at this pub in Camden Town, up near the artist's shop, called . . . what was it called, something to do with polar bears or the moon. All sorts used to go there, anyway; painters and American forces people, and in the Blitz days, lots of the Ministry film set. Sort of unofficial club. We were all there one night, anyway, tight as ticks – The North Pole, the place was called, that was it – and I remember, some silly ass was playing "In an English Country Garden", over and over again. And in she came. She was with some American press people. They didn't stay long: I think she realised straight away that it wasn't the place for her, that she was too . . . Belgravian, you might call it. And so she spoke to the Americans and they looked around them for a bit and smiled and nodded at everyone and then they all left without buying a drink.'

They continued in silence.

'And that was it.' He lifted the collar of his jacket. 'It's chillier this side.'

'They say starboard's the cold side out,' Cato answered. 'Nothing between us and the Arctic Circle.'

A note at his bedside in his father's precise hand suggested that they meet before dinner. Fatigued, Cato looked at his watch. He had an hour. Treading off his walking shoes and dropping his sports jacket to the floor, he laid himself face downwards on the quilted bedspread. He closed his eyes. The glazed chintz was cool against his face, and his breathing, gentle against the pale cabbage roses, was soon aligned with the muted drum of the engine. Slowly, as the bedspread received him and grew warm, a parade of pale figures processed before the dark cyclorama of his closed eyes. Some of these were recognisable, some were grotesque, none was quite coherent. His father was there, in uniform, as was his mother and a third figure whose face, though shadowed, Cato knew to be assembled of cowrie-teeth and horsehair and spitted bone. They passed by and then receded, to be replaced by others who in their turn briefly revealed themselves and dissolved. And then there were the half-strangers, the forgotten or once-seen, the figures from the newspapers, the film extras, the people from down the road. And as always, they were unsurprised to be there, as Cato himself was unsurprised by their bizarre adjacencies.

Finally, as he knew they would, the Lilliput girls arrived. Sonia appeared first, then Astrid, Heather, and finally Trixie. Urgency crawled at Cato's groin, his eyes opened, and heart steadily pounding, he raised himself from the warm impression in the bedspread.

From the wardrobe, he took his empty overnight case. Reaching inside it, his fingers felt between two unstitched layers of pigskin lining, and drew out a worn manila envelope. Returning to the bed, he switched on the wall-lamp, turned down the bedspread, and loosened his trousers. Arranging himself on his stomach, he drew the first of the Lilliput girls from the manila envelope and laid her on the pillow.

The Lilliput girls had originally been scissored from a clutch of postcard-sized magazines that Cato had discovered behind a lavatory cistern in the Cleeve infirmary. To begin with, he had carried the girls around with him everywhere, had never left them unattended. He had stared at them for minutes, for hours, and had analysed their every shadowed blur, every graded tone-change. Sometimes he had held them at arm's length, allowing them to contract into black-and-white coherence: at other times he had pored over them with a magnifying glass until their contours dissolved into blurred and random-seeming dot-fields. Since the ship's departure, he had not had the chance to take them out. They had waited for him, though, patient and hidden, as he knew they would.

Indulgently, and with the knowledge of better things to come, he examined Sonia. Of all of them, in recent weeks, he had had perhaps the least time for Sonia. She was French, as the Eiffel Tower visible through the shuttered window behind her indicated, but she was also spoiled, passive and overweight. Of all the Lilliput girls she was the fairest-complexioned, and perhaps in this fact lay Cato's equivocal feelings for her. For while her attitude suggested a certain mature accommodation, her heavy body was of such a uniform paleness as to be all but featureless in reproduction. Her breasts, most disappointingly of all, were of a marmoreal and magnifying-glass-defying blankness. Despite these deficiencies, however, Cato retained a certain affection for Sonia, and from time to time still permitted himself her compliance.

The curiously named Astrid, described in the magazine as an Annamite princess, was quite another kettle of fish. Where Sonia was pale, fleshly and cheerful, Astrid was slender, dark of skin, and unsmilingly serious. She knelt on sand, naked but for the sarong at her waist, and plucked gently at a long-necked instrument made from a gourd and what Cato very much feared to be a broomstick. Behind her, not quite in focus, swayed coconut palms. Cato was very fond of Astrid. Of all the Lilliput girls it was Astrid he would have married, given the choice. He knew that she was no princess, that her father was more likely to have been a Lascar seaman than the king of Siam, but it would not have mattered. They would have lived in a hut roofed with palm fronds, her hair would have smelled of coconut, and every night, as the velvet darkness fell, he would have gently unwrapped the leopardskin-print sarong from her small dark-pointed breasts and borne her to the palm-fronded floor.

Conscious of his increasingly rapid heart-beat, of the vacuuming sensation behind his breastbone, Cato closed his eyes. Slowly, he recited the first ten lines of the second book of the *Aeneid* and a substantial section of the Pangbourne bus timetable. For the two minutes that followed, counting off each second, he lay with his eyes closed, and finally the pounding receded. He had – as Dr Wheeler and others had made unequivocally clear – to be careful.

Checking his watch – he still had forty minutes – Cato exchanged Astrid for Heather. The potency of Heather's allure was something that Cato would have been hard put to it to explain. She was the oldest by some years of the Lilliput girls, and – at first sight anyway – easily the least exotic. For a start, with her pinched, rather severe expression and her permanent wave, she was obviously English, as was the standard lamp at her side and the heavy velour armchair in which she sat. The occasional table at her side seemed to further confirm this domestic identity, supporting as it did a blurred portrait photograph, a pair of reading glasses, and a gas-mask. Despite an uncanny resemblance to the sterner of the two assistants at the local public library, however, Heather was quite calculatedly unbuttoning her blouse. As she was not, as it happened, wearing a brassière, this action had the effect of releasing to the pale daylight a pair of disproportionately large breasts. Her gaze at this moment was thoughtful, complicit rather than come-hither, and seemed to indicate a perverse enjoyment of the incompatibility of her actions and her surroundings.

Cato had always been fascinated by Heather. She suggested a world whose existence he had long suspected, a world in which only the most threadbare of curtains – and those liable to be twitched away at any moment – hung between the ordinary and the bizarre. And she *did* look like Miss Corbishley at the library, than whom, it had to be faced, no one could be more ordinary. (On several occasions over the previous holidays the intensity of his stare had unnerved Miss Corbishley. 'What's *wrong* with that boy?' she had demanded of her colleague as Cato, clutching himself through his flannel trousers, had fixed her with a basilisk stare.) His movements on the bedspread now one with the rise and fall of the *Carmelia*, Cato lifted Trixie from the manila envelope. Trixie, Cato could tell from the voluminous hydrangea bush before which she stood, was tiny. A pocket Venus. But not quite a Venus, for there was something detectibly malign about Trixie. Her attitude, hard little breasts out-thrust, hands flat on tight-trousered hips, simultaneously invited and repelled. It was her face, though, vixenish, witchy and – Cato imagined – yellow-eyed, which was somehow her most potently sexual characteristic. She threw herself at him, challenged him with her half-naked body, and yet that evil little face suggested that the consequences of accepting her would be unimaginably dark.

For two long minutes, Trixie held him with her eyes. Where was she? Cato wondered. Where was that scrubby hydrangea growing? In the grounds of a French château, perhaps, or outside some sandswept East Anglian bungalow? He would never know. All that he knew was the potency of her invitation, and the fear, and the approaching dark. He released her, as the darkness clutched his chest, and closed his eyes.

He remembered standing on the Pang bridge, many years ago, with his father. Below them, trout hung in the current like shadows, tilting upwards from time to time to dimple the surface-film. The insects the fish were taking, Reginald had explained, were Mayflies. Like others of the *Ephemeridae*, these insects lived only for a day. They rose to the surface in the morning sunshine as pupae, hatched at midday, selected a mate, and in the evening, their dance of love complete, fluttered to the water and expired. It was curious, Cato mused, the order things took. He feared pain, and he wished not to die. And yet for a collection of lithographic dots on cheap paper, he unhesitatingly risked all. He knew the illogic, but was helpless before the imperative.

He returned to Trixie. After a time, a steady and measured time in which all else went from his mind, he found himself looking at her eyes. They were the flat cold eyes, he saw, of the hamadryad. They willed him to her, willed him to her venom, to exhaustion and death. His eyes closed, but hers, shining, remained, and now the dark coils at his chest held him tight, held him to the hard hot fanged little body which, as he entered it, was suddenly and terribly ice-cold. Pinpoints of light, neon-pale, leapt before him.

There was a click, a slight draught.

'Ah. I'm sorry, sir.'

The voice, as if from a great distance, was that of Herbert, the cabin steward. His heart cold, his fingers blued and slowed by shame, Cato crumpled the magazine cuttings under the pillow.

'Shall I . . . come back later, sir?' asked Herbert levelly.

'Um . . . if you would, please,' managed Cato.

The door closed. Miserable, and with still-shaking fingers, Cato rebuttoned his trousers. Desultory flaring lingered at the edges of his vision. Herbert, he reminded himself without conviction, was only a servant.

And really, Cato supposed, he should be saving himself. The night before they had left, he had made a solemn vow before his grandfather's Great War service medals. An implausible vow, he knew, given his age and state of health, but a vow no less. Before landfall, he had resolved, before the hospital and the gas and the knife, he would feel a real woman's body against his own. Even if it killed him.

At dinner, Max drew out Pierre on the subject of his work.

Hesitantly at first, as if fearful of seeming blasé, Pierre described working with Leslie Howard, Margaret Leighton and a number of others – Jack Priestley's was a recurring name – of whom Cato had not heard. Loelia's mood seemed to have returned; she ignored Pierre, and between Max and herself there passed no communication of any kind. Instead – the object of Jerry Farrell's frank and staring curiosity – she toyed darkly with her food. Her silence was of the kind that drew constant attention to itself, made all conversation self-conscious.

'The Ministry got us everyone we needed, serving or not,' explained Pierre in the direction of Reginald, who, having now conceded Pierre's existence, nodded. 'The more important the actor, the easier it was. They weren't by any means all happy about it, though. Some of them actually got rather shirty about just how willingly their units let them go.'

'Gone With the Wind Up,' said Farrell, speaking for the first time.

'That's what they said about the ones who stayed in Hollywood,' said Pierre. 'Yes.'

'Don't suppose you ever came across a fellow named Smedley-Brown?' asked Farrell, blotting his eye. 'Frightfully funny chap. Mortarman in the North Bucks. Captured in '40. Spent the war in a prison camp in rubber tits and a wig.'

'I don't think I ever came across a Smedley-Brown,' said Pierre carefully, 'No.'

They addressed their food.

'Have you left your mother at home?' Loelia suddenly asked Cato, her black eyes glittering. The soup-spoon paused half-way to Reginald's mouth.

'She was killed in a car accident,' said Cato. 'In '44.'

'Ah,' said Loelia, nodding slowly and turning to Reginald. 'I'm sorry.'

'That's all right.' Father and son spoke simultaneously, and their eyes met in something like complicity. Max gave his wife an abstractedly tolerant look, as if she were a mental patient he was reintroducing to society.

'Well, *I* didn't know . . .' she began, banging her glass to the tablecloth.

But Max had turned to Cato. 'I've a book in the cabin you might care to have a look at,' he said. 'Written at the end of the last century, about poisonous snakes. I'll send it over to your cabin.'

Cato, smiling, nodded.

'It's a collection of case-histories from before the days of anti-venins,' continued Max. 'The treatments then were pretty much kill or cure. You might enjoy it.' He reached for his glass, and Cato wondered if his use of the expression 'kill or cure' was intentional. With a start he realised that the voyage, barring foul weather, was almost half-complete. It seemed only just to have started.

He thought of his vow of – of whatever was the opposite of chastity. Sitting in that vast dining room surrounded by the best part of five hundred strangers it seemed blush-making, ridiculous, impossible to fulfil. He felt obliged, nevertheless, to go through the motions, to have some sort of a crack at the whole thing. He had a vague impression that there were bars on Atlantic liners which always contained women of a certain disposition, women who sat for hours before a succession of gin-and-limes and could be relied upon to start a conversation with a stranger. Cato looked around him. He certainly couldn't see anyone remotely answering that description in the staid, middle-aged crowd. Most of the women present seemed to manifest a sort of powdered, chiffoned doughiness that represented the exact antithesis of the *femme fatale* of his imaginings. Loelia Amber, he admitted to himself, was nearer the mark; there was a real sense there of the . . . At the same time – and even as he thought it Cato felt guilty of disloyalty towards Max – there was something repellent about Loelia, about the powdered wax of her skin and the copper-wire hair and the giddy, dangerous little eyes.

And Ayrest? Well. Ayrest. Ayrest MacLean. He pronounced her name silently to himself as he raised the glass of Vichy water to his mouth. She was the stuff of which dreams were made, all right, but not the dark Lilliput-girl dreams that he was determined to make flesh. She was so beautiful and self-possessed and alone that there was an infidelity, somehow, in even thinking of her in those terms.

He drained the glass, and touching his pocket for his passenger list and plan of the ship, felt a reassuring crackle.

When his father had departed for the smoking room, Cato nodded his apologies to the others and left the dining room by the main staircase. There was a 24-hour bar he had decided to investigate, and although it was too early yet to put his plan into motion, he wanted to be alone to consider his strategies.

The staircase, he soon found, was steeper and harder going than it had looked. As he reached the top his chest tightened, and for a moment he stood unmoving at the balustrade. Slowly, he reopened his eyes. Before him, the gallery was deserted, its tenebrous gloom augmented rather than dispelled by the concealed cornice lighting and by the illuminated columns which stood amongst the empty tables. It was also, but for the muted strains of 'In the Mood' issuing from the ballroom at its far end, silent.

He seated himself half-way along, with his back to the windows and the shadowed olive drapes. Opposite him, on the panelled wall, hung a large dark painting of wildfowl flighting over an estuary. It seemed to Cato that he had spent much of his life in such mute surroundings, in staff-rooms and waiting rooms and consulting rooms: in places between places. Hard upon this impression, as usual, came the guilt: the knowledge of his own ingratitude and of the disappointment that, to his father, he undoubtedly represented.

He thought of the girl. Hard to imagine her here, moving amongst the heavy upholstery and breathing the silent air.

She would be in her own world, a jollier if undoubtedly sharper-edged place. She was probably less than a hundred feet away.

Forgetting her, he touched his pockets. Usually he carried a paper-backed book with him, in case, as tonight, he was compelled to rest for any length of time. He considered returning to the cabin for *The Case of the Gilded Fly* and, estimating the distance, turned his head to the staircase. There, an elderly waiter caught his eye, and, tray beneath arm, silent on the heavy carpet, proceeded slowly to his side. Cato, who wanted nothing but did not wish to give the impression of having wasted the man's time, ordered an Indian tonic water and, as an afterthought, a packet of Senior Service.

As he waited, the first couples made their way down the gallery towards the ballroom. If they were aware of his presence, they showed no sign of it. One group included Pierre and Loelia, she laughing animatedly with a man in a white tuxedo, he trailing at the back, smoking.

The waiter placed tonic water and cigarettes before him, indicated the matches which stood, heads-up, in a frosted glass model of the ship, and withdrew. As, glass in hand, Cato blew a first long plume of smoke, the tonic water caught the light of the silver-bronze pylon at his side, and turned a radiant, pearlescent blue. Beyond the ballroom doors, a boogie-woogie thumped and shivered. Cato sensed the parade before him quicken, hurry as if chilled towards the rectangle of light at the gallery's end. He settled to wait.

In the thirty-six hours since he and Reginald had joined the *Carmelia*, Cato had made a point of acquainting himself, slowly but surely, with the interior architecture of the ship. The rich, he had discovered, and especially the older rich, did not wish to spend their days and their evenings climbing stairs. In consequence, lifts had been situated at strategic points, and these had enabled Cato to move around the *Carmelia* with comparative speed. Planning was necessary, of course; he had to pace himself with care so as not to find himself on the Boat Deck, say, with only half an hour in which to get back to the cabin and dress for dinner. (The latter operation, allowing for two rest stops on the way down, a bath, and fifteen minutes to get his shirt-studs and bow-tie right, took ninety minutes.)

The largest and dullest of the decks, he had discovered on these cautious wanderings, was the Main Deck. Here, their pillared reflections shimmering in the brown linoleum, were to be found the main hall, the shopping arcade, and most of the other public rooms. Their decoration tended to the institutional and the unaccountably depressing. Cato had opened one heavy door to discover lines and lines of empty whist tables reflected to infinity in the machine-polished flooring, and the sight had induced something close to despair.

Above the Main Deck were the Promenade and Boat Decks. These, housing an elaborate complex of lounges and salons, were effectively a Cabin Class preserve, and it was in one of the Promenade Deck galleries that Cato sat and waited. Within walking distance of his position were the ballroom, a library, a writing room, and several cocktail bars. On the deck above him, aft, was the private restaurant, the Riviera Grill. Surrounding these amenities on the outside were hundreds of yards of salt-bleached promenade, the lower of the two decks glass-windowed against the weather, the upper, beneath the lifeboat davits, open to the night sky.

It was along the Boat Deck that, a few minutes after eleven o'clock, Cato made his way. It was all but deserted – after-dinner saunterers tended to prefer the shelter of the Promenade Deck – and he had little fear of running into any shipboard acquaintances. As he approached the aft area his step slowed, and he touched his pockets for his cigarettes. Outside the heavy outer door, he folded the plan back into his pocket, took a deep breath of salt air, and stepped inside. He found himself, as he had calculated, in the corridor outside the Riviera Grill. A murmur of conversation was audible from the restaurant, as were isolated snatches of jazz piano. The bar was at the end of the corridor on his left.

He stepped into a peach-lit cell, into whirling cigar smoke and a burst of raucous laughter falling away to silence. He had an impression of jowls and drinks suspended, of gaping query, and saw immediately that there was nowhere to sit.

The bar was tiny. In a window seat around an oval table crowded with bottles, glasses and ashtrays were pressed a dozen male figures, all of them, it seemed, identically flushed and whisky-eyed. Immediately in front of Cato a man turned from the bar with a pair of martinis, revealing an unoccupied stool. Conscious of the continued inspection of those behind him, Cato claimed the seat, laying his cigarettes and matches before him.

To his left, staring straight in front of her at the rows of spirit bottles, sat the only woman in the room. She was about thirty-five, Cato guessed, blonde, firm-jawed, and with a profile not unlike that of the actress Christine Norden. As he watched, she crushed out a cigarette in an ashtray and took another from a tin in front of her. She placed it in her mouth, but made no move to light it. Several moments passed, and then – conscious of the cinematic nature of the moment – Cato lit a match and held it towards her. Like an oriental dancer, she moved her head sideways to the flame, remaining in profile. Beyond her, several drinkers watched with surreptitious amusement. Cato lit a cigarette of his own, and shaking out the match, caught the barman's eye. Halting a customer's story with an upraised finger, the barman raised an interrogative eyebrow. Cato drew on the Senior Service.

'A champagne cocktail please, and . . .'

Her glass, but for a maraschino cherry, was empty. Now or never. The cigarette smoke, fluttering, betrayed the tiny shake of his right hand.

'Can I buy you a drink?'

The hubbub died as surely as a switched-off wireless. Cato was aware of the attention of the entire room. Her profile did not waver, but she regarded him from the corner of her eye.

'Thank you,' she said eventually and with glacial care, 'I'll have the same.'

The barman nodded.

For a minute, Cato imitated the woman's attitude, staring sphinx-like at the raffia donkeys and the matelot dolls and the bottles of Parfait Amour. As the preparation of the cocktails neared completion, however, and still she remained frozen, he began to steal furtive glances. Her face, he saw, was very perfectly painted, the eyebrow darkened with the finest and softest of pencils, the mascara sparing, the lipstick exact. There was a tension, an icy control around the visible corner of the mouth, but otherwise it was as if she presented him with her photograph, impeccable and unmoving.

'Who are you?' she asked, in the same careful voice, her lips hardly moving.

'My name's Cato,' he ventured.

'Cato,' she said. 'Ah.'

The barman placed the champagne cocktails in front of them. Around them conversation had resumed, but Cato was conscious that he remained the object of the room's attention.

'You're ill,' she said. 'I can tell it about you.'

'I'm fine,' said Cato, watching the bubbles pouring upwards from the sugar-lump in his glass. 'What's your name?'

'My name?' she said. 'You're asking me that?'

'You know mine,' he countered reasonably, and tried without success to blow a smoke ring.

'I asked who you were,' she said, in the same tightly controlled voice. 'Not what your name was. The two are quite different.'

With satisfaction, Cato recognised that the conversation was taking an intellectual turn. Comfortable with his cocktail and his cigarette and the lateness of the hour, he felt the warmth of self-congratulation rise within him.

'Well, I'm travelling to New York to see some people. After that, I'm not sure. I may continue to Chicago to see a zoologist, or I may push on to Los Angeles where I know a poet. Then again, I may just . . . stay in New York.' Something within him, he discovered irritatedly, refused to allow him to release his hold on the whole truth.

'That's where you are. Not who you are.' Her smoking stub joined a dozen others, all cork-tipped, all smudged with the same shade of lipstick, in the ashtray. She did not look down. The profile, the photographic study, remained unaltered.

'Perhaps if I tell you who I am,' she continued in her curiously mannered voice, 'you'll tell me who you are. Now what do you say to that?'

Cato took a large swallow of his drink. He felt fine. He caught sight of himself in a small mirrored panel behind the bar. With his narrow, shadowed face and his razor-cropped hair and the cigarette at his lip, he thought, he looked like one of the bleaker and less transient of the French intellectuals. '*Aux yeux de l'avenir*,' he murmured to himself, appreciative of this new identity, '*il n'y a de beau que les existences malheureuses*.' He drank again. 'I say yes to that,' he said.

The moment, the half-moment before she turned, he glimpsed her reflection, blurred and distorted, in another of the mirrored panels. But as the flawless profile became full-face, he saw that the distortion was not the mirror's. On the side that had been concealed from him there was no cheek; instead, suture-dotted flesh twisted inwards beneath the bone, dragging down the eyelid and lifting the upper lip from her teeth in a clownish grimace. Patiently, if warily, like a hermit crab poised at its shell, the undamaged side of her face held its smile.

Cato felt his blood thicken. There was a long silence, and he was aware in the silence of a vast amusement, a crowding expectancy on the part of the bar's other occupants. It was as if he had been the object of an elaborate leg-pull and now had to show himself a good sport.

And then, damning them, Cato found himself rescued. Rescued by the surprising expedient of imitating his father's unbending courtesy. Holding her gaze, he inclined his head. 'Please,' he said. 'Tell me about yourself.'

Her expression unfroze a degree. Cato suddenly saw the whole of her: the crossed legs beneath the tweed skirt, the yellow pullover, the slender gold chain at her neck, the long manicured hands. The others, the drinkers, oyster-eyed and wet-lipped, seemed to withdraw, disappointed.

Her story was simple enough. She lived with her parents in Cambridgeshire, and had been engaged to a flier who, shot down over France, had been held in a prisoner-of-war camp. One evening, as she was crossing a railway bridge on the way to post some letters, a munition train had exploded in a siding. She was lucky to have survived. The doctors had done what they could. At the end of the war her fiancé had been released but on his return had broken off their engagement. Since then her parents had died and left her a little money. She was travelling alone.

As she spoke, revealed details of her life, the embarrassing portentousness of their first exchanges returned to Cato. In the light of the specific details that she had just given him (Soham post office, Ely Hospital, bronchitis) his original posture and intentions seemed grotesque. To return to them would have been impossible.

And yet, and yet. There had been a moment – several moments – before she turned, when he had thrilled to the untruth of the situation. As, possibly, had she. He drained the second champagne cocktail, watched the smear of dissolving sugar.

'I have to go,' he said. He was already on his feet.

'When do I hear your story?'

'Another night, perhaps.'

'How many more nights are there?'

We're back in the play again, thought Cato, and felt a crawl of curiosity at his loins. 'I suppose that depends on the sea.' She had not, he realized, told him her name.

The barman inclined apologetically.

'That will be one pound four shillings, sir.'

Cato, carrying no money, was appalled. He had no idea that he was expected to pay cash. He slapped his pockets, helpless, and the room's attention swung to him like a cloud of flies.

'Look, can I . . .?' Maybe, he thought, he could sign something.

'That's all right.' She laid a hand on his arm and nodded to the barman, who withdrew. Desperate to be gone, Cato stared for a moment into her calm, distorted features. Gently, she lifted her hand and returned her attention to the raffia donkeys and the matelot dolls and the bottles of Parfait Amour.

An hour later he was still at the Boat Deck rail. From a distance, from the Cabin Class salon and the ship's radio diffusion system, came fragments of orchestral dance music. Behind him, the lifeboats and the ship's upper parts were whitely illuminated, her raked funnel-stacks a dying-ember scarlet against the enfolding darkness. Below, beyond the wash and the frayed sigh of their passing, the sea extended into blackness.

Tonight there was no horizon, no ocean of stars, only the dark ranges of the Atlantic. With his barathea sleeve Cato brushed a wind-tear from his cheek, and a ghost-image of reflected light leapt against the darkness of the sea. He was cold.

Something, though, some formless longing released by the encounter in the bar, held him at the sea-damp rail. And finally, as he watched and waited, the sea became land, became the endless wind-dulled plain of his longing, calling and calling and calling.

# 3

*Illustrative cases*

## No. 1

Reported by Dr James Lafrenais (*Indian Medical Gazette*, October 1874)

Bite from *Naja Hannah* (King Cobra). Toxaemia. Death in 190 minutes.

On a night in May, at approximately 3.00 a.m., a man named Jadul Das, a male cooly aged thirty-eight years, was bitten by a cobra while sleeping on the verandah of the Collector's bungalow at Berhampore. From the patient's description, in which he made particular point both of the snake's alleged length ('twice the length of a man') and of his having observed yellow 'Shiva-ite' chevrons at its throat, the culprit was almost certainly *N. Hannah* rather than the commoner *N. Naja*.

Upon Dr Lafrenais's inspection at 4.00 a.m. and upon the washing-off of pastes applied by the *hakim*, a healer 'of known repute' who had first attended him, there were found to be two indistinct fang-marks a little more than an inch apart over the anterior border of the deltoid. From these oozed a clear serous fluid tinged with blood. The patient complained of a burning pain to the area of the integument immediately surrounding the bite but manifested no further symptom or distress, answering clearly all such questions as were put to him. Although sensible to the potential danger of his situation he expressed full confidence in the pastes and 'snake-stone' of the *hakim* and refused any further treatment beyond Dr Lafrenais's inspection.

4.15 a.m. The patient complained of a feeling of intoxication and some giddiness, but was able to walk unsupported. Despite the prayers of his wife, he continued to decline all persuasions to proceed to hospital or to receive treatment *in situ*.

4.30 a.m. The patient complained of increased unsteadiness of vision. Upon examination by Dr Lafrenais his conjunctivae proved to be the seat of ecchymotic haemorrhage. The patient summoned the *hakim* who insufflated dried bile of chicken into the patient's nostrils and applied compresses of mud to his (the patient's) eyes and abdomen.

4.40 a.m. The patient indicated some unease, swaying on his feet and removing the compresses of the *hakim* from his eyes. He complained of an increased sensation of burning around the site of the dorsal punctures and vomited three times, the *ejecta* consisting of chapatti, a little bile-stained water, and some glairy mucus. Upon his commencing some minutes later to urinate in his clothes and to pass (with difficulty) a frothy mucus stained with red blood from his mouth and nose, permission for Dr Lafrenais's intervention was obtained from the patient's wife, the *hakim* being dismissed by the constable.

4.45 a.m. After dosing the patient with whisky (4 oz.), Dr Lafrenais immediately and freely excised the site, now tumefied, and in the hope of reducing a supra-lethal dose to a sublethal one, injected a saturated solution of permanganate of potash. Powdered crystals were also rubbed in and the wound packed with the same and dressed with cyanide gauze. The patient took a little water. The pupils at this juncture were not dilated, contracting when exposed to the light of a lamp, and there was no embarrassment of the respiration. It became apparent, however, that pain had become a prominent symptom.

4.50 a.m. Spasmodic twitching of the lower limbs. The patient voluntarily reclined and a charpoy, or native cot, was brought. The patient complained of an oppression of the chest, and liquor ammoniae (mxxx diluted with mxx of water) was injected under the skin of the forearm. Conscious of the paralysis rising through his legs the patient began to exhibit symptoms of nervous depression and was administered sweet-ened black coffee.

5.00 a.m. Distressing nausea; the patient vomited four times (*ejecta* consisting of tenacious brownish mucus, bile and coffee) and became increasingly restless and fearful, his head falling from side to side and his hands executing plucking gestures. It was apparent that par-alysis had risen to his chest. He was still able to talk, but indistinctly, as if under the influence of liquor. His jaw was beginning to fall, and viscid saliva to dribble from his mouth. Liquor ammoniae (dil. as previously) was injected into the basilic vein and a similar dose given by mouth, but this latter was swiftly regurgitated through his nose. At this juncture Dr Lafrenais advised the patient to complete such fare-wells of his wife, fellows etc. as he might consider appropriate, as comprehensible speech would shortly be beyond him. These, with some difficulty, the patient achieved, all but the patient's wife then being removed to a distance by the constable. The patient's bowels acted once in his clothes.

5.10 a.m. The patient's speech became incoherent, and his pulse and respiration accelerated. Dr Lafrenais injected liquor ammoniae mxxx (undiluted) into the left saphenous vein and ordered ammon. carb. (10 gr.), rum (2 oz.) as an enema: no effect. As paralysis finally overtook the patient's lingual and labial muscles he attempted for some minutes to communicate his distress through signs, continually striving at the same time to remove with his fingers the frothy and viscid saliva which clung to his mouth. His countenance became increasingly livid as a result of distress and of defective aeration of the blood; he appeared to be quite conscious, however, and to be suffering little or no paralysis of the arms.

5.20 a.m. The patient's respiration became slow and difficult. His head was turned on the left side with the left hand held to the mouth, from which dribbled frothy and viscid saliva. He passed urine in his clothes. The external jugular vein of the left side was laid bare and liquor ammoniae mxxx (undiluted) injected, but without notable result. A rattling sound issued from the patient's throat and it was observed that his extremities had become cold.

5.25 a.m. Patient died of asphyxia heralded by convulsions in the presence of his wife, the constable, the Assistant Surgeon, and Dr Lafrenais. Consciousness was retained until the final cessation of breathing, with heart-beat continuing for two minutes longer.

Post-mortem was not allowed.

*Addendum*: A week after this incident a hamadryad of ten feet and eight inches, displaying treble yellow chevrons at the throat, was killed by a *mali* (native gardener) some thirty yards from the Collector's bungalow.

As Cato read this account for the second time he found that he could picture every element of the drama. Its location, in his mind, was the moonlit clearing in front of the bungalow where Myrna Loy visited George Brent in *The Rains Came*. As well as Jadul Das, Cato imagined, there would have been others sleeping on the verandah, taking advantage, perhaps, of the Collector's absence (it was safe to assume his absence; the man was not mentioned from start to finish, and the point of a Collector, surely, was to be out there, up-country, collecting). The night would have been one of restless heat, broken sleep and the insistent peep of insects (the rains coming, but not yet, not yet), and the sleeping men lying more or less parallel beneath the cane furniture, their feet towards the clearing and the banyan trees.

Das would have lain at the end of the balcony, a little separate from the others, deep sleep evading him. He would have shifted on the planking, muttering perhaps, flinging out an arm, and felt the tiny red-hot stabbings beneath his shoulder that were suddenly not of a dream, not the claspings of some formless dream-wife but a waking and convulsive nightmare, holding fast. He would have moved to rise but fallen back, speechless with fear, held by the terrible coiling strength that his hands could not reach or grasp. And then the others stirring, sitting up confused around him, but only Das seeing the creature's great dark hood, its black moonlit eyes, and, at its throat, the sign of the god of death.

It would have been the constable who fetched Lafrenais. Cato saw an officious and overweight figure, unshaven for a week, sleepily pulling on the shirt bearing his insignia of office. He would probably have sent a boy ahead, a runner, to the doctor's bungalow, and met Lafrenais and the Assistant Surgeon (whom, being unnamed, Cato assumed to be an Indian) half-way. Lafrenais himself Cato imagined as a temperate, sandy-haired ex-Rugbeian, older-looking than his twenty-eight years, and liable to sunburn. He saw him making the journey on horseback, saddlebagged, and with the Assistant Surgeon following on foot.

On his arrival at the Collector's bungalow Lafrenais would have been grateful to the *hakim* for reassuring his patient, although the constable would have been all for shooing the healer away at once. Das's wife would have been there (although Cato did not see her as having slept on the verandah but near by, beneath the banyan, perhaps) trying to persuade her husband to lie down, to rest. And Das knowing that as long as he stood, as long as he retained his faith in the *hakim* and the power of the snake-stone to draw venom, he lived. But that faith ebbing, and he and Lafrenais both knowing, even as he described the hamadryad and its size and the duration of the bite, that he was a dead man standing, that the story would end in that same clearing at dawn, with the weeping of his wife, the silence of his fellows, and birdsong.

As Cato's eyes closed, the book fell from his fingers. He jerked awake to discover himself regarded by a pair of sage-green eyes.

'I'm sorry,' he said, self-conscious. 'I nodded off.'

'Don't apologise,' said Ayrest MacLean. 'Nodding off is what we're here for, surely.' She lifted the book, which had fallen between their chairs. '*Terrestrial Venomous Snakes of Bengal and the North Eastern Provinces.* Goodness. Have you ever been there? India, I suppose it is?'

'Yes, it is. And, no. I haven't.'

There was silence, and she closed her eyes. For the first

time that day, Cato was aware of the vibration rising from the engines.

'Have you seen it yet?' she asked. 'That snake you were telling me about. The one that's going to Chicago?'

'Yes,' said Cato, 'Mr Amber – Max – took me. A twelve-foot King Cobra.'

She narrowed her eyes. 'That sounds most terrifically deadly.'

'It is. That's what I was reading about, in fact, a . . .'

'You'd better not tell me the details.' She smiled distractedly. 'I might never sleep again.'

At that moment, steaming like a horse, Jerry Farrell burst into their presence. Undammed sound rushed to Cato's ears.

'Twenty-five times round the Prom Deck,' he gasped, lowering a small cast-iron radiator to the deck and his hands to his serge-battledressed knees. 'Five miles.' Sweat dripped from his nose and hair to his brown plimsolls.

'Running?' asked Cato.

'Absolutely. Cabin steward fixed me up with the pipework. Same weight as a mortar baseplate, see?'

Straightening, he peeled off a cricket pullover and threw it to his chair. 'Where's the old man?'

'Playing bridge, I think.'

'Really? Bit early in the day, isn't it? Mind you,' he rubbed at the crimped eye, now winking involuntarily, 'that Corcoran fellow plays the devil of a weak no trump.' He kicked at the radiator. 'Now where, I wonder, shall I stow the old baseplate?'

Smiling her excuses, Ayrest MacLean left them, and Docherty materialised at the rail. The horizon, Cato noticed, had a definite swing to it.

'Freshening,' remarked Farrell. 'Got a drop of that neck-oil, Seamus?'

Wordlessly, Docherty handed him a large silver flask and the baseless glass.

Cato looked out beyond his blanketed knees. The sea

was a dark petrol grey, unbroken. There was a broad rise and fall to it, however, that he had not seen before.

'What time are you seeing the PT instructor?' Farrell asked Docherty.

'Twelve o'clock,' said Docherty without enthusiasm.

'I've entered him for the boxing,' explained Farrell. 'Glaswegian fellow looking for a bout. Big old bugger, but I'd say Docherty has the beating of him. Coiled spring, you see.' He pulled a towel from round his neck, where it was looped like a damp cravat. 'Here.' He threw it to the Irishman. 'You'll need this. Some fancy footwork, too, if this sea gets up.'

The noon whistle blew, and he drained the baseless glass.

As the *Carmelia*'s bow rose and fell and the wind found his eyes, Cato's apprehension gradually turned to elation. He felt fine, and the ship was doing what she had been built to do, breasting the North Atlantic with shrouds singing, the smoke flat to her stacks, and the scalloping wake of the past behind her.

'Bloody marvellous!' said Farrell at the rail next to him, and for once Cato understood exactly what he meant.

With the morning's sudden increase in weather, most of the Cabin Class passengers had retired to the covered Promenade Deck beneath them. Those remaining were for the most part standing in ones and twos at the rail rather than attempting to read or sleep in their chairs.

'Yes, it's . . .' Farrell's lips continued to move, but if there were words, the wind took them. Cupping an ear, Cato leant towards him, but Farrell, his expression thoughtful, was silent. Cato's gaze fell. Farrell's hands were at the thick serge and khaki buttons of his battledress trousers, and as Cato watched, disbelieving, he drew out a fistful of penis.

Not knowing what to say, appalled but unafraid, Cato said nothing. Retreating a pace, he looked around, but nobody was watching, and he realised that he was sheltering

Farrell from the view of the other passengers behind them. Farrell now had both hands on the rail, his sex hanging at disconsolate half-mast from his trousers. He looked as if he was thinking about something else.

'Look,' started Cato, 'Please. You can't . . .'

'No one around, old boy,' said Farrell vaguely. 'Don't mind, do you?' Releasing the rail with one hand he attempted, staring at the sky and with a few absent-minded strokes, to further prime himself.

'Jerry, someone's going to . . .'

'Just trying to crack a stand, old lad,' said Farrell, frowning distractedly. 'Doctor's orders. Dropped a bollock and sundry pipework, do you see, on the wadi line above Suda Bay.'

Concentration returned to his features, the crimped eye blinked rapidly, and then, as Cato looked anxiously around them, he shook his head.

'Looks like you're right, though. Bit blowy.' Bundling himself philosophically back into his trousers, he buttoned the khaki with heavy fingers. 'Hungry, too. Wonder what's for lunch.'

Reginald was not in their cabin when Cato, the carpet now plunging beneath his feet, closed the door behind him. The motion of the ship had not increased since the wind's getting up at midday, but seemed to have settled at a regular rise and fall. Twin columns of sea-light swung from the portholes across the ceiling, the panelling popped and groaned, and the ivory hairbrushes rocked at the raised edges of the dressing table. A trio of roses in a wall-sconce looked particularly vulnerable, and Cato moved to pour their water down the sink. In the bathroom there was a strong smell of Essence of Limes, and shards of broken glass trembled on the tiled floor.

There was something in his condition, Cato knew, something stricken and dysfunctional, which called out to the more abstract hurts of his elders. It was a peculiar and

unsolicited freemasonry, that of distress, but it was one
which had afforded him certain understanding. Even had
he been able to find the words, it would never have occurred
to Cato to mention the Farrell incident. He was surprised
by it but at the same time he was unsurprised. And to
avoid the man, of course, was impossible. Like his familiar,
Docherty, he never came at you across open ground.

The lift descended four feet. Beyond the gates, 'A' deck
rose to the height of their shoulders, and then they gasped
to a halt.

'Fuck's-sakes-not-a-bloody-gain,' breathed Tudor.

Through the gilt-painted grillework of the gates and the
gap in front of their faces, Cato saw the movement of
legs, feet, shoes. 'Least bit of a sea, the bugger packs up,'
continued Tudor. 'I hope you're not too hungry.' He
pushed at a button, and Cato heard the distant ringing of
a bell.

'What happens?' asked Cato.

'Counterweight,' explained Tudor vaguely. 'Loss of
equi . . . balance.'

'No, I mean, what usually . . . how do they fix it?'

'Engineers,' said Tudor.

Cato nodded. 'Not much we can do, then.'

'Wait,' said Tudor. 'Jus' wait.' He passed the back of a
hand across his nose. 'Bet you wish you'd walked, now.'

Cato shrugged. 'I don't mind waiting.'

'Last time it happened, that actress . . . what was her
name, from *Bomber's Moon*? Edna something . . .' He
removed his cap, and took a stick of chewing gum from
the lining.

'Felton,' said Cato. 'Edna Felton.'

'That's the one. She was in this very lift with her poodle,
goin' down to the restaurant. Now the thing with
poodles . . .' he folded the gum into his mouth and jabbed
once more at the alarm button, ' . . . is their insides go
funny at sea. They can't shit.' He chewed for a moment.

'Anyway there we were, Miss Felton tappin' her fingers t-r-r-r-k, t-r-r-r-k, t-r-r-r-k on the wall, and suddenly, no word of warnin' . . .'

Cato silenced him with an upraised hand. The feet and legs in front of the lift gates had dispersed to reveal, slumped in a banquette several yards away and in an attitude of high irritation, Loelia Amber. She was not alone, but appeared to be arguing with a second, male figure. This figure was closer to the lift gates, and only the lower half of a pair of black corduroys, an inch of mauve silk sock and two cracked brogues were visible. Cato, however, recognised these easily enough.

'Just give me *one* good reason,' Loelia was saying, sucking furiously at her cigarette. '*One.*'

'I can't,' said the voice of Pierre, from above them. 'Don't ask me why, but I can't. You'll just have to . . .'

Loelia batted away the suggestion with the hand holding the cigarette and closed her eyes. Cato heard the tiny creak of leather as Pierre began to pace.

'Look,' started Loelia again. 'If it's . . .'

'We can't go there,' said Pierre, 'and there's an end of it.'

'But . . .'

Several other figures swept into the low rectangular frame of Cato's vision. Three feet from his face, the cracked black brogues turned sharply towards him.

'Max, darling, at *last*,' continued the voice of Loelia, easily. 'I'm famished.' She stood up. 'Let's take the stairs, this damn lift seems to be taking ages.'

'Do you like to listen, then?' asked Tudor, probing with chewed fingers at his acned chin.

Cato folded his arms and leant back against the mirrored wall of the cage. 'What I like', he said, 'is to know. When you're sick, you see, people tell you things. They think you don't count. But then you want to know the whole story.'

'Like a spy?' asked Tudor.

Cato considered. 'Yes.' He smiled. 'Like a spy.'

With a sudden rattling shudder, their descent recommenced. Tudor returned the gum to the interior of his cap. At the restaurant level, he held the doors open for Cato. 'Listen,' he said, 'do you want to come down Alamein tonight? It's Pig's Follies. Should be a good 'un.'

Cato nodded. 'Okay.'

'Nine, then?' asked Tudor quickly. 'Top of the lift?'

'All right,' said Cato.

In the dining hall, fiddle-edges had been raised on the tables and cloths dampened to prevent the sliding of plates and glasses. The waiters moved with practised ease between the tables, the passengers more carefully, apologising with nervous laughter as they steadied themselves. Around the tubular glass fountain (which had been switched off, and now stood a smoky and purposeless grey), the jellies trembled and the dwarf palms swayed.

Beneath the balcony, the Parkes and the Ambers sat in silence. For the first time since embarkation, Cato found that he had no great appetite. This had less to do with the rolling of the ship than with a disinclination for the company of his fellow-diners. He wanted to think. For try as he might, he could find no innocent explanation for the conversation he had overheard. It was not so much the words spoken, as their complicit tone. And if he was as pleased as ever to be in possession of secret knowledge and impressed – in a horrified sort of a way – by the idea of Pierre as unscrupulous seducer, he was appalled by the idea of Max as deceived husband. Watching him now, watching his small elegantly made hands at the heavy cutlery, Cato felt a surge of pity. From time to time his eyes crept to Loelia where, at her husband's side, she sat impassive, unreadable.

'What do you think?' asked Reginald eventually.

Cato, starting guiltily at this apparent reading of his

thoughts, forced his attention from the Ambers to his father.

'There's a film', he said, handing Reginald the schedule, 'in the main lounge. I think it's supposed to be pretty good.'

'*The Four Feathers*,' read his father suspiciously. 'What's . . .?'

'The Sudanese War, I think. Omdurman.'

'Ah,' said Reginald. 'Fuzzy-wuzzies.'

'And so on, yes. And in colour.'

'Well, let's give it a try, then. Got the plan?'

Cato nodded, glad that with his father temporarily released from his bridge game, they were to spend some time together.

In the three years since Claudia's death, Reginald had seemed to talk very little. He had never spoken much about his work at the War Office, and lately had only seemed at any kind of ease when encouraged to expand upon technical or political matters. The last time Cato could recall real animation on his father's part was when, a month before, the car had blown a gasket. They had broken down outside Wallingford. His father had rolled up his sleeves, revealing London-pale forearms, pushed the car to a lay-by, laid out spanners and wrenches on a groundsheet, and improvised a repair which had elicited the congratulations of the ex-REME mechanic at their own garage. Somehow the exercise had combined the instructional and the unpredictable in perfect measure, and later, as they had sat grease-fingered before glasses of cider outside The Locomotive, their silence had been an easy one, no more and no less than the silence of a summer's day.

A film had been a good idea. The vast carpeted silences of the Boat and Promenade Deck interiors were not encouraging of conversation, and neither father nor son was much drawn by the hearty egalitarianism of the Sports Deck. Cato had thought of suggesting a walk beneath the lifeboats, but feared slow progress and slower conversation. The thing that was all but silencing them was that both the future and the past had somehow been placed off limits. Only Cato's survival could create a future for them to refer to, and only the creation of a future would release them from the unmentionable past.

Unfortunately, it seemed, a sizeable proportion of the present was also off limits. He would dearly have loved, for example (over a cigarette and a whisky, perhaps) to pick over Loelia Amber's furies, affectations, and presumed strayings. But such discussion, he knew, such *gossip* – and the word would carry its full malignant charge – would simply not be countenanced by his father. Similarly beyond any conversational pale was the business of Mrs MacLean. Cato had seen his father's eyes follow her along the deck and surreptitiously seek her out in the dining hall. Without overwhelming embarrassment, however, there could be no shared appreciation.

In a quiet way, nevertheless, Mrs MacLean was already the talk of the ship, and was discreetly but insistently courted at every turn. Cato wondered if he would mind if his father were to take his place amongst her suitors, and rather to his surprise, found that he wouldn't. Perhaps he would wake in his hospital bed high above New York City (the operation, in his imaginings, always took place at the top of a skyscraper), to be greeted by the sight of his father and Mrs MacLean waiting together anxiously with grapes and books and flowers. The more Cato thought about it, the finer and crazier an idea it all seemed.

The actual business of the operation and of the waiting for it was harder for his father, Cato knew, than for him. Cato was pretty sure, most of the time, that he no longer feared death. He was bored with his halting frailty and his endless spectator status and the inevitable flicker – part pity, part fear – in the eyes of strangers. He was ready, he was fairly certain, for something new. If that something new turned out to be death, if under anaesthetic and to

the sound of American accents he was whirled to infinity
– well, so be it.

If he died, though, and this he knew for certain, his
father would never recover. To die would be to let him
down just once too often.

The film was good. Watching it, however, was not easy. The
projector had been set up at the back of the lounge on a
trestle table and shuddered, blurring the picture, with every
rise and fall of the ship. Late arrivals – Jerry Farrell
amongst them – tripped over wires, causing a number of
unscheduled intermissions, and the grinding whir of the
projector rendered several of the love scenes inaudible. To
Cato, however, who had seen more films in school gymnasia
than he had in public cinemas, none of this was a cause
for particular irritation. With the exception of an
uncomfortable sequence in which the brigadier-general
expressed his concern about the manliness of his fifteen-
year-old son ('I don't mind telling you, Doctor, I'm worried
about him . . .') Cato enjoyed the film enormously. There
was patriotic whooping from the front rows as the Khalifa's
dervishes finally broke before the crashing load-and-volley
of the British square, and a satisfactorily sentimental silence
as John Clements finally folded June Duprez in his arms.
As the credits rolled and the projectionist picked his way
towards the light-switch, Cato glanced surreptitiously at his
father. He found, as he knew he would find, an unblinking
impassivity.

'Those were the days, what?' said Jerry Farrell, closing
on them, his radiator clasped under one arm, as they waited
to leave.

'They were indeed,' said Reginald. 'They were indeed.'

'Fellow was telling me, they filmed the whole shooting-
match on a piece of land the size of a pocket handkerchief
in Borehamwood.'

'Remarkable,' said Reginald.

They made their way up the main staircase to the Promenade Deck, where Farrell departed them. The swell had subsided a little, but the dim silence of the galleries indicated that a number of passengers had retired to their cabins and remained there. The grand saloon, usually a popular tea-time rendezvous, was all but deserted, the grand piano silent on its distant podium. As Reginald and Cato entered, a steward was moving between the linen-covered tables, ensuring, with a light shove to each, that the fittings were firmly bolted to the floor.

'Expecting a bit of weather?' Reginald asked him, as they seated themselves.

'Safe than sorry, sir,' said the steward. 'Could be a grumble or two ahead.'

'I see. How are you feeling?' Reginald asked Cato.

'Quite all right,' said Cato, 'really.' He looked around them. Slowly, from the distant far end of the room and heralded by the faint rattle of bone china, a second steward approached with a trolley. They sat in silence as tiered dishes of scones, cakes, and cucumber sandwiches were laid before them.

'Good film, I thought,' said Cato, watching the steward's unhurried departure.

'There was a moment I particularly remember,' said Reginald after a moment, thoughtfully touching his moustache. 'When what's-his-name . . . Faversham has resigned his commission and the regiment has sailed for Egypt and he goes to explain himself to Ethne.'

'Yes,' said Cato.

'You remember a box is delivered, the box containing the white feathers.'

'Yes.'

'Well, I wonder if you noticed exactly what Faversham did. He bowed to Ethne – nothing . . . ambassadorial, just an inclination of the head to excuse himself from her immediate vicinity – took the box over to a small table, laid it down, found a paper knife, and opened it.'

'I remember,' said Cato.

Reginald lifted his gaze to the pale skylight. 'Well, that's what's changed between then and now. If the story was taking place today, he would simply have torn off the brown paper where he stood and . . .' he shrugged, 'dropped it on the floor.' He lowered his eyes to Cato's, and leant a degree or two towards him. 'He wouldn't have been able to wait, do you see.'

There was a moment's silence.

'I see,' said Cato.

The teapot handle, of some dark wood set in silver, was hot. Cato wrapped a linen napkin around it, and began to pour. The handle slipped inside the napkin and the spout swung downwards, chipping the rim of the cup and spilling the pale tea on the tablecloth and on his father's trousers. Awkwardly, Cato lowered the pot.

'Sorry,' he said.

Reginald shook his head and raised a hand; a steward came over, briefly surveyed the damage, and hurried away for another cup.

'Forgot to tell you,' said Reginald, pressing his napkin to his thigh. 'Spot of good news.'

Cato turned to him, surprised.

'As I expect you've noticed, I've been playing some bridge with one or two of the other fellows. Well, to cut a long story short, I seem to have won quite a decent amount. Enough to . . . well, a good four figures, anyway. That fellow Corcoran and a chum of his called Villiers, more money than sense in my opinion. They do themselves pretty well – staterooms and malt whisky and so forth – but it's got to the point where in all decency I can't take any more off them.'

'That's . . . terrific, Dad.'

Cato was greatly heartened. It was more than he could hope for that he might be told the actual sum – 'not talking about money' was as important to Reginald as 'not talking about work' or 'not talking about other people behind their backs' – but there was considerable entertainment in the idea of his father emerging from a smoke-filled state-room with a roll of someone else's cash.

'I thought we might treat ourselves,' said Reginald. 'A slap-up bean-feast in the Riviera Grill on the last day, what do you say?'

'Rather!' Cato smiled. There was very little else, he realised, that his father could have offered him. Perhaps not the easiest of occasions to look forward to, though. The last meal.

The steward approached, carrying a tray. At the same time, Cato saw Mrs MacLean. Moving soundlessly towards them from the entrance, emerald-brooched and alone, she gave the impression that the room's shadowless depths had been created expressly to serve, on this single occasion, as her backdrop. She had once been a fashion model, Cato remembered.

Intercepting her gaze, wondering whether their Boat Deck conversation constituted an acquaintanceship (or whether, for that matter, it had even taken place at all) Cato stared at her uncertainly. She responded with an oblique smile, and Cato, a napkin unconsciously clutched in his right hand, found himself rising to his feet.

'You must be Colonel Parkes. How do you do. Ayrest MacLean.' Her outstretched hand moved past Cato's table-napkin towards the still-straightening figure of his father.

'Reginald Parkes. How do you do.' Releasing her, he touched his tie uncertainly and indicated the third chair. 'Would you . . .?'

'That's most kind,' said Ayrest, easily, and Reginald nodded to the waiting steward.

'So,' she inclined her head interrogatively after the three of them had sat in silence for some moments. 'You're the father.'

'Yes,' said Reginald gravely, 'I'm the father.'

She opened her crocodile bag and laid a black enamelled cigarette case on the table. 'We're neighbours once removed, I believe. On deck.'

'Have a sandwich,' said Cato. 'They're very good.'

She smiled, and shook her head. At the far end of the room, distant beyond the empty tables, a tail-coated figure seated himself behind the piano and began to play.

'Now, what's that tune?' asked Reginald, gravely.

Ayrest MacLean laughed. 'Oh . . . it's from that . . .' She closed her eyes and steepled her fingers. 'What was its name, that *silly* show, I *saw* it for Heaven's sake.'

'Portugal,' frowned Reginald. 'Something about Portugal.'

'*The Lisbon Story*,' offered Cato flatly.

' "Pedro the Fisherman"!' said Ayrest and Reginald together, and laughed.

'Four years ago,' she said reflectively. 'It seems like a lifetime.'

The steward placed a fresh pot of tea before them. Ayrest looked from father to son. 'Shall I . . .?'

'Go ahead,' said Reginald.

Ten minutes later, having listened to his father describe his work at the War Office in terms so vague as to be all but incomprehensible, Cato made his apologies. With what he hoped was a meaningful bow, he left them to the scones and the walnut cake.

In addition to the Promenade and Boat Decks, which were entirely reserved for Cabin Class passengers, there were outposts of privilege deeper in the ship. Higher-paying passengers could descend by lift to the lower parts and continue to enjoy a number of facilities from which all but they were excluded. These – a hairdresser, a swimming pool, and various gymnasia, hammams and tepidaria – Cato had identified on his plan, but had not yet visited.

To this end, five minutes after leaving his father and Mrs MacLean in the grand saloon, he made his way down a short flight of stairs, through a double glass door, and into the gallery above the 'C'-deck swimming pool. Both pool and gallery were deserted, but a vestigial echo seemed

to hang in the air as if the last swimmers had just that
moment departed. From the glass ceiling above his head,
gouts of condensation dropped heavily to the water's surface. A faint steam rose.

For several minutes Cato stood looking down, wondering
if he dared go into the water. He was not allowed to swim,
but the pool was temptingly beautiful, its walls a dark
riverine green, its floor the dull gold of sunlit water over
sand. The swell outside had subsided, and the warmed
water rocked gently from end to end.

He decided, finally, on a ritual descent of the ladder. He
had no swimming costume, had indeed never owned a
swimming costume, and so decided to risk it in his underpants. Genuflecting on the damp gallery floor, he unlaced
his walking shoes. As he did so he heard a door close on
the level below. The girl – he thought of her now simply
as the girl – stepped into view, followed by two others, a
fattish one and a definitely thin one. The girl, her hands
at the chinstrap of her rubber cap, was wearing a bathing
costume and sandals; the others, hesitant behind her, were
fully dressed.

'Come *on*!' ordered the girl. 'Joan. *Mavis*. S'all right.'

Unseen, he watched as she removed her sandals, picked
her way over the wet tiles to the shallow end of the pool
and climbed the steps to the top of the chute.

The splash echoed shockingly. 'Come *on*!' shouted the
girl, surfacing. 'It's lovely!'

The other two looked at each other.

'We got nothing to . . .'

'Pardon?' shouted the girl, unpopping her chinstrap
and lifting the earflap.

'Got no bathers.'

'Come in your vest and pants,' said the girl, wiping her
nose on the back of her hand and pushing her hair back
under the cap. 'No one's going to see.'

'No towels . . .' began the thin one, but the girl had
launched herself into an energetic breast-stroke. Her

companions looked at each other doubtfully. Slowly, the fattish one began to unbutton her cardigan. In the gallery above, Cato remained on one knee.

Behind him, there was a sudden draught. Cato turned to find himself inspected by a broadly built man in flannels and jersey.

'Afternoon, sir. Looking for the changing rooms?'

At the sound of his voice, there was a scrambling from the poolside, followed by a sharp cry of pain. The broadly built man glanced over the balcony and, followed by Cato, swiftly descended the steps to the pool. The fattish girl had slipped, and was lying whimpering in the pool-wash, blood swimming at her knee and elbow. Like a cod on a slab, thought Cato. A big mauve cod.

The thin girl, eyes wide with anxiety, looked from one to the other of them. 'We wasn't going in,' she whispered. 'Honest.'

'That's all right,' said the pool assistant. 'Let's just have a . . .' He prodded at her, gently articulating the joints. 'Nothing broken.' He raised her to a sitting position. 'What's your name?'

'Mavis Kippax.' She sniffed, slowly buttoning the sodden cardigan.

'Well, why don't you come to my room, Mavis, and we'll see what we can do to patch you up. As for you, young lady,' he turned to the thin Joan with a wry smile, 'I suggest you cut along back to your quarters.'

She gaped briefly, and turned on her heel.

'Walk!' he called after her. 'Don't run.' He turned his attention to the pool, where, having watched the proceedings with waning interest, the girl had resumed her leisurely breast-stroke.

'It's Okay,' said Cato, 'she's . . .'

The assistant nodded. ''Course, sir. Come along then, Mavis, we'd better have a look at that knee.'

He led her limping away.

The girl swam to the side to watch them go. 'You comin' in, then?' she asked Cato.

'I haven't got a costume either,' said Cato.

'Why d'you take your shoes off, then?' she asked, reasonably.

'Floor's wet,' answered Cato, lowering the shoes to the blood-smeared tiles.

'Tell you why,' she continued in the same tone. 'It was so's you could watch us undress and if anyone asked, you were taking your shoes off, is why.'

'I wasn't,' said Cato, pushing his hands defensively into his pockets. 'I mean I was. Taking them off. Because of the floor.'

She pinched her nose and smiled. 'I saw you.'

'Didn't say anything if you did.'

'Why should I? Wanted to see what'd happen, didn't I?' Turning, she appeared to stand on her head. Her feet disappeared beneath the water, and Cato saw her glide strong and greenish-pale over the quartzite tiles. A minute later, she surfaced, folding her arms on the edge of the pool. As the water ran from them, the tiny fair hairs jumped upright on her forearms.

'Goose bumps,' said Cato.

She regarded him levelly. 'You were down before, weren't you. On our deck. Night before last.'

'Yes.' He tried to squat, to speak to her face-to-face, but it hurt his knees. He had to keep standing up. Water washed and swirled from the pool, soaking the turn-ups of his trousers.

She lowered her eyes to his bare feet.

'You looked bad. You still look bad. Come into the water.'

Would it be worse, he wondered, to refuse, or to be discovered to be unable to swim? He *wanted* to go in. And lots of people couldn't swim. He wasn't strong, though. He didn't look much in his Aertex pants. He might drown.

'Okay,' he said.

She watched as he undressed and piled his clothes on

one of the low poolside walls. Somehow he understood that it was part of the challenge that he didn't retire to the changing rooms. Snaking the belt from his trousers, he buckled it over the waist of his underpants.

'I'm afraid I can't swim terribly well.'

In answer she lay back in the water and pointed to the badge sewn at the hip of her navy-blue costume. 'Life-saving,' she said. 'Bronze.'

The swell had not noticeably increased outside, but a progressive momentum seemed to be building in the pool. The water was now swinging from end to end, breaking loudly over the tiled surround. At its centre, the girl's head and shoulders rose and fell.

'Buck up, old chap!' she shouted, in what he realised – although not immediately – was an imitation of a public-school accent. 'Jolly old dip, what?'

Carefully, he stepped on to the ladder. This was in the shallow end, well within his depth, but it was also now bearing the brunt, every ten seconds or so, of several tons of rolling seawater. If he lowered himself more than a few rungs he risked being swept against the end wall. At his chest, the snake tightened its coils. Light played around the head of the girl.

'Come in deeper,' she shouted, beckoning. 'To the middle.'

In the middle, he guessed, at the fulcrum point, the disturbance was least. At the same time it was certainly more than six-foot deep. The wave, as it drew back, was now exposing several feet of wall at the deep end, and all of the wall at the shallow end. The mass and crash and spatter of it – his underpants were already hanging drenched from his belt, frightened Cato very badly indeed.

Lowering himself to a sitting position on the edge of the pool, he felt the swing of the water at his legs. She was no more than four feet from him, riding the wave. Turning, he lowered himself on his hands as far as his waist. The golden floor was suddenly dimly, unreachably distant below him, and with the last of his strength he hauled himself back, keening with the effort, to a sitting position.

As he slumped blue-fingered on the tiles, light and water bursting around him and the snake clenching furiously at his chest, the girl very faintly smiled. She rose and fell, treading water, seemed to crouch, and then, arms extended behind her, leapt into a reverse dive.

For a moment, shining and unbelievable, she hung on the wave, and then she slipped behind it, feet last, and he could no longer see her. He struggled to rise, but the floor pitched, and water rushed towards him. He felt himself rolled two, three, four times, felt the seawater press at his throat and his shoulder crack hard. Struggling to rise, retching, he saw a shoe sail past him over the tiles. He stared after it, not immediately recognising it as his own.

'Up you get, son!'

Arms lifted him to a standing position, and, a hand at his back, bent him over. He spattered his feet with a pint of seawater, bile and cucumber sandwich and finally, gasping, straightened. The girl was nowhere to be seen.

'Thought we'd lost you there, son,' said the pool attendant, regarding him thoughtfully. 'You'd better come and get a nice warm bevvy inside you.' He gathered up Cato's clothes. 'I'll take these. You seem to be missing a shoe.'

Cato hesitated, looking towards the pool.

'I'm draining her off tonight,' the attendant said. 'I'll find your shoe.' He walked Cato to a small well-heated office smelling of Knight's Castile Soap and decorated with photographs of athletic young men in the attitudes of Greek statuary, and handed him a towel.

'I'm Denton, by the way. You'd better get out of those wet things. Cocoa?'

Twenty minutes later, still missing a shoe and with his trousers damp at his calves, Cato made his way along the gallery towards the 'C'-deck foyer. The pool was awash beneath him, and the attendant had announced his intention of placing it out of bounds for twenty-four hours. Beyond the glass exit door, seated cross-legged on the carpet, he found the girl. In her sandals and home-made clothes she looked gawky, inappropriate. Her eyes were pink from the water and the ends of her hair were damp and blunt. 'I waited,' she said, regarding him flatly.

'I lost you.'

'I don't expect you looked, especially,' she said.

'Come with me,' said Cato. 'There's something I want to show you.'

Wordlessly, her swimming things in a satchel at her side, she followed his single-shoed limp. Beneath their feet the deck rose and fell. Slowly, holding tightly to the guide-ropes, Cato led the girl down to 'D' deck, along the working alley past the glory-holes, and down the greasers' rail to the 'G'-deck hold.

'It's hot,' she said.

Cato felt for the light-switch. The girl looked around her at the cargo creaking and straining at its ropes, and followed him forward. The cage, covered by its tarpaulin, stood at the centre of the hold like a monument. Cato motioned the girl to her knees before the padlocked grille, and as he had seen Max do, tapped at it gently.

There was nothing. The girl, apparently intent upon showing no curiosity of any kind, waited expressionless. Cato repeated the action. Again, nothing.

Bending, Cato squinted past the padlock. Perhaps – and this seemed the likely answer – the hamadryad was asleep. He drew a box of matches from his pocket, and, still crouched, struck one in front of the wire. Deep beneath the canvas shade, the match's flame found two tiny reflections. At the final moment before he had to drop the match, the reflections moved.

'What is it?' she asked eventually.

'King Cobra,' said Cato. 'A twelve-footer. Female.'

'Is it yours?' she asked.

He shook his head. Silently, questing, the hamadryad

poured from the darkness before them. As coil after molten coil revealed itself, Cato smelt the metallic damp of the girl's hair.

'Poisonous?' she whispered.

'Deadly,' confirmed Cato.

'That's . . .' she shook her head. 'I never seen anything like that,' she conceded. 'Never.'

The small plated head of the hamadryad came to rest before them, lowered itself on to a tyre-like coil. Cato lowered his head until it was a foot from the snake's. The girl, watching thoughtfully, sat back on her knees. Before Cato had had time to think better of the idea – before, almost, he knew that he was going to do it at all – he had pushed two fingers between the wire bars and was stroking the smooth dry back of the hamadryad's head. Unmoving, expressionless, the snake submitted to the caress. Cato continued until he could hold his breath no longer, and carefully withdrew his fingers.

The girl smiled.

'So what's your name, then?' she asked.

He told her.

'Cato? That's never a proper name?'

'It's mine,' said Cato. 'What's yours?'

'Philippa,' said the girl. 'Pretty stupid too.'

'Philippa's not bad,' said Cato. 'What are they like, then, down where you are?'

'Who?' she asked, suddenly suspicious.

'Oh, your . . . people. The people with you.'

'They're all right,' she said, running a wary finger beneath her nose and sniffing. 'What are your . . . *people* like.'

'Oh . . . all right,' said Cato, pausing. 'Actually, pretty bonkers really, if I'm honest.' Turning to sit cross-legged, he peered down at his shoeless foot.

She smiled again, and looked away. 'You're ill, aren't you?'

'A bit, yes,' said Cato.

She nodded. 'They let you go where you want, though?'
He spread his hands and shrugged.

'Haven't seen you down at the pool before,' she said, pinching the dark ends of her hair.

'Haven't been there before,' said Cato.

'It's my favourite place on the ship,' said Philippa. 'I'm always there.'

'And you've never had any . . .?'

'Never chucked me out, no. Won't now, neither,' she said thoughtfully, 'after you told that inspector bloke I was with you. Cabin Class, I am, far as he's concerned.'

'Well,' said Cato. 'Why not?'

'I wouldn't have had you down as Cabin,' she said. 'More like Tourist, I'd have said.'

'Oh, really?' said Cato, irritated. 'And why's that exactly?'

'You look around.' She shrugged. 'Like it's all new to you. Like a Tourist.'

'If I wasn't going Cabin,' said Cato, 'I'd rather go Third.'

'Then you're stupid,' said Philippa evenly, and reached for her satchel. 'I ought to go.'

'Do you know the way?' asked Cato.

She stared at him for a moment, climbed to her feet, and began to walk to the staircase.

'Wait,' said Cato, struggling to a standing position.

She hesitated and then ran, her footsteps echoing on the ironwork above.

This time, when Cato closed the cabin door, he double-locked it. Dropping his jacket to a chair, he hurried to the wardrobe and took out the manila envelope. The late-afternoon light from the porthole illuminated his pillows. Treading off his shoes, he climbed expectantly on to the cold chintz of the bedspread and laid out the Lilliput girls before him. It was not long before he dismissed idle, marble-breasted Sonia and, with greater regret, Astrid, the Annamite princess. Heather, as always, he dwelt on for longer, but despite these attentions she seemed to be evad-

ing him. Who, he wondered vaguely, was the subject of the
curiously blurred photograph on the table at her side. Was
it some absent husband, rendered faceless by betrayal? Her
face, thoughtful and collusive as she unbuttoned herself,
suggested as much. Cato closed his eyes and saw Max and
Loelia Amber at the deck games. He re-examined Heather
in her velour armchair, but somehow the moment portrayed
had become lifeless, frozen without past or future.

He turned to Trixie, but something had happened to
Trixie. The desperate haste with which he had scrambled
her under the pillow had distorted her. The venal little
face was now crumpled across one side. Crumpled like
the face of the bar siren, the woman from Soham in Cambridgeshire who had paid for his drinks and whose name
he had never asked.

He looked from one to the other of them, removed Sonia
and Astrid once again from the manila envelope and laid
them alongside, but it was no good. He closed his eyes,
and slowly, as his mind emptied, the parade began again.
For a time those passing by were strangers, hurt or
wounded mostly (the Soham woman again), but then more
familiar forms began to appear. Ayrest MacLean, dressed
as she had been for tea and wearing the emerald brooch,
paused to regard him, and in something like self-
consciousness, he lay still until she dissolved. Beneath him,
the rise and fall of the sea grew more forceful.

Finally, and displacing the others, came the girl,
Philippa. She came, he saw, from the ocean, from the sea
become land. She hung on the wave, was carried for a long
single moment and then, feet last, slipped beneath it. This
time, though, naked, she held him to her, held him against
her pale body, its long muscles contracting and releasing
for them both, and as they streamed downwards together
to the darkness, breathing the glimmering sea, breathing
the darkness, he could taste the salt at his mouth.

And then, as if from a great distance, but impossible to

ignore, came the telephone. Unwilling, blinking in the light, he surfaced, and she slipped away.

'Hello?'

'Cato?' In the background, voices, laughter.

'Hello, yes?'

'It's . . . Dad. Just spoken to Dusty. He said you'd got into a spot of trouble in the swimming pool. Are you all right?'

'Yes, I'm fine. Really.'

'Righto, then.' There was a pause, during which, Cato knew, his father was weighing up the pros and cons of tearing him off a strip for being in the swimming pool in the first place.

'I'll be up in ten minutes or so to change. Sure you're all right?'

'Yes, Dad.'

The phone went dead. Cato rubbed his eyes, rolled on to his back, and felt a cold flush of embarrassment. With her flat hair and flat face and flat chest – flat eyes in fact – she wasn't even pretty, let alone nice or . . . He saw her sitting cross-legged on the carpet by the glass door in her sandals and her cheap, formless clothes, he saw her awful friends, and then the ship lurched and he smelt the sharp dampness of her hair, and he wondered.

'Said she wanted to lie down,' said Max, lowering the dinner menu. 'More loss of appetite than actual sea-sickness.'

'Well, I hope she feels better soon,' said Reginald.

The steady rise and fall of the ship had been replaced by the rounder and more disturbing combination of pitch and roll, and the dining room, its palmy vastness creaking around them, was no more than a quarter full. A pianist picked his way, as the podium rose and fell beneath him, through 'Lamplight'. Table-cloths had once again been damped and safety ropes, along which newcomers made unsteady passage, had been strung from pillar to pillar. At those tables which boasted a full complement of 'good sailors' – and only Loelia was absent from the table beneath the balcony – an enforced jollity was the rule. They ordered lavishly, as if to banish any thought of sickness, and the waiters, responding, performed with urbane dispatch.

'You're not married, are you?' Max asked Pierre, as the fish course was dispensed.

'Not me,' said Pierre, trapping an errant new potato with his fork.

'Ever been close?'

'Not really,' admitted Pierre. 'It's only comparatively recently that I've been able to keep myself in any kind of comfort, let alone . . .' He shrugged.

Max nodded. 'I wonder how long you'll last in Hollywood. Unmarried, I mean.'

Pierre smiled. The room seemed to hang suspended in the air for a moment and then, with a crash of glass and china, fell flat. A moment's complete silence was followed by a round of uneasy laughter. To no more than mild amusement, the pianist began to play 'What Shall We Do with the Drunken Sailor?'

Pierre cleared his throat. 'So how long is it since you . . .?'

'About eighteen months,' said Max. There was silence, and Cato guessed that, like himself, Pierre had assumed the Ambers to have skirmished their way through many years of marriage. 'We met in the Blitz.'

They watched him in silence. From behind Cato, as the room dipped sharply downwards towards the pianist, came the further tinkle of falling cutlery and glass.

'Long courtship, old boy,' said Farrell. 'Five years.'

'I don't think either of us thought we'd get married,' shrugged Max. 'You know how it was. We were just good chums, really. Not especially . . .' He shrugged, emptied his glass, and raised a hand to the waiter, who sidled expertly towards him. 'And of course there was the war,' continued Max. 'Until '43, or so – and I saw the figures on this – you were more likely to be killed going about your business in London than you were as a member of the services.'

'I think, old boy, it probably depended on what you were doing in the services,' said Farrell, levelly.

'Statistically, I mean,' said Max, as the waiter returned the bottle to the ice-bucket. 'On average. But as a result, as I'm sure Pierre will confirm, we were all behaving very strangely.'

'That's true enough,' said Pierre.

'Tell me, for example,' said Max, 'what you think about this. I was walking home from the zoo one lunchtime – it was a Friday, summer, in '41 – and outside the house in Regent's Park Road I saw, parked but with its engine on, a brand new Vauxhall Ten. Now, it was still seven or eight months before they did away with the petrol ration altogether – that wasn't until the next March, as far as I remember – but a new car was already a fairly unusual thing to see. Well, I must have stared at it for a full minute before I saw that the window was being wound down. It was a woman – handsome enough, smartly dressed, perhaps forty – and she called me over and asked if I wanted to get in. I said yes. The inside of the car, I remember, smelt very strongly of her cigarettes, Pashas, the Turkish ones. "I'm going to the Isle of Wight," she told me, as if this was the most ordinary thing in the world. "If you want to come, I'll see that you're back by Monday morning." '

Cato surreptitiously glanced at his watch. It was almost nine o'clock.

'Well, to cut a long story short,' continued Max, 'that's what we did. We drove to Portsmouth, the car was put on a boat, and we ended up in a large white hotel outside Bembridge. I think I had three and sixpence on me. After dinner, we were sitting on the terrace and she suddenly took my hands. "What's that smell?" she asked. "Formaldehyde," I said. "I've been performing an autopsy on a gibbon."

' "You'll have to sleep in your own room," she said, and I did. The next morning I washed my hands several times with the hotel soap and then – there was a geranium on the windowsill, potted – rubbed the leaves into my hands and washed them again. After breakfast we were on the terrace, and same thing, she took my hands. This time she didn't say anything, just lit another Pasha.' He spread his fingers modestly. 'Bingo, one might say.' Max looked around him to total silence. Cato avoided his father's eye.

'I pointed the hotel out to Loelia as we passed it the other day,' Max continued. 'You could see it clearly. And, do you know?' he smiled and shook his head. 'She wasn't in the least bit interested.'

Tudor was waiting at the lift. Cato would have liked to have changed out of his dinner-jacket into something more appropriate to the lower decks, but there hadn't been time. Besides, he would only have had to change back on his return.

They descended in silence. Tudor led the way, maintaining a tactful pace along the galleries and down the lurching stairways. Finally, descending through the emptying decks, they reached the steel door and the clamour and cabbage-smelling humidity of El Alamein. On previous visits Cato had sensed a clattering urgency, but tonight was different. There was an almost formal restraint about the groups who made their way towards the Pig and Whistle, a controlled and low-voiced excitement. All of them ignored the ship's pitching roll. Tudor backed Cato and himself into an opening by a shell door, and as each crew-member passed, identified in a low sing-song the various store-keepers, trimmers, quartermasters, commis-waiters, linen-men, platehousemen, greasers, plumbers and donkeymen. Many of the restaurant staff were still wearing dinner- and mess jackets, and Cato felt less out of place in evening dress than he had feared he might. He hoped above all hope that he would not start to feel seasick.

'You're lucky,' said Tudor, steadying him as the corridor swung downwards. 'Best concert group tonight. DOTS.'

'Dots?'

'D-O-T-S. Daughters of the Sea. You get different groups, see, do the shows. The main three're the Belle Boys, DOTS, and the Milly Molly Mandies. This trip out's the DOTS show, going back's the Millies, next out's the Belles. Works like that.'

'No women coming?' asked Cato. 'Stewardesses or . . .?'

'No Tabbies allowed down the Pig,' said Tudor. 'Alamein's a men's deck.'

'Except for the concert group,' said Cato.

'Well . . .' Tudor smiled, licked a fingertip, touched his eyebrows, and pulled a comb from a back pocket. 'You'll see.' He ran the comb through his hair and buffed his toe caps against the back of his serge trousers. 'In?'

'After you,' said Cato.

He followed Tudor through the low steel doorway. Inside, packed four-deep around the steel walls, and shoulder-to-shoulder on benches and metal chairs, waited some two hundred uniformed and shirt-sleeved men. On the floor in front of the chairs sat the bellboys, cross-legged. Forward of them, beneath a shuttered dart-board, a small space had been left clear, at one side of which stood a battered upright piano. The air was thick with smoke, soapy-sour with beer, tight with expectancy.

Every eye, as he entered, turned to Cato. Their regard was friendly, however, and space was swiftly made for him between two seamen on one of the benches near the back. As the ship rose and fell, he felt himself safely immovable. A bottle of beer was passed to him; he craned forward but could not identify the giver.

At some invisible signal, a hand reached to the electric light-switch. Half-darkness and complete silence fell over the waiting rows of men. Only a single low-wattage bulb suspended over the dart-board remained lit. A stout figure in pantryman's whites took his place at the piano, and

Dusty Hay, his cannonball head shining, stepped into the dim circle of light.

'Evening, gents!' He paused, rolling easily with the ship, 'You are all . . . *gentlemen*, aren't you? No . . . *ladies* present?'

The question, clearly a familiar one, was greeted with cries of 'No!', 'Never!' and in one case, 'Get off!'

Dusty silenced them with a raised hand. His manner was that of the ringmaster, gravelled and polished. The discreet upper-deck servant might never have existed. 'Gentlemen, that being the case, it is my very great pleasure to present to you – in the brand new DOTS revue "Girls at Sea" – our very own, our lovely Miss . . . *Davina*!'

Through the steel entrance door – now curtained – and into the light, stepped a monstrous simulacrum of a woman. Six feet of loosely worked flesh had been packed, not easily, into a sequined fish-tail gown, and over the rouged and wattled features, in horrible approximation of a Eugene wave, crouched a lard-white horsehair wig. This vision was greeted with stamping and raucous applause.

'Evening, boys! Bit rough, isn't it? Still,' she pursed her lips and raised an eyebrow as the pianist brought his hands down in a shuddering major chord, 'I've never minded *rough*!' Her voice was a mahoganied bass. Cato felt the shaking of shoulders on either side of him. 'We've got a decidedly *bona* little show for you tonight, boys, so a big strong hand please – you know how they love it – for *Eth* and *Barrietta*!'

Through the black curtain scrambled two further figures, less massive than Davina perhaps, but similarly – and similarly implausibly – coiffed, bosomed and sequined. They placed a beringed hand each on Davina's shoulders, Eth (or possibly Barrietta) wobbled, Davina rolled her eyes – 'Lost yer sea-lals, girl?' – and the pianist banged out the lead-in to the show's first number.

Girls at sea!
Whirls at sea!
Ruby lips and choo-choo nose and curls at sea!
You really can't imagine
The trouble we take
The slap we use, the schickels,
And the mirrors we b-r-e-a-k . . .

Girls at sea!
Whirls at sea!
Oggle-riah, fancy bats and pearls at sea!
We're really very nice girls,
We promise we are
And nice girls all love seafood
Love a jolly Jack T-a-r . . .

In the roar of laughter greeting these words, the seaman
to Cato's left – a sharp-featured man with a broken nose –
turned to him. Through the whooping and stamping, Cato
strained for the seaman's words. ' . . . the lingo?' the man
shouted, ' . . . the old parleyare?'

Cato shrugged and smiled.

'Not to worry.' The seaman removed his roll-up and
called across to his companion. 'In a dim light, eh!'

'This *is* a fuckin' dim light,' grinned the other.

Girls at sea!
Whirls at sea!
Dorothys, Deannas, Judys, *Merles* at sea.
There's some girls love a villa,
a castle in Spain,
But my delight's a glory-hole
in El Ala-m-e-i-n . . .

As the steel floor rang with the stamping of four hundred
feet, Cato realised that he had not touched his beer. He
tilted the bottle backwards.

'That's the way, son.' The broken-nosed seaman handed him a tin.

'Smoko?'

'Thanks,' said Cato.

'Ain't they gorgeous?'

Lighting up, Cato nodded and gave a thumbs-up.

'Gentlemen,' Dusty joined the applause, 'The one, the only, the Daughters of the Sea.'

Steadying themselves, Eth and Barrietta withdrew into the darkness, and Davina, like a great frilled lizard, drew herself up to her full six feet.

'Thank you, Dusty dear. What a dolly, dolly omi you are . . . D'you know, boys, I first met Dusty in the tunnel of love – he was building it! Seriously though, boys, we had mala trouble getting here, *mala*. We're sharing a suite you see, right next to that camp Mrs MacLean everyone's talking about. Well, tonight, see, eight of the soirée we've got the riah up and we're trolling out for a sparkle when drop-drawers sticks her eek round the door and says Davina pet I need your dress sense I've this pash on for the purser we're meeting in number-three lifeboat and I don't yet know his taste. You soon will pet, I thought – vada the naf palone – so I says to her have you got anything dark and rough, yes she says I've got me Cocoa Channel . . .'

Cato listened uncomprehending, the gassy beer rising in his throat.

'Captain looked in this morning,' continued Davina. 'Lovely man, just popped his face in – said I want you three palones up on the bridge sharpish. Well it was!'

There were several more minutes of this oblique material, a second bottle found its way into Cato's hands, and then, abruptly, Davina sat down. In the quiet following the applause, the pantryman began to play the Warsaw Concerto theme from *Dangerous Moonlight*. The quiet became silence, broken only by the creak of chairs as the floor pitched beneath them. The men sat tight in the warm beery dark, thigh to thigh, shoulder to shoulder, unmoving, and Cato was suddenly happy to be there, unquestioned, amongst them. With the music's end, fanning herself, Davina rose heavily to her feet.

'All right, powder-monkeys, that'll do, dry yer eyes – it's us again. Barrietta, dear, you've got the passenger list, give us a vada who's on board.'

'Well, dear,' started Barrietta, stepping into the light, 'apart from the lovely Mrs Mac, it seems that we have Mister Ed "Dimples" Nelligan the boxer . . .'

'Ooooh, *bona*,' interjected Eth, (who as soon as she – or he – spoke, Cato recognised as Herbert the room-steward), 'I do love a ringside position!'

'We've got the gallant Major Farrell, D.S.O. . . .' Barrietta went on.

'Ooooh, *lash* me to the mast,' begged Eth–Herbert, 'an erect guardsman, I just *adore* a man in ribbons . . .'

'And – *quelle surprise* – we've got Mr Corcoran.'

'Ah, Miss Cork-Tip,' said Davina. 'Queen of the flush and the rubber. So who's she travelling as *this* time?'

'Own name, dear,' said Barrietta. 'No more titles. That nice Lady Walberton saw *pink* when she found that Naughty Corky had pinched hers to sucker a Yank. Really got her wild up, poor pet. She's a peer, after all!'

A cold void seemed to expand within Cato. '*Naughty Corky*,' he repeated to himself, unhearing of the patter which followed. '*Sucker a Yank?*' There couldn't be more than one. When, finally, his attention returned to the stage, the Daughters of the Sea were delivering a spirited if knowing rendition of 'Three Little Girls from School Are We'. This proved to be their finale, and five minutes later, with the national anthem sung, the lights were switched on.

'Enjoy it?' asked the broken-nosed seaman as, beer bottles in hand, they got to their feet.

'What I understood of it,' said Cato, suddenly dizzy, 'yes.'

'It's the parlare, see,' said the seaman, winking at his

companion on Cato's right. 'I might say, see, you had a *bona lucoddy* . . .'

'Button it, Squeezer,' amiably cut in a third, older man. 'Give us those bottles, son.'

'Thanks,' said Cato, steadying himself. 'Who should I thank for them?'

'Pig's blessing, son.' The seaman passed the bottles to a boy carrying a beer-crate. 'Who was it brought you down, now?'

'Um . . . Tudor. The bellboy. Can I ask you something?'

'Fire away.'

'Who was that Corcoran they were talking about?'

'Corcoran? Corky Corcoran? Professional sharp, what we call a boatman. Why, have you met him?'

'He's playing bridge with my father,' said Cato.

'Ah,' said the seaman slowly. 'Right.' He nodded, frowned, and wiped his hands uneasily on the backs of his serge trousers. 'I think . . . I think you'd better speak to Davey Garnett. Squeezer, could you . . .?'

'Now?' asked the seaman with the broken nose.

The other nodded. Cato, gesturing to Tudor to wait for him, followed Squeezer out of the Pig. In the crowded corridor the seaman turned to him. 'Tell me something, son. Is you one of the hunters,' – his face cracked into a smile – 'or one of the hunted?'

Cato stared at him, and after a long moment the other shook his head and, still smiling, turned away.

Cato followed him into a neighbouring glory-hole. As he stepped inside he realised that he was in a miniature green room. Garish costumes swung limply from a rack, a mirrored counter held greasepaint sticks, eyeblack, and several dirty glasses, and the air was thick with cheap lilac scent. On a chair before the mirror, smoking, and somehow overwhelmingly male despite the wig and the powder and the quilted pink dressing gown, sat Davina. Behind him, in flesh-coloured brassière and towel, Herbert was unhooking Barrietta's mauve fish-tailed gown. In the confines of the tiny steel-walled room the three men appeared shockingly oversized; the cloying, powdered sweat-smell enveloped Cato, and unbalanced by the rearing of the ship, he stepped backwards.

'Come *in*, dear, what a pleasure.'

It was Herbert who had spoken. Cato, mute, turned to Squeezer, who braced himself against the door-jamb and coughed. 'Young gentleman wanted to ask Mr Garnett about Mr Corcoran. Seems 'is dad's . . .'

Davina looked up.

'My father's playing bridge with Corcoran,' said Cato, belatedly finding his voice.

'Mr Blunden said the gentleman should speak to you,' said Squeezer. 'That you'd know the score, like.'

'How could I, dear?' Davina turned pensively to the mirror and patted at his wattle with the back of a plump hand. 'I'm not playing.' He turned to his fellow-performers. 'Who's she think I am?' he demanded petulantly, 'Old Moore?'

Behind him, Eth and Barrietta turned away, sniggering.

'On the other hand,' Davina continued gravely, leaning forward for a closer examination of his heavy-pored features, 'I can always accommodate a gentleman caller. So why don't you leave him here with us?'

Squeezer nodded and withdrew, and Garnett leaned heavily back in his chair.

'Now, first things first. Eth, run and fetch your mother a bevvy, there's a good girl. Gin and It.'

'Crystals?' asked Herbert.

'Nanti, dear, as it comes.' He turned to Cato. 'What about a drop for you, ducks?'

Cato shook his head. 'No thanks.'

'No? Chorus girl's breakfast, then? Cup of tea and a fag?'

Cato discovered that that was exactly what he did want, and Herbert, covering his damply muscled shoulders with a mohair shawl, left the glory-hole.

'Now then,' said Garnett, 'off with the riah . . .' Carefully, he removed his wig to reveal a nylon stocking-cap kirby-gripped to blue-grey hair, ' . . . and let us turn our attention to Mr Corcoran. They're playing bridge, you say. Sure it's not poker?' His voice had changed, Cato noticed, had assumed a brisker and more official timbre. He looked concerned, and not in the least ridiculous.

'Bridge, my father said.'

'How did they meet?'

Cato told him all he knew.

'And where's the game taking place now?'

'Corcoran's cabin. Suite, actually, he's got.'

'And who are the other two?'

'Other two?' asked Cato.

Garnett looked at him patiently. At that moment Herbert re-entered with a tray.

'Thanks, dear,' said Garnett, something of his earlier manner returning. 'Now, have we got a decent ciggy for Mr . . .'

'Parkes,' said Herbert. 'Cato Parkes. He's one of my "A" deckers, aren't you, pet. Take the bevvy and I'll have a vada in my croccy-bag. I've got a Passing Cloud somewhere.'

'Thanks,' said Cato, 'that's . . .'

'Shush, dear. *Noblesse oblige!*' He lowered the tray and handed Barrietta a glass of advocaat. 'There you go, girl. Tart's custard!'

'Mmmm. Chin-chin!'

Garnett, detaching himself from this exchange, slowly began to work cold cream into his face.

'Let me explain to you', he said eventually, 'about boatmen. They work in teams – card-sharps like Corky usually in teams of three, sometimes with a girl – and hit one mark per crossing.' He wiped his lips with a greasepaint-stained towel and sipped minutely at his drink.

'Your dad'll win to start with, probably go on winning for the whole trip, get more and more confident. Last moment, though, when land's in sight and he's flush with their money, one of the three will suggest a last game. Poker, this time, or red dog. Well,' Garnett looked up, his saurian features now an oily clay, 'put yourself in his position. Not easy to say no. Besides, these men are his friends. He's taken their money, he's drunk their whisky, he's spent most of the crossing in their suite . . .'

Cato blew on his tea. A pall of cigarette smoke hung above them.

'The final game never takes more than a few minutes. At the end of it the mark's handed back all the seed money and is reaching for his cheque book. He's not quite sure what's happened to him except that it's happened very, very fast. Horrid, really. I remember seeing one passenger – lovely man, American – standing at the rail as we docked at Pier Ninety. He was white as a sheet, and his mouth was hanging open. Couldn't move. Just stood like that for . . . I don't know how long. He'd just been taken by the Girl with the Waxen Arm for twenty-five thousand.'

He shook his head. 'And there's nothing we can do about it. We know most of the boatmen, and those we don't are easy to spot. Any passenger books into a stateroom with no more than a suitcase you can be sure he's on the cross, but . . .' He shrugged.

'What should I do?' asked Cato, steadying his cup and saucer on the counter.

'You're probably still Okay,' said Garnett. 'We've a fair way to go yet. Your safest bet, truth be told, would be for your dad to hand back the money he's won and call it a day. Corcoran's boys'd get the message all right, and you wouldn't have them after you for the seed money. Depends how rough you want to play.'

Cato nodded. As if in response to Garnett's words, the ship hung motionless, and then meeting the sea dead-weight, sheered hard to starboard.

'Old girl's a bit snappy on the roll tonight,' observed Garnett, reaching forward for the counter. 'See you've got your sea-legs, though. Good boy.' He buried his head for a moment in the towel. 'I bet you one thing,' he said. 'I bet your dad's the soberest, most sensible bloke you'd ever hope to meet.'

'I suppose he is,' admitted Cato. 'I'd always thought, though, he was a bit . . . well, foxier.'

'The *Milly*'s the Royal Albion's flagship, son. The boat-men are the cleverest in the world. Your dad isn't the first and he won't be the last.'

Cato nodded again. 'Well,' he hesitated. 'I'm sure you're . . . I'll get on up. Thanks for the advice.'

'If it's come on top already, get a word down. The name's Davey Garnett, I'm the Captain's Tiger.'

'I will, thanks, Davey. And thanks for the show.'

Garnett winked. 'Just a bit of camp, dear.'

Cato knew as soon as he turned into his own corridor that something had happened, that there had been an event. Light shone from the hooked-open door of the cabin, and in the low entrance, arms braced against the movement of the ship, stood two women in the white aprons and back-swept veils of nursing sisters. As he approached, they turned towards him.

'Are you the son?' one of them asked.

Cato nodded.

'Your father's had a wee accident. Nothing serious, but . . .'

Cato, conscious of the smoke and beer of the Pig hanging sourly about him, stepped between them. At his father's bedside, a uniformed Montmorency was returning surgical articles to his Gladstone bag.

'Ah,' he said. 'Cato. I'm afraid your Dad's taken a bit of a knock. Slipped and cracked his head.'

Reginald seemed to be asleep. He was in pyjamas, and his head had been bandaged around the crown and under his chin so that he looked like a motor-racing driver or a parachutist. A large safety-pin – a baby's nappy-pin – stood upright at his ear.

'He's concussed,' continued Montmorency, steadying himself against the wardrobe, 'and I've had to put in half a dozen stitches. What he really needs is a good night's sleep and a couple of day's rest.' He snapped the bag closed, and rubbed his eyes. 'Just to be on the safe side, I'd like to have Moira stay in here tonight. We've moved your things down the corridor to another cabin.'

Cato looked more closely at his father. His breathing was inaudible, he smelt faintly of spirits, and he was very pale.

'He'll be fine,' repeated Montmorency, the long pessimistic features appearing to contradict him. 'Fine.'

Cato nodded. Pulling open the wardrobe door he saw that his clothes and cases had been removed. Surreptitiously, he felt in his father's dinner-jacket for his wallet and transferred it to his own breast pocket.

'Right,' he said. 'Well. Thank you very much. Do you have any idea where I'm supposed to go?'

The new cabin was thirty yards further forward, was smaller than the first, and only contained a single bed. Otherwise it was the same. The same Bible, clothes-brush and ashtray lay against the raised edges of the dressing table, and the air was damped by the same smell of furniture polish and bath salts.

Locking the door, Cato opened his father's wallet. He counted over twelve hundred pounds. Pocketing twenty of them, he laid the remainder next to the manila envelope in the lining of his overnight bag and left the bag ostentatiously opened and empty in the wardrobe. The wallet he placed on the dressing table.

At the knock on the door, he started guiltily. Montmorency stood outside, holding his Gladstone bag.

'Fancy a breath of air up top?' Self-consciousness shadowed the suggestion.

'Um . . . yes, why not?' Cato unhooked the cabin door.

'Probably our last chance for a day or two. They'll be closing the decks if this swell gets any worse, and after a day tending seasick passengers, frankly . . . You're Okay, by the way, aren't you?'

'Yes,' said Cato. 'Fine, somehow.'

He followed Montmorency along the heaving, falling corridor to the main staircase. This staircase, which ascended from the Main Deck, was centrally divided, the inner stream ascending directly to the Sports Deck – a wind-blown area between the funnels, marked out for deck games – and the outer, reserved for the Cabin Classes, giving on to the Promenade and Boat Decks. Cato had used the staircase once or twice, and had found himself stared at – whether out of envy at his privilege or pity at his halting progress he was unsure – by those on the public side of the rail. Tonight, though, there was nobody. Montmorency waited for him at the top of the staircase.

'That question you asked me, old son. About surgical procedure?'

'Mmm.'

'Still want to know the answer?'

'I think so,' said Cato, reaching for the guide-rope. 'Yes.'

'Well, I'll tell you,' he said, 'on the condition that you forget all that hacksaw-through-the-sternum nonsense, and that you don't mention . . .'

'I promise,' said Cato.

'It makes me angry,' said Montmorency. 'They tell you nothing, and the human imagination being what it is, you imagine the worst.'

Cato, reaching the top of the stairs, said nothing.

'You're anaesthetised,' said Montmorency decisively. 'The incision,' he drew a spatulate finger between the third and fourth rib of Cato's left side, 'is made here, and the ribs are clamped apart. The surgeon then clears the lungs out of the way and makes a small incision in the left atrium of the heart. Atrium?'

'Yes,' said Cato.

'Right. The surgeon then pokes his finger through the hole that he's made, and with his fingertip feels for

143

the mitral valve. In your case this valve is too small, and not enough blood is getting through to the lungs. So the surgeon just . . . pushes it open with his finger.'

Slowly, Cato nodded. He smelt the thin larder-smell, saw black blood congealed like snot at the nostrils of hares, dripping from the beaks of pigeons. 'And then?'

'And then that's it. They patch you up and pack you off home. Who's your surgeon?'

'A Mr Tod.'

'Lawrence Tod, eh? Well, you're in good hands.'

'So everyone says. To be honest, I've not thought about it much in the last couple of days.'

'That's good,' said Montmorency, peering through a porthole at the grey, pitching sky. 'Keeping busy, then?'

'Oh, not really,' said Cato. 'One thing just seems to follow another.'

'Good,' said Montmorency. 'Good.' He nodded at some length, as if the darkening seascape had confirmed some privately held theory. 'Well, I hope that tells you more or less what you wanted to know. I always say an operation's a bit like a day out at Sandown Park. To come out a winner you've either got to know all of the facts or none of them. Shall we . . .?' He pushed at the heavy door. The wind, angry, resisted them, and then they were outside.

For a moment, Cato's eyes refused what they saw. The *Carmelia*'s white-lit superstructure was so massive – and her roll, in consequence, so slow – that it seemed as if the horizon itself was tilting on its axis. Only when he found himself swung several paces across an apparently level deck and pitched hard against the guard-rail did his senses adjust and the pale night skyline return to the horizontal. The weather was bearing down on them from the starboard side, from the Pole, and the *Carmelia* was listing hard to port. Slowly, as her forepeak reared and bowed to the black water a hundred yards ahead, she righted herself. White spray leapt about her shoulders and then, once again, she started to roll. She seemed to go over and over and then, as the wind screamed through the shrouds and around the deck-houses, to go further still. Only the lessening pressure of his body against the rail told Cato that the slow climb to the vertical had begun again.

'I'm surprised they haven't roped off the decks,' shouted Montmorency. 'Usually when they put the rolling lines out, they close 'em off.'

'How long do you think it'll go on?' asked Cato.

'Oh, I doubt this'll let up till tomorrow at the earliest. See a few more cuts and bruises by then, I'm afraid.'

They were standing, sheltered from the wind, behind a boiler vent.

'See up there,' Montmorency pointed upwards. 'That was a gun position. All the vents had twenty-mill Oerlikons mounted and a couple of blokes up. You can imagine the fun they had in a high sea.'

'Were you the ship's doctor then?' asked Cato.

'More than one of us,' said Montmorency. 'Full surgical team in those days.' He shrugged the uniform jacket around his shoulders and looked at his watch. 'Better get below. I'll look in on your dad. Don't stay out too long.'

'Thanks,' said Cato. 'I won't.'

As Montmorency closed the entrance door behind him, Cato stepped from behind the vent and cautiously began to move along the rail to the forward position from which, two days earlier, he had watched the Hampshire coast recede. He settled himself, finally, against a lifeboat winch. As the ship reached the furthest point of her vertiginous outward roll, he found himself suspended, not over the decks below but over the racing, illuminated sea. For a moment, leaning outwards, he imagined the whole vast, lit-up mansion-block a yacht, imagined that it was only his weight which carried her down.

Between the bridge and the forward funnel a pale, fluttering movement caught his eye, and he straightened self-consciously. At first, he was uncertain of what he had seen. The floodlights washing the funnel threw the surrounding deck-fittings into a greater darkness, and he had to squint to penetrate their beam. Gradually he made out the head and shoulders of a man, who, several yards away and half-concealed by a life-belt locker, appeared to be holding a woman by the forearms against the steel-plated exterior of the bridge. The man, who had his back to Cato, was all but invisible in dark evening dress. It was the faint movement of the woman's hand beyond the shadow of the locker that he had seen. She must be cold, thought Cato, irrelevantly. Her head jerked spasmodically from side to side as if she were having a fit. Shielding his eyes against the floodlight at the base of the funnel Cato saw that the woman was wearing a strapless evening dress of some pale material. It was too dark behind the locker to make out her features. He tried looking away to the side, the unlit side, and for a moment, at the edge of his vision, saw her more clearly. He looked at her and looked away, looked at her and looked away, but finally he could make no more of her than a dark assembly of features. The man shifted, gathered her forearms above her head, and holding them with one hand against the steel wall, began to slap forehand and backhand at the shadowed face with the other. The woman's dark head continued its twitching, loose-necked movement. Beyond the wind, Cato could hear nothing. It was as if he were watching a poor-quality silent film.

Belatedly, it occurred to him that he was witnessing some kind of assault, and that despite its soundlessness, its curious ritual quality, this assault was happening only yards from him. Carefully, withdrawing from his position against the winch, he edged along the dark rail towards the exit.

Inside, he hurried down the outer stairs to the Boat Deck, where, at the head of one of the galleries, he knew there to be a telephone. Pulling out his passenger list, hesitating only briefly, he dialled the number of Jerry Farrell's cabin. Farrell answered immediately.

'Jerry, it's Cato. Cato Parkes. I wonder, could you come

to the head of the main stairs, by the Sports Deck exit. Someone's being attacked.'

'On my way,' said Farrell.

He arrived less than a minute later in pale blue pyjamas and cricket pullover, carrying something that looked like a chair-leg.

'I'm terribly sorry,' began Cato, 'I didn't know you'd . . .'

'Don't worry, old man,' said Farrell, cheerfully. '*Semper Paratus* and all that rot. Where's the scrap?'

Indicating silence, Cato led him on to the pitching deck and along the rail. Although highly visible in his pale clothing, Farrell moved with the agility of a cat. Together they edged forward to Cato's earlier position and crouched behind the winch.

Over the few minutes of Cato's absence, however, things had changed. The male figure still had his back to them, but his hands were now beneath the woman's evening dress which, like a pornographic ceramic shepherdess Cato had once discovered in his parents' wardrobe, she was holding up around her waist.

'Ah,' said Farrell, quite loudly. '*That* sort of scrap.'

Mortified at his misconstruction, completely at a loss for words, Cato made to withdraw, but his arm was stilled. Below them, as the ship reached the furthest point of her roll, the white spray leapt up and fell soundlessly away.

The man seemed to genuflect, and then to raise his head to the woman as if in prayer. In turn she parted her legs further, lowering herself down the steel wall to meet him. One hand released the bunched material at her waist and found his hair. Once again Cato moved to stand, but the grip on his arm tightened. Beside him, shifting his weight, Farrell reached into the fly of his pyjama trousers and commenced an urgent stroking. His heart sinking – and terrified, now, of discovery, of implication – Cato looked away. Any lingering curiosity he might have felt was dispelled by the presence of Farrell and that mad jacking fist. The ship pitched, cracking Cato's head against the engine casing and sending tears to his eyes and the shadows swinging.

'Ease springs a minute,' said Farrell, his dancing hand slowing to a thoughtful halt. 'That's the bloody zookeeper's wife. And that chancer Watson.'

Behind the pain of the knock, a horrible certainty flooded Cato that Farrell was right.

'Look,' he said, 'please. I really have to go. My father . . .'

'Oh . . . Righto, then.' The grip at Cato's arm loosened a notch or two and then tightened again. 'Sure you won't stick around?'

'I think not.'

'Okay, then. Off you push. Now I'm padded up, so to speak, I might just . . .'

Cato crept past him and made his way back along the rail. A trickle of blood blew across his forehead and he blotted it away with his cuff.

As soon as he opened the door, he realised he'd come to the wrong cabin. His father stirred and groaned, and the nursing sister looked up from her armchair.

'Sorry,' mouthed Cato. 'I forgot.' As he went out, he paused to look at Reginald. A line of blood-spots had seeped through the crown of the bandage, and he was breathing with a faint whistle. The sister stood, put down her knitting, and walked over. 'What've ye done to yersel'?'

'Oh, I just banged my head. It's . . .'

'Gi' us a look, then, under the light.' She was about twenty, with soft, determined eyes. Reluctantly, fearful of her kindness, Cato closed the door and followed her.

'Aye, well,' she told him two minutes later, returning a bottle of witch-hazel to her bag. 'Ye'll live.'

'Is he really Okay?' He nodded towards his father.

'Dinna' ye trust us?' She smiled.

'Of course.' He touched the still-damp lump on his forehead.

'Go on wi' ye, then.'

In his own cabin, Cato began to undress. The beer and the knock had given him a headache, but he felt unhappier than a headache would have warranted.

He tried to wash the blood from his dress-shirt, but an obstinate brown stain remained. Stepping backwards from the sink as the ship reared beneath his feet, he trod on the trailing cuff, from which he had not removed the link. There was a crunching sound, and when he lifted the shirt he found that the black oval face of the cufflink was snapped.

The cufflinks had been a birthday present. His father had taken him up to town for the day; they had lunched at Ley-On's in Wardour Street, taken in a matinée of *Pink String and Sealing Wax*, and had then sortied forth rather aimlessly to look for a present. With five o'clock approaching, no present bought, and Cato's nervousness increasing by the minute, they had found themselves outside a gent's outfitters in Cecil Court, off St Martin's Lane. The links had lain amongst a dusty assortment of carded braces and garters beneath a display of suiting material. When the assistant handed them to him in their cheap little box Cato could see that they were second-rate but also – he was acutely aware of the limitations of his father's position – that they were easily affordable. He had pronounced himself satisfied, and the box had been handed over and paid for. Examining the cufflinks at home, he had determined, despite the too-thin enamel and yellow electro-plating, that they would become loved and familiar objects. They hadn't; instead, they had come to symbolise all the things that, over the years, his father had been unable to provide or to enjoy. And sitting on his bed with the twisted link and the stained shirt in his hand, seeing once again the scrubby-moustached features beneath the nappy-pinned helmet of bandages, Cato felt tears at his cheeks. For he knew that these unenjoyed things were in their turn symbolic of an obstinately grounded integrity, and that inseparable from that integrity, finally, was unreachability.

# 4

Around him, the panelling creaked and shuddered in an agony of strain. The bedhead fell away, was caught and swung upwards. For a moment, the ship righted herself, and then – and Cato imagined the great screws screaming, biting on air – she crashed stomach-emptyingly into the void.

Above him materialised a swinging, illuminated sky-sign. A face, ivory-white and in the form of a monocled, cigar-smoking balloon glass, rose from a starched and disembodied shirt-front.

MR BRANDYMAN, read the sign. Make Friends With MARTELL.

Cato forced himself awake, and reached sightlessly for the bedside table. The luminous hands of his watch indicated either ten past three or quarter past two. Above him, above the dark and angry ranges of sea, the monocled balloon-glass face of Mr Brandyman reappeared.

Make Friends With MARTELL.

Cato knew himself to be asleep, and knowing that he knew, thought himself awake. 'Where are the Vermilion Lancers,' he asked aloud.

'Quartered close,' said Mr Brandyman, his voice like death. 'Quartered close and mobilised. What do you wish?'

'I wish to ride,' said Cato.

The Brandyman, no more than a suspended skull now, removed the cigar, nodded, and grew faint. Cato found himself on the sea-become-land, a smoke-darkened plain over which blew an infinity of charred papers, printed forms, and typewritten requisitions. Around him, he heard the jangle of stirrups, the snort and snicker of excited horses. Dust rose: he was in the saddle, moving from the trot to the canter and then with the smoke at his eyes and his lance levelled, to the gallop. Shouts, now, screams, whipped away behind the drumming hooves and all around him the other riders spattering into scarlet and falling away as they met the crashing load-and-volley, load-and-volley, from the darkness ahead.

And then, like a film arrested, everything was still. Riderless horses hung suspended at the gallop, sabre-strokes blurred in mid-descent, and all around, stilled so that he could pick them from the air, the pitted, drop-cast balls of shot. Cato reached out before him but as he did so an ochred varnish formed over all that he saw, became a craquelure, separated, and was whirled away in fragments on the fretting wind of the plain.

He found himself folding, quite comfortably, to the ground. Charred papers blew in front of his face, the braid facings of his scarlet coat parted and he saw that his chest was laid open. Briefly, above him, he saw the fading sky-sign figure, saw amusement touch the cadaverous features and then a familiar darkness fell, the knives moved cold within him, and the needles drew their clotted threads.

They moved him after that, as they always did, carried him over uneven ground on a stretcher covered by a stained and sticking sheet.

> The nights were very bad,
> and patches of night, dressings,
> applied to the pale day . . .

The lines came to him fully formed. He repeated them, fearful of forgetting, but the violent swinging of the stretcher prevented his holding to the words and they drifted away like smoke.

He woke to a dawn in which the tattered remains of night still flapped and lingered. Beyond the streaming armour-plated glass of the porthole, sea and sky joined in a blurred grey. In the wardrobe he could hear the trunk and the suitcases thumping hollowly backwards and forwards.

He lay in the wrecked bed for a time, trying to escape the dread which accompanied wakefulness, but the rolling of the ship made further sleep impossible. He reached for his watch, which had fallen from the bedside table to the carpet, but it had stopped. He dressed, and telephoned for Herbert. The steward told him that it was half past seven, and Cato ordered breakfast to be served in his father's cabin.

He discovered Reginald somewhat tetchily submitting to the ministrations of the barber, who was darting around him to the roll of the ship like a prize-fighter. From her armchair the nurse, Moira, watched with slow amusement.

'How is the patient?' asked Cato.

'Well enough.' She smiled. 'Ask him yersel'.'

Reginald, around whose mouth the barber was at that moment manoeuvring his blade, remained silent. Only when talcum powder had been applied to his chin and the razor and strop returned to the barber's bag did he bid Cato a rueful good-morning.

'Quite a blow,' said Cato, turning to the portholes.

Reginald gingerly touched his head. 'Damn stupid of me. Should've known better at my age.'

'I meant outside,' said Cato.

'Hey? Oh, see what you mean, yes. I . . .'

'It's been a fair old storm for June,' said Moira, peering carefully between the curtains. 'Worst's over now, though, I'd say.' She gathered her things together, and moved to Reginald's bedside. Timing her movements as the barber had done to those of the ship, she changed his dressing and bandage. With the work complete, and the safety-pin once more in vertical place at Reginald's temple, she left, promising to call in later in the morning.

In his dispensing of the breakfast, Herbert made no reference, by word or by look, to the scene of the previous night in the Pig and Whistle; Cato, however, thought he detected a faint cosmetic residue about the steward's pinkish features.

'You gentlemen are in a minority for breakfast,' Herbert told Reginald. 'There's still a fair old swell.'

No one, thought Cato, could speak of anything but the weather. It governed them absolutely. 'Do you think it'll clear up?' he asked the steward.

'Certain to, sir. Blow itself out by lunchtime. I'd drink a spot of that tea, sir, before you put it down.'

For several minutes, father and son breakfasted in silence. Finally Cato looked up from his tray at the dressing table.

'Dad,' he asked, 'do you know what a "boatman" is?'

Something in his son's expression made Reginald lower, and then fold, the morning's copy of the ship's newspaper.

Slowly, omitting only the precise nature of the revue he had watched, Cato recounted what he had discovered. His words were followed by a long silence, during which his father's expression changed not at all.

'And this man Garnett,' Reginald finally began, 'is the . . .?'

'Captain's Tiger,' explained Cato. 'I think some kind of senior waiter.'

'And he named Corcoran by name.'

'Several of them did. They recognised him from other crossings.'

For a dozen further heart-beats, one hand absently steadying the breakfast tray in front of him, Reginald sat in disbelieving silence.

'A card-sharping gang,' he said eventually. 'Well I'm damned. Well I'm ruddy well damned.' He shook his head, winced, and looked up. Grimacing, he touched the tips of his fingers to his incisors. 'It looks as if I have you both to thank.'

Cato shrugged. 'Garnett didn't seem to imply that was necessary,' he said, warily. 'And I . . . well, the whole thing was complete chance. It's Tudor we should thank.'

'Tudor?'

'The bellboy who invited me down there.'

'Extraordinary name,' murmured Reginald. 'Imagine christening your son Tudor.'

'Not much odder than Stewart,' said Cato.

'That's true,' said Reginald vaguely. 'That's true . . . My *God*, what a chump I've been.' He made as if to shake his head and, remembering his injury, closed his eyes.

At the dressing table, Cato poured a second cup of tea.

'You've done damn well,' said Reginald. 'Damn well.'

'It wasn't really me,' said Cato.

'You pushed on,' said Reginald, in a tone of voice that Cato had not heard before from his father. 'You followed up. You secured the truth – probably at the cost of some embarrassment – in an entirely alien situation. To be frank with you, I'm impressed. Damn impressed.'

Cato's eyes widened. 'It occurred to me', he said, not quite trusting his voice, 'that perhaps you shouldn't . . . show yourself around the ship too much.'

'No fear of that, old boy.' He folded his arms over his pyjamaed chest, and immediately unfolded them as the tray on his knees shunted to starboard. 'I'm staying put right here. Only another thirty-four or -five hours and we'll be in New York.'

'Should we perhaps let the purser or somone know the situation?'

'Tell me what you think,' asked Reginald.

Cato took a long draught of the not-quite-hot tea. 'Well,' he began, 'as things stand, they – Corcoran and Co. – don't know that we know what we know.' He paused, ordering his thoughts. 'That being the case, our holding on to the winnings seems only natural, as does our remaining . . . politely disposed towards them.' He looked at Reginald, who nodded without expression. 'If we inform on them,'

Cato continued, 'the purser or whoever we speak to has a choice of taking action or of taking no action. We have to assume from the fact that Corcoran is known to the below-decks crew that he is also known to the officers. From the fact that he and his . . . gang have been allowed to operate, we have to assume that the officers – ship's authorities – are unwilling or unable to prevent them from doing so.' Reginald nodded again and Cato, anxious to hold fast to his argument, closed his eyes. One by one, fully formed, the phrases presented themselves. It was as if they were not of his own devising, that he was simply the instrument of their release.

'If we report the gang's activities,' he continued, 'any action that the authorities take is contrary to our direct interests. Whether we are named or quoted or not, Corcoran's people will know – since we have been their only targets – who has complained. They will be forced into an attitude of hostility, and our hanging on to their "seed" money – which is what, despite Garnett's advice, I assume we intend to do – will be a challenge to which they will feel that they owe it to themselves to respond. So, no,' he said, stilling with one hand a silver milk-jug's slide towards his lap, 'we keep *stumm*.'

'And future passengers, future victims?' asked Reginald, almost impatiently.

'We have no case against Corcoran and Co., who, whatever their intentions, have – so far – done us no harm. Nothing short of barring them from the ship for life would have any effect on future passengers, and nothing we could do or say would achieve that end. Taking their money, on the other hand, might slow them down.'

'And the moral position?'

'There is no moral position. To intend is to do. Their intentions are to do us harm, and release us from any obligation to respond other than in kind.'

For several minutes they sat in silence. Finally, effortfully, Reginald lowered the breakfast tray to the floor.

'And just who, may I ask, taught you to reason in that way?' His voice came from beneath the bed. 'It doesn't sound much like the authentic voice of Cleeve – "*Damus plus quam pollicemur*" and so forth.'

'I think', said Cato slowly, suddenly tired, 'that you did.'

Reginald, righting himself and rearranging the bed-clothes before him into a series of parallel folds, slowly nodded. 'I was afraid you'd say that.' He touched his fingertips thoughtfully to his incisors. 'You do know, don't you, what I do?'

'Pretty much,' said Cato.

'And what do you . . .?' asked Reginald.

'I think that it's what – if everything works out – I'd . . .'

'Like to do?'

Cato said nothing.

'The world, someone once told me,' said Reginald, 'is divided into prosecution and defence counsels. A matter, I suppose, of how you view the instincts of your fellow human beings. I have always known myself to be a pros-ecutor, just as I always knew your mother to be a defender. Until recently I always thought you were a defender too. Now I'm not so sure.'

'What would I have to do?' asked Cato.

'Oh . . . finish Cleeve, go up to Cambridge, probably read a bit of history or some modern languages . . . But let's see. You may well decide between now and then that you don't want to spend your life in a Whitehall office, that you'd rather be a doctor in Winchester or a solicitor in Cheltenham or a barrister . . .' Unable to think of further professions or locations, he fell silent.

'I won't change my mind.'

'Well, we'll see. Just don't go around talking about it all.'

'Dad!' Cato protested.

'Well, don't. That's lesson one.' He lifted the telephone receiver and held his hand over the mouthpiece. 'Lesson two', he continued sternly, 'is never play bridge with strangers on an ocean liner.'

With no particular destination in mind, Cato made his way to the Promenade Deck. The lifts, to his surprise, were in service – he had imagined that they would only function in good weather – and he shared the ascent with a clergyman with a badly cut cheek and a heavily bandaged ankle.

'Bathroom floor,' explained the priest apologetically. 'Frightful cropper.'

Cato followed the limping man from the lift and out to the covered promenade. The sea, leaping soundless and grey-brown beyond the windowed screen, had a routed, disorganised appearance, as if in flight before the wind. Standing at the streaming glass with his collar turned up and his hands on the rail, Cato knew a sober but certain exhilaration. He looked around him and saw that the promenade, its diminishing perspectives pale in the glass-dulled light, had assumed the formal composition of a painting. Somewhere at the edge of his memory swam a particular painting, a particular wall, and as he turned back to the plate-glass he remembered the blustering but unimportant seascape that had overhung the empty mantelpiece of the Wimpole Street waiting room. Part of his present exhilaration, he realised, lay in the knowledge that there would be no more stifling waiting rooms, no more yawning dread, no more deferral of pain and fear. The moment was almost here, and all the necessary decisions were already taken. He knew that his chances stood no better and no worse than at evens (he had read Rutherford's letter upside-down at the breakfast table the day it arrived) and he also knew that the greatest test of his discretion was to keep that same knowledge from his father. It would, of course, have been interesting to discuss the whole thing – Cato guessed that Reginald had sent men into the field with far poorer chances of survival – but it would not have been kind. For his own courage, he realised, corresponded exactly to his father's vulnerability.

In the corridor, Cato found himself reeling, not uncomfortably, from wall to wall. The sensation recalled his first experience of drunkenness. The strain of remaining on his feet made progress around the ship at least twice as exhausting as it was in calm weather, and it was with relief that he reached the door to the library and reading room.

Inside were a dozen or so passengers, including the priest, who was now drinking brandy. At a corner table beneath a bookcase, Pierre Watson was reading to Ayrest MacLean. As Cato approached, he looked up.

'Another survivor,' said Pierre without inflexion. 'Glass of Mumm?'

'I think I will,' said Cato, lowering himself to a leather-covered armchair as Pierre waved in the direction of the steward. 'Thank you.'

He noticed that, in common with several other male passengers, Pierre was unshaven. Two or three of those present appeared to have sustained minor injuries of one sort or another, and all were cheerfully ignoring the notices requesting silence. For Cabin Class passengers, they looked almost raffish.

The exception, of course, was Ayrest MacLean. In the past, Cato had never particularly noticed women's clothes except as sternly nondescript barriers to cold and immodesty, but from his first sight of Ayrest he had noticed, and covertly examined, everything that she wore. The individual garments were always extraordinary – swirling Tanagra straw hats, tight pongee jackets, balloon or Zouave-draped skirts – and she never repeated a single element of any ensemble. Today she was wearing a fitted tussore jacket over a long accordion-pleated black skirt. Beneath the table, twitching in mild ennui, were a pair of pointed black Spanish pumps. Cato had never before encountered such insouciant elegance and, blinking away as fast as it came the image of his mother's flat shoes and brown Woollands coat and skirt, he was deeply, sensually, impressed.

Pierre, it occurred to him, was attempting to make a sartorial impression of a different kind. Pierre always wore the same clothes – rumpled black corduroys and white shirt – and today he had added to these a paisley cravat. The effect, combined with his unshaven and habitually wild appeerence, was almost operatically Bohemian. Beside the pair of them (and in his sports jacket and pressed flannels and brown Waukeezee shoes) Cato felt distinctly provincial.

'Have you seen the rest of the ship?' asked Pierre. 'Frightful devastation. The Art and Science frieze broke off the wall in the Long Gallery – or at least the Art part did – and in the main lounge a Lalique vase weighted with lead shot fell on Mrs Klampmayer.'

'Who's Mrs Klampmayer?'

'I'm not sure,' said Pierre, rubbing at his chin. 'A fellow in the bar was telling me.'

'Mr Watson,' said Ayrest MacLean, 'was reading me some of his poetry.'

Pierre smiled self-consciously. The ship pitched, the books in the shelves strained against the cords holding them in place and the steward, deftly balancing a tray, climbed the room towards them. In order to avoid spilling the champagne, they all drank immediately.

'Perhaps you'd read some more?' enquired Cato, lowering his glass.

Pierre turned to Mrs MacLean. 'Well, if you're sure you . . .?'

'No, no.' She gave a small distracted wave of her cigarette. 'Please.'

Pierre paged through the notebook which lay in his lap, and then lifted it long-sightedly to arm's length. It was the same gesture, Cato noticed, that he habitually employed in the restaurant with the menu.

'A short one, then. This is called "Fall".' Darting a look

at Ayrest, who was examining the stem of her glass, he began to read:

> There is a single beat,
> when trailing empty air, the talons tighten,
> fall,
> to racing consequence.
>
> Again, no real choice,
> as pinions move, a gasp, and softly fold
> the feathered palm. To cast unhooded, flush
> at empty air
> to swing oblique, or tightening, watch
> the patient dulling of a gaze?

There was a moment's silence before Cato understood that there was no more to come. 'Are you interested in falconry?' he asked in a kind of panic.

'Not *per se*,' said Pierre, a little tersely. 'But I hope the poem's about a little more than falconry.' He ended the sentence on an interrogative note and inclined his head.

'I'm afraid I'm frightfully stupid about modern poetry,' said Ayrest, recognising her cue. 'Could you sort of . . . *explain*?'

'Well, what I think it's about,' said Pierre, turning to her, 'and of course what I think it's about and what you think it's about needn't be the same thing at all . . . What I think it's about is that moment of absolute commitment to a course of action. The moment, for example, when the Spitfire pilot or the falcon give themselves over absolutely the business of attack, and in so doing render themselves absolutely defenceless. The same thing, of course,' and he frowned at the notebook, 'applies to the lover . . .'

'Defenceless?' she murmured. 'Do you really think so? Or are you talking about a woman?'

'A man in love can be defenceless. Is defenceless. No?'

'I've heard it said so.' She leant forward to extinguish

her cigarette. 'But I must say', she raised her eyes to Cato, 'I find it a perfectly extraordinary idea.'

Cato, unable to respond, blinked, and looked at Pierre.

'I mean,' she continued, 'is it really the worst thing in the world to have "no" said to you?'

'Perhaps . . . it can seem so,' said Pierre, closing the notebook with a snap.

She regarded him for a moment, her face still, and then looked away. 'I'm sorry, I'm being disagreeable.'

'No!' Pierre's head darted forward solicitously. 'No, you're not, not at all.' He turned to Cato for confirmation, and Cato, mute, shook his head.

She looked from one to the other of them, amused, and closed her eyes.

It was the wrong thing, at that moment, to have done. The ship rolled violently to port, precipitating her from the polished chesterfield towards the heavily laden neighbouring table. Cato, whose first instinct was to save his drink, and who in nearly seventeen years of life had never made a sudden movement towards a woman, discovered himself impelled from his seat. As his glass fell to the table and shattered, his hand closed around the ivory silk of her sleeve. For a moment the continuing roll held them in frozen tableau – the boy braced against the forward impetus of the woman, the man holding the notebook to his chest and the tulip glass high in the air – and then, to the nervous laughter and hubbub that followed each more than usually violent motion of the ship, they righted themselves.

'Thank you,' Ayrest said to Cato. 'I almost feel that I caused that myself. As if I took my eye off the wheel.'

The steward hurried forward to clear the debris, returning unasked a minute later with a full glass. A typewritten page, much annotated, had fallen beneath the table from Pierre's notebook. Surreptitiously Cato read the first lines:

Again, and far from dawn,
The dull, familiar sidings of unease,

The villas where the ticker men once cheerioed
   anaemic girls,
and now the phones are dead

Walk, walk the xxxxxxxx

'Could you pass us that?' asked Pierre, blotting his cham-
pagne-damp trouser leg with a napkin, and indicating the
loose page.

'Yes,' said Cato, 'of course. Is the poem finished?'

'Holding out on me, rather, as a matter of fact. I wrote
the first quatrain in ten minutes flat at Croydon Airport, the
morning after a raid. I must have spent ten hours on it
since. How's the old man?'

'The . . . Oh, Dad. He's fine. At least, he isn't really. He
fell on the stairs last night and cut his head. He had to
have stitches.'

'Oh, I say,' said Pierre absently. 'Poor old chap. Do
convey my . . .'

'So he won't be coming tonight,' said Ayrest.

'Tonight?' asked Cato.

She smiled. 'Don't tell me you don't know what's on
tonight?' she said. 'It's the Last Night Ball.'

'Will that still be happening?' asked Cato, who remembered some mention of the event in the ship's newspaper.

'My dear boy, why on earth not?'

'Well, all the damage. And half – more than half – of
the passengers ill, and . . .'

'The storm will have blown itself out long before then.
And I doubt there's any permanent damage to passengers
or ship.'

'Well, my father certainly won't be coming,' said Cato,
smarting a little at 'dear boy'.

'And you?'

Cato imagined himself at an outer table, alone with Vichy
water and Senior Service, as elderly couples foxtrotted
around a lurching floor.

'I don't dance much,' he said.

'Even so,' she pleaded. 'You really have to come. Both of you. Everything leads up to the Last Night Ball. Nothing's quite the same on these crossings afterwards. Cato, are you sure we can't persuade your father to bestir himself.'

'I'm really not sure he's up to it,' said Cato (with her use of his name, all was forgiven). 'His head is bandaged. He's had stitches.'

'In that case,' she declared, snapping open her bag and taking out a passenger list, 'I shall go and convey my sympathies to him *en personne*. Any messages?'

Cato shook his head and Ayrest stood, gathered her gloves, and strode with easy mannequin composure from the room.

When she was gone, Pierre moved to the chair that she had occupied and around which, just detectibly, hung the faint freesia suggestion of her presence. As Pierre passed him, pensively removing a cigarette from the battered silver case and tapping it against his thumbnail, Cato was aware of the man's heavy corporeal odour flooding the space that she had occupied. The second and third fingers of the writer's hand, he saw, were stained a dark, nicotined orange.

'I hope I didn't . . .' he began.

'No, no . . .' said Pierre vaguely. 'Not at all.' He offered Cato the cigarette case, but Cato didn't feel like smoking.

'I don't know about you,' said Pierre, 'but I'm beginning to find this weather rather bloody.' He rubbed his eyes and ran a finger around the junction of the paisley cravat and his unshaven neck. 'I'd marry that woman tomorrow, you know.'

'Where's she going?' asked Cato.

'What do you mean, where's she going?'

'I mean, to New York or Hollywood or Minneapolis or . . . or Pennsylvania or where?'

Pierre looked at Cato as if at a prophet. 'I . . . don't know,' he said. 'I've really no idea.'

'Are you in love with her?' asked Cato, emboldened by the champagne.

'Are you?'

'I like her clothes,' said Cato. 'She gets on well with my father.'

'Well, there's intemperate passion for you. Are you going to this Last Night hootenanny, do you suppose?'

'I don't really dance,' said Cato.

It was as Pierre had said: in the main lounge a ton-weight section of the phosphor-bronze frieze surmounting the stage proscenium had detached itself from the wall and fallen to the carpet below. In the course of its passage it had cleft in half a large circular table, splintered elements of which remained beneath the burnished grouping of lyre-playing Orphei, eurhythmic Columbines and comedy-masked satyrs. The effect of the whole – the sheared mounts and the dusted outline on the wall, the frozen figures amongst the matchwood on the carpet – was disconcerting, and it seemed to Cato, as he passed through, that the vast, empty room remained charged with the elemental violence of the storm. At the back of the unlit stage, in obedience to some earlier-published programme, a shadowed pianist was picking out 'Drop me off in Harlem' on the concert grand. The number became Ellington's 'Black and Tan Fantasy', and then abruptly stopped. There was a muted and dusty resonance as the piano-lid closed, and the tail-coated figure disappeared amongst the black side-curtains.

In the gallery beyond, Cato saw Tudor somewhat awkwardly carrying Snorkly-Porkly.

'Party's injured herself,' explained the bellboy, as the dog's eyes revolved, glossy and selfish.

'My father said to thank you.'

'What for?'

Cato explained.

'A boatman might make what . . . twenty crossings a

year,' said Tudor. 'Staterooms, champagne, hairdressing . . . they're the line's best customers. Them and the commercials. So up go the warning notices and after that it's buyer beware. So where you off, then?'

'I thought I might go to the Main Deck.'

'I'll see you down.'

'Are your shoes too tight?' asked Cato, as they made their way towards the lift.

'Pigfoot,' answered Tudor. 'From carrying loads on the roll. Shopping?'

'No, just . . .'

Cato had a reason for descending to the Main Deck, but it was not one he wished Tudor to know. As they stood in silence in the gilt-painted cage, the smell of dog-fart rose around them.

'Main Deck,' said Tudor neutrally, as the lift gasped to a halt. Cato wondered if he expected a tip. Perhaps all Tudor's friendliness was calculated towards a fat gratuity at journey's end; perhaps he laughed about him, laughed about his sickness and slowness with the other bellboys. Champagne rose sour at Cato's throat and he felt himself grow pale.

'Thanks,' he said, walking away from the lift without looking back.

'Sir,' he heard Tudor's quiet response. He noticed that the swell had lessened.


The Third Class promenade, the most forward area of the public areas, was tightly packed. Passengers here were much closer to the sea than they were on the Boat Deck, and as the foremast stays moaned in the wind above them a fine spray darkened the teak beneath their feet and ensured that the capstan and the bollards and the handrail shone wet. The passengers – the majority mackintosh-wrapped but a hearty few in shirt-sleeves or pullovers – stood angled forwards in disordered parallel, their hands to their hats and bowed (or so it seemed to Cato) to the future and to the land that lay ahead.

The wind pulling at his hair, he turned up his collar, buttoned his sports jacket, and angled his way forwards. He apologised as he went, but – with the wind whipping away his words – doubted that he was heard. A bearded man smoking an upside-downturned pipe raised his eyebrows as if to say 'no rest for the wicked', a Negro couple with a child ate egg sandwiches on a hatchway, and a woman in a grey gaberdine coat frowned to see Cato hatless, but he couldn't see the girl. Philippa, he corrected himself, repeating her name. Philippa. Eyes narrowed, he leant forward into the pillowing wind.

He wanted quite badly to see her. It wasn't that he thought her beautiful: she wasn't. It wasn't that she was clever: she wasn't remotely. What she was, was forcefully and physically and outspokenly alive. And there was something about his fellow Cabin Classers – and he craned up at the great white-painted superstructure towering above him – that wasn't quite present, wasn't quite alive. They disengaged themselves, somehow, by their elevation, by their irony, by their weariness.

And the worst of it was just how well – with what fluent obliquity – he spoke his own lines amongst them. In the days that were to come, he knew, he was going to have to fight for his life. And unless he could stand four-square – rid himself of this fogging detachment – he would lose the fight. What he wanted was to enter the anaesthetic subterraneum like Theseus, unravelling a thread as he went so that, with the Minotaur dead and bloody at his feet, he might find his way back from the darkness. Somehow he felt that the girl, with her uncompromising physical presence and her terrible truthfulness, could arm him, could charge him with life for what was to come, could stand and wait at the end of the thread in the light.

She wasn't there.

Inside, he looked without hope into the Third Class

dining saloon. The room was empty, and despite the knowledge that this was where she ate her meals, sulked, or barged her noisy way between tables, he could not quite suppress a shudder at the room's utilitarian lines, at the endlessly multiplied glass tumblers and paper napkins and stern acres of disinfected linoleum.

And the swimming pool, as he had half-expected it would be, was locked.

His progress along Alamein was almost guilty. Stewards and kitchen staff passed him, ignored him, grumbling about the hell that the weather and the attendant seasickness was playing with catering schedules.

'Hello-allo. It's Sunny Jim!'

Denton, the pool attendant, a silver police whistle suspended from his neck by a leather thong, was lounging cheerily half-in and half-out of the entrance to the Pig and Whistle, attended by a powerful smell of liniment.

'Saw you at last night's concert but couldn't reach you. Understand Mr Garnett snapped you up. I've got your shoe.'

'Thank you,' said Cato, surprised. 'Thank you very much.'

'Why don't you sit down in here, and I'll cut along and get it from my office. Unless you'd fancy a good rub-down, of course? The pool's closed, but I can do you a vibro or a Turk and Electric?'

'Not this time, perhaps,' said Cato.

'Coom down to t'boiler-'ouse, ye can 'ave the 'ole fookin' lot fe' nowt,' came a voice, followed by laughter, from inside the Pig.

'I'll wait here,' said Cato. 'Thanks anyway.'

Denton hurried heavily away, his rubber-soled shoes squeaking on the metal floor, and was back less than a minute later with a damp brown-paper package (a curious servitude, thought Cato, in this act of wrapping). As he handed it to Cato, there was the sound of a muffled report.

Frowning, Denton walked to the doorway leading down to the hold. As he opened the door the sound was repeated. This time, however, it was louder, and followed by a brief metallic whine. Someone was hammering.

'Hang on a tick, son.'

In the absence of Philippa, Cato had decided to seek a final silent audience with the hamadryad. Tomorrow, he supposed, she would be gawped at, crowded around, and swung to the sky over some Manhattan pier, but today, for an hour, she would be his. He wanted, just once more, to kneel in the warm half-dark and await her dark streaming approach. She was beautiful, she was unpitying, she called to him, and she was death.

Frustrated for the moment in his purpose of solitude, Cato followed Denton down the spiral staircase. At first he could see very little. As he descended into the weak yellow light of the hold, however, he saw that a small, hunched figure knelt by the hamadryad's cage.

Ignoring Denton, and recognising from the foot of the stairway the astrakhan coat and the headscarf printed with Airedale dogs, Cato crossed the plated floor of the hold towards Loelia Amber. On the floor in front of her, shockingly large, lay a service revolver. A plaited red and yellow lanyard was attached to a ring at the end of the butt, lending the heavy weapon an impractical, ceremonial appearance. Loelia's eyes were closed; her hands were clasped tightly in front of her, and she was rocking backwards and forwards on her heels in a series of minutely controlled and barely perceptible movements. She seemed to be praying.

Staring at her for a moment, Denton knelt, gently lifted the revolver and thumbed open the chamber.

'Two rounds discharged,' he murmured to Cato, as if attempting to impose procedural order on to the situation. Upending the weapon he poured four blunt-nosed bullets and two empty brass cartridge cases into his hand and transferred them to separate pockets.

'Do you know who she is?'

Cato nodded, but did not answer. Inside the unpadlocked cage his eyes had found the darkly heaped form of the hamadryad. Where the neat little coffin-head had been, however, there was no longer a head, only a bloody fascicle, a wrenched cluster as of an electrical cable hacked through. On the steel floor of the cage two shallow gouges shone bright as nickel, and two thumb's-width holes admitted a pale seep of light through the soft metal side-wall.

'*Naja Hannah*,' he murmured. He felt the wholly unexpected approach of tears. I slept too little last night, he thought. I'm not free of my dreams.

'Hannah,' said Denton. 'Hannah?' He turned to the cage, peered inside, and jumped back, jerking up the unloaded revolver in front of him. 'Mother of God . . .!'

'It's dead,' said Cato. 'Shot.'

Slowly Denton reapproached the cage and, glancing once at Loelia, closed the small gate with a touch of the gun-barrel. Wonderingly, he looked from the pistol in his hand to the silently rocking woman and then again, suspiciously – as if it might merely be feigning death, simulating head-lessness – at the inert, shadowed form of the snake.

'Madam.' Tentatively, Denton touched her shoulder, but she made no response. With the look of a man disinclined towards further involvement but through whose mind phrases like 'material evidence' were passing, Denton weighed the revolver in his hand.

Cato wondered briefly if the pool attendant would let him take charge of the weapon – perhaps fire a few rounds over the side of the ship – and regretfully dismissed the idea as unlikely. Reaching inside his jacket for his fountain-pen and passenger list, he underlined Max's name and the telephone number of the Ambers' cabin, and handed the list wordlessly to Denton. As an afterthought, he added Dr Montmorency's card. Denton nodded, hesitated, and gingerly reached inside the broad pockets (revolver-sized pockets, thought Cato) of Loelia's astrakhan coat. Finding no further weapon, and satisfied that he had done all that might reasonably be expected of him given the circumstances, Denton pocketed the Webley and started towards the staircase. The heavy pistol with its sharp cocking lever must have been awkward to carry in the flannel trousers, for after a few paces he lifted it out and carried it by the butt.

When Denton had gone, Cato genuflected at Loelia's side and whispered her name. When she did not respond he touched her hands, but they were hard and tight, their interlock unyielding. Helplessly, like a dog nosing at the corpse of its master, he stroked her curling lambskin shoulders, and then a sharp and familiar smell touched his nostrils and he heard a dripping sound beneath her coat. Urine pooled around her shoes, was drawn back and forth by the ship's movement, and Cato rose hastily to his feet.

He withdrew to the edge of the dim corona of light and seated himself on a trunk. From the darkness at his back came the uneasy creak of rope and crate and the gritted shift of cargo and from beyond these, softened by distance into inseparability from all else that he heard and felt, the drumming whirl of the ship's heart-beat. He was at the centre – the epicentre – of an incomprehensible event, and he enjoyed the sensation. Perhaps, the thought occurred to him, he might ask Max if he could have the hamadryad's skin.

Montmorency was the first down. He stood his Gladstone bag carefully to one side of the hamadryad's cage, glanced at Cato and at the dead snake, and moved to Loelia's side.

'Mrs Amber,' he said quietly. 'Mrs Amber, it's all right. I'm a doctor.'

He looked up at Cato. 'Has she spoken?'

Cato shook his head.

'Mrs Amber, you have to tell me. Were you bitten?'

Cato's mouth opened. The possibility that she had been bitten had simply not occurred to him.

*Bite from* Naja Hannah *(King Cobra). Toxaemia. Death in 190 minutes . . .*

'Mrs Amber,' continued Montmorency. 'Try and speak to me. Did the snake bite you? Show me your hands.'

He reached out his hands to hers and attempted to separate them. When she resisted he ordered that Cato bring him a torch from the Gladstone bag. As best he could, ignoring the urine at her feet, Montmorency examined Loelia's hands, forearms and ankles.

'No visible puncture marks,' he murmured. 'Unfortunately, that doesn't . . .'

He took a shallow tin box and a small bottle from the Gladstone bag. Condensation from recent boiling blurred the glass barrel of the hypodermic, and Montmorency shook it out hard before selecting one of the shorter needles. Laying the needle inside the bottle, he drew a small amount of the pale liquid into the syringe.

'Give me a hand,' he ordered. 'Put an arm round her shoulders. Hold her still.'

Cato held her, heard the tiny whimpers of her exhalation as Montmorency, crouching in front, held the syringe briefly to the electric light. Then he removed the needle, pulled down the lower lid of her right eye and, with a hand which only barely perceptibly shook, allowed a single drop of the anti-venom to fall into her conjunctival sac. As he withdrew, breathing a little more heavily than usual, there came from above the sound of leather-soled shoes on the iron stairway.

Followed by Denton, Max Amber approached them. Briefly, his regard flickered from the huddled group around Loelia to the unpadlocked cage. Bending before the wire gate, he reached inside for the headless snake, and then, appearing to think better of the action, allowed his hand to fall. For a moment he looked at the hand, at the sapphire ring, and then he withdrew his arm and turned. Lifting the knees of his trousers – and carefully avoiding the wet imprints of the soles of Cato's and Montmorency's shoes – he knelt before his wife.

'Is she bitten?' he asked, simply.

'I'm not sure,' said Montmorency.

Max reached over to Loelia and tried to raise her head with his hands. Mutely, her eyes tight closed, she resisted him. Cato's arm still loosely encircled her shoulders, and he felt her tauten at her husband's touch.

'Is that the serum I gave you?' asked Max, nodding at the loaded syringe which Montmorency had laid in the lid of the tin box.

'Yes, sir, rehydrated. Can you tell me precisely what primary symptoms we might expect?'

'If she . . .?'

'Yes.'

Max considered. A muscle worked in his jaw. 'Intoxication, weakness in the legs, profuse salivation, incontinence . . .' He shook his head, turned back to Loelia, and, unseeing of Cato at her side, took the lobe of her ear and, grimacing, drove in his thumbnail until his hand trembled and blood beaded on his nail. When she made no reaction, he wiped his fingers with a handkerchief. 'What are you waiting for?' he asked.

'I'm waiting for her to tell us whether she has been bitten,' said Montmorency levelly.

'And if she won't?' asked Max, pocketing the handkerchief. 'If she can't?'

'I've tested her for sensitivity to horse serum. I'll need to wait for a result.'

'And how long's that going to take? She could be . . .' He turned sharply away, and examined his hands. 'Do you have any idea of the potency, the volume of neurotoxin a . . .'

'I have to know,' said Montmorency.

'Look, just give me the syringe. Please. I'll give her the bloody injection myself.'

'I can't do that, Mr Amber. Besides, it has to be injected in solution.'

'I know that. Have you got any saline?'

'Yes, sir.'

'Well, do it. Inject her now, I beg you. Please. I'll take full responsibility.'

*. . . Patient died of asphyxia heralded by convulsions in the presence of his wife, the constable, the Assistant Surgeon, and Dr Lafrenais. Consciousness was retained until the final cessation of breathing, with heart-beat continuing for two minutes longer. Post-mortem was not allowed . . .*

Cato's knees and hamstrings were aching painfully, but for fear of dismissal he dared not shift his weight or make any other movement which might call attention to his presence. At the edge of his vision, awkward in stillness like a bad actor, was the large pale figure of Denton. Cato switched his gaze.

'I killed her.'

At first only Cato heard her murmur. Her eyes remained closed and she did not move. He leant nearer. The others closed quietly in.

'I killed her. I killed the *Naja*.'

Montmorency spoke first. 'Never mind all that, Mrs Amber. Just tell us if you were bitten.'

'I shot her,' said Loelia. 'She was asleep.'

'Were you bitten by the snake, Mrs Amber?'

She began, soundlessly, to weep. Her hands remained clasped and the tears ran down her cheeks. Montmorency looked at Max, who twitched up his trouser-knees and crouched urgently before her. 'Loelia . . .' He hesitated, and looked around him. 'Did the *Naja* . . .?'

'No!' she said patiently, as if this were a point she had been trying to explain for hours. 'No, no . . .' Her voice fell away.

'Are you sure?' asked Max, his voice roughening. 'Show me your hands.'

'She was asleep,' repeated Loelia. 'Sleeping.'

She suddenly sat backwards, knees apart, into the pool of urine, and the tweed of her skirt rode back to reveal darkly sodden underclothes.

For a moment no one moved, and then Max wrenched his wife to her feet, drew back his sapphire-ringed hand, and slapped her. The blow was inaccurate, glancing her cheek, but somehow the more violent for its ineptitude. Frowning, her knees shaking beneath her coat, Loelia touched her face.

'That's enough, sir.' Montmorency's hand closed over Max's slender wrist before he could deliver a second blow.

Paralysed until that moment by surprise, Cato took several steps backwards. His heart was beating painfully, and obscure motifs appeared to be flaring around the figures of Montmorency and the Ambers. He closed his eyes and, as his chest tightened, the image of Loelia's sodden, satin-webbed loins rose before him. Somehow, he negotiated his halting way back to the trunk where he had sat earlier. When he looked up, Loelia's face was in her hands.

'It hurts,' he heard her exclaim plaintively. 'My eye hurts.'

'Show me,' Montmorency ordered.

She raised her head.

'It was to . . . snap her out of it,' said Max, dragging a hand tensely through his hair. 'I thought . . .'

'That inflammation isn't a result of your slapping her, Mr Amber,' said Montmorency, reaching into his bag. 'It's from my serum test, which seems to be positive. Your wife is allergic – hyper-allergic, in fact – to horse serum, so I'm . . .' He tilted her head, and Loelia stood unresisting as he placed a single drop in her eye. 'There, adrenalin chloride, that should do it.'

'Is that better, dear?' Max asked, as she stood blinking.

She ignored him, and felt at her sleeve for a handkerchief.

'Perhaps we should return to the cabin,' Max persisted, taking her arm. She wrenched it free, and walked unassisted and in silence towards the staircase. Max followed her and Denton raised a palm to indicate that he would accompany them.

When they had left, Montmorency lowered himself on to the trunk next to Cato. 'Are you all right, old son? You looked a bit groggy there for a moment.'

Cato nodded. 'I'm fine. A bit . . .' he shrugged, and beat his chest in a vague gesture of *mea culpa*. 'What on earth was happening there?'

Montmorency locked his bag with a key on a chain. 'Most of it, who the hell knows?' He shook his head, and patted his pocket for cigarettes. 'The gun, for example, where did she get that? Did she smuggle it on to the ship, or does it belong to someone else . . .? And why shoot the snake? Jealousy? Target practice? To get her husband into trouble? I doubt she has much idea herself. I'll go up to her cabin and give her a sedative in a minute, but all that I can really do, if I'm honest, is try and hold her together until she's out of my charge.' He tapped a cigarette on the trunk. 'Unhappiness, you see. Nothing any doctor can do about that.'

'They're at our table,' said Cato. 'They don't really get on. And I think she's been seasick.'

'I'll tell you something,' said Montmorency without emphasis, 'and this is God's own truth. If I'd gone ahead and given her that injection when he asked me to – if I'd given her even a hundredth of it – she'd be lying dead on the floor there by now.' He pointed. 'Fatal anaphylactic shock. Rare condition, of course, to be that susceptible, but you always test for it.'

'But surely . . .?' began Cato.

'Yes,' said Montmorency. 'He's a snake man. He'd have known.' Pausing, he sent a large smoke ring wobbling through the dusty yellow air. 'And so of course would she. What we've just seen – perhaps seen, I should say, because we'll never know for certain – is a man . . . encouraging the death of his wife.'

An hour later, in the dining room, Cato stirred mechanically at his coffee. He felt a crushing dispiritude. It was not just the retributive events of the morning, it was his father's injury and the girl's absence and the broken cufflink and the shortness of time: it was everything.

Even the *Carmelia* had changed. What he had formerly perceived as grandeur now stood revealed merely as an overbearing vastness. The mirrored walls of the dining hall, around which the dwarf palms stood wilting guard, served only to multiply the room's half-emptiness. At its centre an unidentifiable ice-carving dripped over a fatigued display of raw crustaceans and carved fruit. The tubular-glass fountain remained greyly unilluminated, and a heavy condensation had formed on the skylight.

Beneath the Odeon sweep of the balcony, Reginald's absence had pressed Pierre Watson and Jerry Farrell into unwilling conversation.

'So it's Hollywood, then?' Farrell was saying. His British Warm overcoat hung from the back of an unoccupied chair.

'So it seems,' Pierre answered.

Beyond Farrell, Docherty – who appeared to have been upgraded to Cabin Class – was consuming his lunch in concentrated silence.

'What is it exactly that you have to . . . offer?' asked Farrell.

'A sense of Englishness, perhaps,' said Pierre, signalling to the waiter for a second glass of brandy. 'They're making a lot of English pictures in Hollywood at the moment – roses, thatched cottages, Dunkirk and so on – and that's come to be the sort of thing I write about. Fearful tosh really – decent, clean-living chaps giving the Hun a bloody nose while brave little women keep the home fires burning – but it does pay the bills.'

A worm of anger began to beat at Farrell's forehead, and the lid trembled beneath his staring eye.

'Mr Docherty, can I ask you something?' said Cato, anxious to deflect the conversation's course.

Docherty, a spoonful of sherry trifle half-way to his mouth, raised his eyebrows.

'That glass you carry about . . .?'

'It's a hunting cup,' explained Docherty, removing it from his jacket. 'You can push it in the pocket of your coat, see. I won it from the Major.'

'It was my grandfather's,' said Farrell, lowering his table-napkin from his eye. 'Rode with the Wicklow. I backed Docherty against a lance-corporal from the Argylls.'

'To do what?' asked Cato.

'Drink four Players' tins of Krassi.'

'Krassi?'

'Greek fire-water we used to get pissed-up on in Crete. Filthy stuff.'

'And you won?' Cato asked Docherty.

'I was the last man standing,' admitted Docherty, 'by a good second or two.'

'Honour of the regiment, I suppose?' smiled Pierre, consulting his watch.

There was a moment's silence.

'Something like that, sir, yes,' said Docherty politely.

'Haven't you got a boxing match coming up?' Cato asked him. He found Pierre's and Farrell's antipathy quite incomprehensible. In some measure, illogically, it made him feel guilty.

'Walkover,' said Docherty. 'Seasick.'

Farrell laughed. He spooned half-dissolved coffee crystals into his mouth from his cup and crunched them noisily between his teeth.

'You'll excuse me,' said Pierre, rising abruptly to his feet. 'I have an appointment.'

They watched him cross the room and mount the staircase.

'What a frightful cunt,' said Farrell. He began, tonelessly, to sing:

> I love to watch Mary make water,
> You can't see her arse for the steam . . .

He upended his cup into its miniature saucer. 'Happy days, eh, Seamus?' He shook his head and climbed heavily to his feet. 'Time and the bogs, however, wait for no man. If Mohammed goeth not to the mountain, the mountain shall most verily and in spades . . .' He shrugged on his overcoat, saluted Cato, and left.

'How long will you and Major Farrell be staying in the United States?' Cato asked Docherty a few minutes later.

'Well, sir, that depends on the success of things. We've no plans, let me put it to you like that, to return. The Major has acquaintances in the Pennsylvania Prison Service.'

'And you're hoping to . . .?'

'Yes, sir. That's the plan.'

'But why . . . America, if you don't mind my asking? Major Farrell seems very much an Englishman at heart.'

Turning away, Docherty flagged down a passing waiter and ordered Kraft cheese, biscuits and more brandy.

'You'll not have heard,' he turned back to Cato, 'but at home, sir, between ourselves, there have been . . . incidents.'

Cato slowly nodded.

'I can see you've more than a fair idea of what I'm talking about, sir. Would I be right?'

Embarrassed, Cato nodded again.

'Well, I can only say I'm sorry for that, sir. The Major's not been himself.'

'You're very . . . loyal,' ventured Cato.

Docherty considered. 'The man took a bullet for me, sir. I went down in the open and the Major left cover to carry me in. Took a nine-mill Schmeisser round for his trouble and left half his bowels and one testicle in a Suda Bay field-hospital.'

Cato grimaced.

'Exactly, sir,' said Docherty quietly.

'And you were hit yourself?'

'I wasn't touched, sir, that was the thing of it. I was –

what's the word, now – shocked you could say, from the bombardment, bleeding from the ears and that, and if I'm honest, more than a little Krassied-up, but no, I wasn't hit. As I remember it I climbed out of my skunk-hole thinking I was in Phoenix Park and walked happy as you like over the escarpment. Twisted my ankle.'

'That's all?'

'That's all, sir. Didn't even break it. Although I might as well have done. Ten seconds in the open and you were a goner for sure with those snipers.' He took the glass of brandy from the waiter and rolled it thoughtfully in his hand. 'No, the man saved my life, no question. And face it, sir, there's no one else has the time of day or night for him.'

Cato slept during the afternoon, and once more dreamed of death. He saw a garden wall with forsythia and japonica and below it the hamadryad, asleep. The hamadryad was headless, but he knew that its motor impulses lived on. As it woke, and moved in a series of wounded, uneven jerks over the lawn towards the white-painted cast-iron table where he sat with his mother, he saw that it was not a snake but an electric cable, a clutch of jacketed wires bound within some frayed brown material.

'When the war is over,' the cable informed them, its cobra-head reforming, 'the grass will grow to a suitable height and then stop growing for ever.'

His mother smiled, unsurprised at this information – although he was no longer certain that these celadon eyes and dragonfly silks were those of his mother – and rested her hand on the rearing, hooded neck of the hamadryad. The hamadryad's dislocate jaws slowly opened beneath her hand, and beyond the scything fangs and the pulsing neurotoxin pillows Cato saw revealed a pearled and shining landscape, a valley of membrane as delicate in its coral-veined tracery as the bottom of the sea.

It was the old topography, of course, so familiar as to

draw tears of longing from his deep memory, and anxious for its unknowing, all resistance exhausted, he inhaled deep and deliberate as the jaws closed over his face.

The last that he knew was the rustle of silk, the scent of freesias, and the parachutes – pink, blue, green, and yellow – falling like confetti from the warm sky.

He woke sour-mouthed and disoriented. It was no recognisable time of day, but the light had gone from the sky, and a coldness had fallen while he slept. The sea, once again, was calm, and he drew himself a hot salt-water bath. If he left the bathroom door open, he discovered, he could lie in the bath and watch the fading sky through the portholes.

He supposed that he probably was going to the Last Night Ball. His father would wish it, it would show Positive Mental Attitude, and there wasn't a great deal else to do. All things being equal he shouldn't have to dance, he could probably just hang around with the chaps. Although Pierre, he thought gloomily – and by the chaps he really just meant Pierre – was probably a brilliant dancer and would be much more keen on steering Ayrest MacLean around than sitting around gas-bagging about modern poetry with a schoolboy.

So much, needless to say, for the idea of his father and Mrs MacLean . . . *joining forces* (he couldn't, even to himself, use the words *falling in love*). Embarrassed and slightly disquieted by the whole fantastical notion of the two of them together and of Ayrest as purveyor of rustling, scented good-night kisses to himself, Cato allowed himself to slide forward in the bath until the hot, pungent salt water touched his chin.

At least, he mused, without his father there, he would be able to smoke at the ball. Idly, and without using soap, he passed a safety razor over his upper lip. The ship shuddered and the salt water stung as he cut himself. With a styptic stick pressed to his mouth, he lay in the bath until the water was cold and the sky through the porthole oyster-grey.

With the insouciance (he hoped) of an aristocrat awaiting the tumbril, Cato touched eau-de-Cologne to his jaw and straightened his black tie in the oval mirror. He found his father in high good spirits.

'You'll never guess who has just telephoned? Precisely. Friend Corcoran. Wanted to suggest that we had a rubber or two in here, nothing like bridge for setting a man on his feet again, et cetera, et cetera. I managed, successfully I think, to plead incapacity and a cracked skull, and sent that fellow Herbert over with a bottle of Moët by way of apology. How are you this evening? You've cut yourself.'

It was a long speech for his father, and an exuberant one.

'I know,' said Cato. 'I'm fine. I thought we might have supper together here and then I might push on to this Last Night business.'

'Last Night business? You mean the ball?'

'Mrs MacLean was saying this morning that it wasn't to be missed.'

'Ah, yes. Mrs MacLean. She brought some flowers over this morning. Still in the wash-basin, I'm afraid. Good of her though.'

'What do you . . . make of her?' asked Cato.

Not discomposed, Reginald turned to face him. 'Charming,' he said thoughtfully. 'Nice woman. Not in the least as one might have expected from that bunch of pansies she turned up with.' He prickled the scrubby moustache. 'Turned up with at Southampton, I mean, not this morning. She brought roses this morning.'

'Pierre likes her,' said Cato, pressing his advantage, and for a moment he thought he detected a slight pinkening of the stern features.

'I'm afraid I think that young man's a bit of a phoney,' said Reginald with a certain finality. He reached for the telephone. 'Now what shall we order? I can't remember if you've tried whitebait?'

'I think that time at Overton's,' said Cato. 'Why do you think Pierre's a phoney?'

'What time at . . .?'

'After I saw Dr Martineau.'

'The first time?'

'Yes. But about Pierre Watson. Is there something particular that you don't . . .?'

'No, nothing particular. I'm just not particularly drawn to what poor Farrell calls the cut of his jib.'

'You've talked to Farrell about him?'

'Farrell's talked to me about him.'

'And you agree with him?'

'I believe in listening to the unprejudiced voice. The thing about Farrell is that for all that he's been through, the man's a genuine innocent. He's like that red setter of Rutherford's, all over everyone, friend and foe alike. So when he suddenly and for no good reason *dislikes* someone, you have to sit up and ask yourself why. But judgement reserved, of course . . . Hello?' He spoke into the telephone. 'Yes, I'd like to . . .'

Cato considered the judgement unfair and Farrell probably the worst judge of character he had ever met, but not wishing to prejudice the tone that his conversations with his father had assumed, remained silent. The roles of spymaster and apprentice, he had discovered, allowed for the expression of an irresistible complicity which was all but indistinguishable from love.

Ten minutes later they were addressing trays laden with the Royal Albion Line's crystal and bone-china. Watching his son – half-boy, half-man in his camel-brown dressing gown and pressed dress-shirt – Reginald wondered if he had been right to lay on this luxurious outward journey, whether it might not have been kinder to proceed in a way which had less of the special treat about it, less of the condemned man's final breakfast. Was Cato really tasting the cold Meursault and the small curling fish which, one by one, he was spearing with his heavy silver fork? To

Reginald the whole experience of first-class travel – with which he was by no means as familiar as he knew that Cato might have wished – had come to underline the gravity and drama of the situation. The elaborate meals seemed to be replacing – *en bloc* – other meals that in years to come and in different places he and Cato might have enjoyed together.

They should have gone second-class, he realised, made the thing ordinary, something to be got over with, and reserved the luxury for the return journey. The return journey? He extinguished all but unseen the image of himself reboarding the *Carmelia* alone, of a coffin swung in chains from a Manhattan pier to the hold. Three days, he thought. Less. What could he do? What could he say – what statement of love could he make – that gave no hint as to the possible finality of his words? He had to pretend that there was no question of their having other than years together, no question but that Cato would eventually join him at Ops. Int. or ISLD or whatever the hell the department was called by then. The damnable thing, of course, was that Cato would be so perfectly suited to the life – far better suited, in truth, than himself. For as both father and intelligence officer, Reginald recognised his besetting sin to be a quite deliberately cultivated inflexibility which, even as he watched, he saw himself attempting to transmit to his son. . . . *I'm afraid I think that young man's a bit of a phoney* . . . And Cato, quite rightly, was resisting him, was resisting his conclusions, was thinking for himself. In the oval dressing-table mirror, Reginald watched his son, watched the exaggerated articulation of jaw and cheekbone in the narrow, mauve-shadowed face. The Cleeve barber – a badly shocked ex-sapper – had arrived with his clippers the day before Cato had left the school and had shaved the sides of his head to a manic, spiteful fuzz. The wind and sunshine of the Boat Deck had coloured this a little, but in the wash of the cabin's tube-lights he still projected an egg-shell pallor and fragility. His shirt was loose at neck and wrist, and Reginald noticed that he had ineffectually replaced one cufflink with a collar-stud.

As so often before, he wondered how he could best arm his son for what lay ahead. Every instinct told him to play the thing down, to dissemble, but at the same time he knew that he was not Farrell, that he was not an innocent, and that his own instincts – and for a long moment, his eyes were met by the eyes in the mirror – were not necessarily to be trusted.

The truth? Reginald had no God to offer his son, only the knowledge that he was inexpressibly precious, that his loss – of which there was an almost exactly fifty per cent probability – would leave his father with nothing but echoing corridors and secrets and the slow carpeted staircase to extinction.

'You seem to be light a cufflink, old boy,' he said.

The deck-doors had been unbarred since the afternoon, but few passengers had chosen to take advantage of this. Perhaps the knowledge that this was to be the last evening at sea, that there was more sea behind than ahead of them, had left them uninterested by the sea itself. And there was literally nothing to see. A vapour had fallen, or perhaps risen, enclosing the *Carmelia* in a hushed and skyless cocoon. Only the scalloping wash at the hull indicated their forward movement, but even then, thought Cato, it was equally reasonable to suppose that the ship herself was still and that the ocean was being drawn past her. The perception appealed to him, and as he stood there, fingers sensate at the damp rail, eyes half-closed, the fear which had clasped itself to him for so long dropped away like a bored monkey. He felt weightless, ambiently buoyant. For so long as he stared into the haze, he knew that the gentlest pressure of his fingertips would allow him to rise like the soda-bubbles that streamed about his heart.

And then, with an inrush of memory so intense as to be choking, he was nine years old again. After a golden summer extended far beyond belief and almost to November, winter had fallen like a sword. By the beginning of the January school term the snow was still lying so heavy that, in thrilling contravention of the natural order, most of the boys and staff had been unable to return. Cato, living a mere ten miles away, had been delivered as normal on the first day of term, but for almost a fortnight had enjoyed the exhilaration of school without work, games or discipline. In the dark afternoons, to the carbon-muffled clacking of the secretary's typewriter, he had reread Lawrence's *Seven Pillars of Wisdom* before the staff-room fire, but each morning had brought a fresh fall of snow and a dazzling virgin landscape to be explored in wellington boots and gaberdine mackintosh. These solitary wanderings had led to a strange discovery. Occupying the acre of the estate at the furthest remove from the school buildings was an ornamental stand of bamboo. This miniature jungle was intersected by a stream and a number of flagstoned paths which were explored, colonised, attacked and defended by each succeeding generation of boys. That January, however, frozen snow had formed a solid roof over the bowed columns of bamboo, and Cato found that, with care, he could climb up the outer drifts on to this icy fan-vaulting and be supported. He had been lying there one morning, ten feet above the jungle floor. All was white, and above him the clouds raced against the harder grey of the sky. And then, after a time, it had been him who was moving, racing beneath unmoving clouds.

He had had the sense then that he had now: that he could move outside time, that he could leave himself standing at the *Carmelia*'s rail or pillowed against that icy canopy of snow and watch his life spool past him like a programme in a News Theatre. And as in a News Theatre, of course, you stayed until you were bored, or it was time for your train, or the film came around to where you came in. No particular beginning, no particular end. Cato had seen his own death in this way many times. One of the rules, however – one of the things about the way it all worked – seemed to be that you could never remember what you had seen. You stepped back into yourself and the knowledge blew away like french chalk on the breeze. And that was it. You were in the present again.

As Cato slowly proceeded along the dark gallery carpet, past the shadowed olive drapes and the silver-bronze pylons and the flighting wildfowl, the music – which he recognised as 'A String of Pearls' – steadily increased in volume, and he found his step quickening to its lifting rhythm.

He pushed open the heavy double doors to a scene of scintillant blare. To his left extended a long bar, at which several mess-jacketed servitors, cocktail shakers ablur, attended to the demands of the crowd pressing at its considerable length. Half-way along each side-wall stood a broad silver-leaf pillar of Egyptian inspiration, its finials invisible in each case beneath a giant cluster of white balloons, and between these, at the ceiling's centre, a great glass-and-chromium lozenge dispensed a splintered, bluish effulgence over the dancing couples below. At the moment of Cato's entrance no more than a dozen couples were moving over the shining parquet, and these, like the musicians, appeared to be holding themselves in check, their mood anticipatory, their circlings exploratory. Surrounding the dance floor was a horseshoe of linen-covered tables, perhaps half of them occupied, and beyond it, on a low stage at the room's furthest point, 'The Oceanaires' swooped and swung in restrained unison behind their music-stands.

Slowly, Cato moved through the crowd at the bar. Martini in hand, Jerry Farrell was holding strident court: ' . . . told everyone he spent the war in Port Said,' Cato heard the familiar bark. 'Turned out of course it was Portslade . . .'

At the bar, Cato ordered a whisky, which he drowned, wetting his cuffs, in soda water. Clutching the tumbler, he tried to extricate himself from the throng without catching Farrell's eye.

' . . . shot a snipe in Hove,' the monologue continued, as Farrell's flushed listeners shook their heads and swayed admiringly. 'Marine Parade. High bird, but took it bang in the beak. Wallop. Pavement.' Farrell shook his head, and the staring eye made sudden contact.

'Cato, old boy, as my sainted mother used to say, heave abreast. Meet the Musketeers. Dickie van Kloof, Squiffy Corfe, and . . .' he indicated with his glass a short red-faced man of about sixty, ' . . . Godfrey Pole-Harcourt. We're not talking to Godfrey at the moment, because he's just farted.'

Cato smiled tightly. Pole-Harcourt smirked apologetically. Beyond him Cato caught sight of Max Amber. 'How do you do,' he said, nodding energetically at the Musketeers, 'I'm actually just . . .' He raised his drink and reared his head in Max's direction.

'Ah, right,' said Jerry, 'Jolly good. We'll . . .'

'Absolutely,' nodded Cato, wondering how he could avoid Max. Only by pushing past him, he suspected. He very much wanted to sit down and catch his breath.

But Max had turned away, and was bestowing his silken attentions on a trio of chiffoned American matrons. He appeared, thought Cato, entirely untouched by the bizarre drama of the morning. There was no sign of Loelia.

At the end of the bar nearest the entrance Cato demanded a second tumbler, and this he filled from a soda-syphon. Carrying both drinks he made his way to an unoccupied table which he had identified as offering a good view of both entrance and dance floor. The second tumbler he placed opposite himself as if to suggest a momentarily absent companion. For the time being, all that he wanted to do was sit comfortably, sip his whisky and soda, smoke a cigarette or two, and listen to the band.

The ballroom filled fast. The passengers, as if suddenly aware that tomorrow brought sterner concerns and the journey's end, hurried in with something of the urgency of the city which, less than a day ahead, awaited them. The men were in dinner-jackets – black mostly, but several of the Americans in more nonchalant cream – while the women glittered in lamé and beaded cashmere, shimmered in slipper-satin, rustled in tulle. And for all that most of them – men and women alike – were of a certain age, and for all that few of them were beautiful, the scene had glamour, and Cato knew that it would define for ever his idea of the desirable, of wealth, of the rich at play. A particular smell, heavy and assured, overlaid the room: an intoxicating mix of powder, perspiration, scent, cigar, bay rum and brandied breath. Cato had smelt it at dinner in the restaurant that first night out, and he smelt it now. It was the odour of wealth and position, and it seemed to whirl about the ballroom on the shivering neon blare of the music. And to hear these tunes played by the Oceanaires at full blast, realised Cato, was quite different from hearing them on the wireless. All of those rhythms which, buzzing from the heavy set, had seemed inseparable from the humdrum, from the stifling fabric of everyday life, suddenly found focus, made sense, and he found himself nodding along and tapping his Senior enthusiastically at the ashtray.

A sudden wavering physical reek, and the appearance before Cato's face of the upper half of a pair of unpressed black dinner trousers, heralded the arrival of Pierre.

'Nailed it!' he said, handing Cato a sheet of ship's writing paper folded into four. 'I can finally sell my soul to Mammon with a clear conscience.'

Cato raised his cigarette before his face and briefly studied Pierre through the smoke. The writer's eyes were bleared, his shave was uneven, and the pewter shine of grime was visible at his dress-shirt collar. Beneath one ear a cut had scabbed and cracked like the varnish on an old painting. On balance, Cato supposed that he was glad to see him, even if he wondered at the man's slightly alarming indifference to appearances. *La vie Bohème*, he supposed, although Pierre had seemed smart enough – or at least clean enough – when they'd boarded. Absently, he pocketed the folded paper.

'Usual faces, I see,' said Pierre, extending his legs proprietorially beneath the table and looking around him. 'What a bloody bunch. That madman Farrell, for example, and all his military toadies. Christ.'

A little guiltily, Cato nodded. Agreement seemed the most painless course of action with Pierre, as indeed it did with Farrell. Why did things seem so black and white, so unambiguous, to so many people? And of all people, to a poet. With the exception of school bullies, who were somehow unknowable, he himself could not recall experiencing such visceral and uncontrollable dislikes. If you let people talk about themselves, as most people seemed to want to, they usually ended up explaining themselves. And then they were either more or less interesting, and the facts they presented either more or less profitable. What Cato could not understand was the need to take a position, Agincourtlike, and to hammer stakes into the ground around that position. Easier, surely to say to yourself – Yes. I see. This is how this person is. And this is how this one is. And knowing these things, recognising these positions, to manoeuvre around them, slipping between the pointed stakes, smiling to all. That, surely, was how to get what you want. To smile, to listen, and then to slip back into the darkness with your knowledge held close.

' . . . first crossing, then, all in all?'

For a moment Cato considered telling him about Corcoran, but something in Pierre's wild appearance gave him pause.

'The storm was interesting,' he said, hesitantly. 'The way that things . . . fell away.'

'Interesting, yes,' said Pierre. 'But I found I couldn't use it. Said to myself: Storm at Sea . . . Mid Atlantic . . . Hopes and Fears . . . Pitch and Roll of the Great Vessel . . . This, surely, can be transmuted into a dozen lines, into insight.

Not a bloody earthly, needless to say.' He looked up with sudden sentimental aggression. 'The whole thing transmutes, when you're in the middle of it, into nothing more gilded than . . .' the words slurred, ' . . . broken furniture and spilt wine.'

Cato was suddenly irritated. Pierre had never read a word that he, Cato, had written, but felt free to discuss his own work at really quite inordinate length. As it happened, Cato had never written a line of poetry that he hadn't immediately destroyed as overwhelmingly and shame-makingly sententious, but that, he thought, wasn't quite the point. He took a swallow of whisky and soda and suddenly – and quite clearly – understood what *was* the point. Pierre was trapped within himself. He related all things to himself, and in so doing weighed himself down to the point of immobility. That's why he was stuck.

Pleased with this deduction, Cato lowered his tumbler, enjoying the smoky prickle on his tongue (whisky and soda, he determined, would be 'his' drink). It was all so obvious, he thought. The self was a millstone, to poet, to spy, to all. The spy, especially, must diminish himself to nothing. He must be a nobody, and his concerns must all lie outside himself. That had been the reason for his father's inexplicable lapse of judgement with Corcoran. He had allowed a sense of what he wanted to be true – self, again – to interfere with the dispassionate processes of logic. This argument, of course, led up a thornyish trail, but Cato forced himself to follow it. Was it self rather than dispassion, he wondered, that had led his father to surround them both with this Cabin Class extravagance. Had he acted on the basis of what he wanted, rather than knew, to be the truth about their place in the world? Icily, warily, Cato's future-spy persona admitted this possibility, and Cato himself felt a slow and unexpected sense of liberation. Elated, he held to the feeling, to the realisation that a refuge from the hardness of truth could be found in the fact of its truthfulness.

' . . . be a good chap, and sort us out a . . .' Pierre's words forced their way into his consciousness, displacing the cold, beautiful order of his thoughts. ' . . . can't face the scrum. If you don't mind?'

'Of course. What was it you . . .?'

'Brandy, there's a good fellow.'

Unwillingly, Cato conceded his concentration. As he rose to his feet, he tried recalling it, and the sensation of cool, cerebral release immediately returned. Satisfied, grateful to Pierre for acting as the unknowing agent of his enlightenment, he made his slow, angling way to the bar. It was clever, he thought – and probably practised – the way that the other emphasised that it was the going for the drinks, rather than the paying for them, that was the favour. Could Pierre be short of money? It seemed unlikely for one on his way to Hollywood. And yet his appearance argued poverty as much as it did poetic licence. Mentally, Cato shrugged.

Returning with the brandy, Cato saw the girl. She had not yet seen him, but accompanied by a lank-haired, razor-burnt youth who was obviously her brother, stood peering uncertainly around her. Crêpe-paper streamers arced pink and green over their heads, and both of them started visibly as, at a nearby table and to general hilarity, a cigar was touched to a cluster of balloons. In less conservative company, the girl might almost have looked stylish. If the short evening dress hadn't been cut from parachute-silk, and if the bead-clustered black sweater had been of cashmere, the ensemble might have been mistaken for something clever, by Mainbocher, perhaps. As it was, her searching anxiety, coupled with the visible awkwardness of the young man in the hand-me-downs at her side, marked her out a stranger, wrongly dressed.

'That farouche creature over there seems to be staring at you,' said Pierre as Cato handed him the balloon glass. 'I say, didn't you get one for yourself?'

'I have to be a bit careful.' The quacking squeak of

noise-makers momentarily drowned out the band, and he almost had to shout.

'She's coming over,' said Pierre.

Cato looked up. She was indeed coming over. Pierre climbed to his feet and, unwillingly, Cato followed suit.

'I'm Philippa,' said the girl to Pierre, as Cato stood momentarily tongue-tied. 'Wiss. How d'you do. And this is Len.' She nodded at Cato. 'Cat's got your tongue, I see. Been back swimming?'

'The pool was closed,' Cato eventually managed, with something like anger. Where had she been this morning, when he was searching for her, and what was she doing invading his evening? 'I was in the cabin all morning,' she said, as if reading his thoughts. 'Pinning the frock. There was a notice in our dining room: any male between twenty and thirty-five as could dance and owned a penguin suit could go to the Last Night Function in the Cabin Class. Short of partners, see. So Len's here legal, aren't you Len? He's had instruction of course,' she added to Cato, 'in the ballroom. Foxtrot and that.'

Len nodded uncomfortably, and touched his reddened jaw.

'Not me, of course. Strictly illegal, me.' Now that she was sitting down, Cato saw, she was gathering confidence, gathering steam. Pierre was observing the tableau with wry, heavy-lidded amusement.

'We ran into each other in the swimming pool,' said Cato, by way of mitigation.

'I wish I had been there,' said Pierre ambiguously, directing his regard, with some deliberation, at Philippa.

'He all but drowned,' said Philippa gaily, smiling at Pierre. 'I saved his life.'

The stunning untruth of this statement reduced Cato to open-mouthed silence.

'A true-life heroine, then?' offered Pierre, one eyebrow raised.

'Hear that, Len? I'm a heroine!' She threw her head

back and laughed, showing her teeth. Pierre's smile remained fixed, bibulous.

'Let me get you a drink,' said Cato, seeing an escape route, or at least a respite, from the brother and sister's presence.

'Don't mind if I do,' said Philippa, planting her elbows pensively on the table-cloth. 'Get me a . . . let's see, choose me something nice.'

Cato nodded. 'Len?'

Len looked up in alarm. 'Er . . . Ta.' His eyes darted to his sister. 'Same as what Pippa's, please.'

Cato left them to it, and plunged once more towards the bar. At least, thanks to good old Corker, he had money in his pocket this time. He ordered a brace of stiff Manhattans.

As he sidled unhurriedly back to the table he passed Farrell and the Musketeers. All four were wearing false noses; Godfrey Pole-Harcourt was bending down as if for a beating, and Farrell was holding a flickering cigarette-lighter against the older man's evening-trousered buttocks.

'When I sailed to England in '38,' came the voice of Max Amber in his ear, 'there was nothing like this. The nearest we came to it was a sing-song on deck around the electric fire.' He spoke, as always, as if he was continuing a conversation that had been momentarily interrupted.

'How's Loelia?' asked Cato, and immediately regretted the question.

'Oh . . .' Max's mouth twitched and his eyes swam with good humour. 'You mustn't take things too . . . seriously.' He regarded Cato levelly and raised an interrogative eyebrow.

Cato looked away. 'The hamadryad,' he said. 'I'm sorry.'

Just visible in the eyes, the control, the tiny containment. 'Yes.' Max nodded. 'As you say. The hamadryad.' He frowned at his glass. Cato, weaving a little, took a sip from each Manhattan. 'She had made the same journey as I had, do you see?'

Did he mean Loelia, wondered Cato, lifting both glasses

to allow for the passage of a pair of clergymen, or the cobra?

'She was taken – captured – in Bengal. Shipped to London, to Regent's Park and winter. Not at the same time as me, of course, but . . .' He closed his eyes, and seemed to consider, to attempt to clear his mind. His free hand, in assistance of this effort, made tentative chopping motions. 'Shortly before I left Calcutta,' he recommenced, 'my parents drove me into the country, several hours away, to a place where we all used to go on holiday. There was nothing much there, really – a look-out point, a picnic spot, a tea-room, you couldn't really call it a hill-station – but the climate, after the city, was good. Salubrious, it was described as. Several hundred feet above sea level. Very quiet.'

He was looking at Cato, at a point directly between Cato's eyes, but looking straight through him. 'We stayed for a week; no one else there, much, that late in the year. We went for walks, read books, went to bed early . . . On my last evening, as it was getting dark, I walked by myself to a place we called the Gorge. It wasn't really a gorge, a boy could scramble up and down it easily enough – I'd often done so myself – but it overlooked the plain below. Anyway, I sat there for a while. I was holding a glass of lime-water,' he raised his tumbler an inch, 'with mint in it. After a while, far away, on the horizon, just as the light was going, a train came. It was the *Patna Queen*, I think, the night mail. I saw its lights, and then, miles and miles away as it crossed the plain, I heard that distant rat-a-ta-tat, rat-a-ta-tat, rat-a-ta-tat, and watched it for . . . oh . . . the horizon was endless, you see. Endless, and absolutely flat. Nothing for a thousand miles, and then the Himalayas. And as she whispered past, all those miles away – rat-a-ta-tat, rat-a-ta-tat – her whistle blew, a last long call over the night air. And I knew at that moment that what I had known up to that moment was what the world calls happiness, that

when I boarded the *'Pindi* a day or two later I would never
– could never – return.'

He emptied the glass in a single swallow. 'And of course
I never have. And here we all are, sailing further and
further away.' He shook his head. 'That's the danger of
having known happiness, you see. It makes us terribly
unforgiving of those who aren't quite able to organise it,
who don't instinctively know what its ingredients are.' At
Cato's troubled silence, Max retracted his gaze. 'I'm sorry,'
he said, with a self-deprecating downwards glance. 'None
of this is of any conceivable interest. And I should let you
deliver those drinks before they're completely flat. Excuse
me.' With a quick, tight smile, he disappeared into the
throng at the bar.

'Ah!' said Pierre, as Cato arrived back at the table. *'Enfin.'*
He was lounging back in his chair, hands clasped behind
his head, and clearly had not made much of an effort with
Len or Philippa Wiss who were sitting tensely forward over
the small table.

'Apologies for the delay,' said Cato, with a breeziness he
did not feel. 'Ran into a, um . . .' he turned to Pierre. 'Max
Amber.'

'Ah,' nodded Pierre. 'Max.'

'Yes,' said Cato, turning to the expectant Wisses. 'Now!
Let me . . .'

But the name of the cocktails had vanished from his
mind.

'What are these things called, Pierre, I've completely . . .?'

'Wormwood, I suspect. Dash of gall, perhaps.'

'Whatever,' said Cato, forcing a smile as he raised the
remains of his whisky. 'Cheers.'

'Cheers,' said Philippa dubiously.

Len nodded his thanks.

There was silence.

Pierre saw her first. Cato followed the suddenly attentive
line of his gaze, and failed to hear Philippa's question. At

the ballroom's entrance, looking about her in self-possessed enquiry, was Ayrest MacLean. Against the admiring black-and-white phalanx at the bar, her pale neck and fine-boned shoulders rose with vulnerable assurance from the silvered faille of her ballgown. The tableau had the curiously composed, photographic quality of all her appearances.

'*Qui ose*,' said Pierre, taking a deep breath and climbing to his feet, '*gagne*.' He began to sidle between tables.

'Is he foreign, your friend?' asked Philippa. 'Or what?'

Cato did not respond. He watched as Pierre engaged Ayrest in a moment's conversation, began to steer her back to where he and the Wisses waited and then, at the last moment, diverted her to a neighbouring and unoccupied table. With a brief smile in Cato's direction – which given its brittle courtesy could equally have been directed at Philippa and Len – she seated herself and turned away.

'You see that woman with the Red Indian head-dress,' commanded Philippa to Len. 'Over there. On the chair under the balloons. Go and dance with her.'

With uncertain obedience, Len followed her instructions. The woman in the feather tiara – a matron of uncertain vintage – appeared delighted by the invitation and Len, Cato saw with surprise, danced beautifully.

'He's good, isn't he?' Philippa said.

'Very,' said Cato. 'Unlike me,' he added, to pre-empt any suggestion that he and she attempt to follow suit. From the next table, Ayrest directed at them the swift willow-green of her regard.

'You could be a lot nicer to me,' said Philippa, quite loudly, 'if you wanted.' She stared at him, but he could not, would not, meet her eyes. At no price, he determined, would Ayrest MacLean see him looking into this girl's eyes. She was at a disadvantage, her presence was inappropriate, and she knew it and didn't care, for which he hated her. His discomfort increased by the second. She clearly wasn't going to go.

At the edge of his vision, with a sense of shock, he saw Pierre overlay Ayrest's ringed hands with his own.

'Look at me,' ordered Philippa.

His jaw clamped, Cato turned to her. Her gaze was open, colourless, mirroring nothing of his confusion. She had finished her drink.

'Whatever it is,' she said almost kindly, 'it doesn't matter.'

He frowned, examining her more closely. Her hair was the colour of dried hay, too fine to support so much as a ribbon without kirby-grips. Her eyes were winter-grey, and her lips, despite a dab of pink, were chapped and pale. The faint odour of lavender water hung depressingly about her, like a provincial department store. In moments of her own making, he thought – and he saw her suspended on the trespassed wave – she was beautiful. Obedient to the conventions of others she was beached, pikestaff-plain.

'It doesn't matter,' she repeated. At the next table, Cato saw Pierre rise and lead Ayrest MacLean to the dance floor.

At the same moment, he felt a small percussion to the back of his head. He turned to see – ten yards away – Jerry Farrell's maniacal grin. Farrell was holding up a narrow cardboard pipe, and as Cato watched he placed a compressed ball of pink cotton-wool in one end, and with a puff sent it caroming from the bald head of a steward, who smiled tolerantly. Only when Cato saw members of the purser's staff moving from table to table distributing blow-pipes and ammunition did he comprehend that these fun and games were official. Soon, to shrieks and laughter and the crash and swing of the orchestra, the area around the bar was a battle-zone, with the soft pink, green, and yellow missiles zooming backwards and forwards across the room at head-height. Farrell had assumed command of the principal faction at the bar, and as elderly and non-British passengers withdrew on hands and knees, was loudly organising firing positions and lines of supply.

'Squiffy,' he ordered, 'You take charge of the Argylls and

I'll take the Leicestershires.' He waved his arm furiously at a frail couple who, chins wobbling in confusion, had found themselves in his front line, 'Come on the Green Tigers, buck up!'

Cato, trapped behind the table with Philippa and the clergymen, listened with some concern. 'You're the Germans!' Farrell shouted at them. 'You're Komet and Mars.'

'I'll give him Germans,' said Philippa. 'Give me that glass.'

Reaching up, Cato found Len's glass, which stood, its contents untouched, at the table's edge.

'When I say now, stand up, count to five, and then get down quick.'

Crouching, Cato nodded. Taking a cotton ball, Philippa dipped it carefully into the Manhattan, and loaded her blowpipe.

'Ready?'

'Yes.'

'Okay. Now!'

Cato stood upright, counting aloud. Cotton balls flew past his ear. On the count of three, as Farrell showed himself and his weapon above the linen-clothed parapet, Philippa rose to her feet, and in the same movement, fired.

Her aim was sure. Loaded with neat alcohol to several times its original weight and impelled by the full force of her swimmer's lungs, the projectile took Farrell in his good eye. Blinded, roaring like Polyphemus, he hurled himself backwards into a tray loaded with Nesselrode ice-creams and sherry trifles. With the crash of glassware, the laughter and the exchange of fire ceased. Van Kloof and Corfe, ignoring Farrell's groaning protestations that although he was done for they should press home the attack and finish the job, removed his custard-smeared dinner-jacket, squirted soda water into his streaming eye and led him from the room. On the dance floor, oblivious to the local disturbance, the couples quickstepped on.

As the clergymen dusted down their knees, and Cato

and Philippa took their places back at the table, Pierre folowed by Ayrest moved past them towards the bar. As she aproached, Cato caught Ayrest's eye, saw her tiny frown, saw the vermilion lips unmistakably form the words: 'Rescue me!'

Cato stared. Unseeing beside him, Philippa – her eyes still illuminated by the pleasure of action – reached for the remains of Len's Manhattan.

'Excuse me,' Ayrest enquired, drawing alongside, 'I wonder if I might just . . . borrow this young man.'

Philippa's gaze briefly touched the oyster-grey ballgown, the long silk gloves, and the diamond bracelet. Lifting her head, her eyes emptying, she smiled her assent.

As he followed Ayrest in silence towards the dance floor, not quite believing the turn of events, Cato glanced back at Philippa. She was staring intently into a powder compact, using the mirror to search the crowd behind her at the bar.

'I'm sorry,' Ayrest turned to him as they walked, 'but I'm afraid I just couldn't manage another minute of your friend Pierre and his poetry. Unfeeling, I know, but there we are.'

'Well, I was happy enough to be rescued, too,' said Cato, elated by her complicit tone.

'Perhaps they can console each other,' said Ayrest with an indeterminate smile. The orchestra fell silent, and there was applause.

'I'm not much of a dancer,' said Cato, glancing nervously at the emptying parquet. On the podium the Oceanaires struck up anew, and Cato felt himself swept forward on a laughing, chattering wave. He found himself taking Ayrest's small gloved hand, felt the pale flutter of her shoulder blades beneath his other palm.

> I got a girl,
> in Kalamazoo.
> Don't wanna boast,
> But I know she's the toast . . .

'Just walk,' said Ayrest. 'And sway a bit.' Their eyes were level, and Cato was acutely conscious of the close regard of the other dancers. In his nervousness, he realised, he was squashing her silk-gloved fingers. His other hand pressed damply against her back.

'You are allowed to look at me,' she said quietly.

'I'm sorry,' said Cato, as if this were just one more thing that he had to apologise for, and he turned to her, and she smiled again. The celadon eyes were six inches from his own, the music and the dancers seemed to retreat, and he was suspended in her gaze. The next thing that he knew was that he had driven her jarringly into a talcum-powdered, mauve-chiffoned back. He smiled his apologies, the music rushed back, and he self-consciously recommenced his footwork.

> . . . a real piperoo.
> I'll make my bid
> for that freckle-faced kid . . .

'At the same time,' said Ayrest, amused, 'you do . . . sort of have to look where you're going.' For the first time he was aware of a Scottish lilt to her voice.

'I'm sorry,' repeated Cato, furious with himself. They seemed the only words that he was capable of saying.

'Over there,' she said, nodding over his shoulder. He steered her round. At the table he had left, Pierre and Philippa were intently conversing. Distantly, from the bar, came raucous laughter and the quack and bleep of noise-makers.

'I wouldn't have thought they'd have that much in common,' he said without thinking.

'Oh, I don't know. More than you think, perhaps.'

He was concentrating so hard on not treading on her feet or steering her into one of the other couples that a crawl of sweat had started to his temples. As they stepped and turned he stole quick downward glances at her, mapping with febrile and not-quite-believing hunger the pale fall of her neck and the translucent, powder-dusted tendrils at its nape. At any second, he thought, this could end. A smile, a laugh, a small ironic bow – do give my regards to your father – and that would be it. He'd have another drink perhaps, a cigarette or two on deck with a blanket round his shoulders and his shoes eased from his feet . . . Every sensation, then – every faint, freesia-smelling moment, every soft flexion beneath his fingers – must be remembered, must be added, like an aerial photograph to a patchwork of intelligence, to a whole, to a composite memory he would never release. Ayrest, he said to himself, enjoying the soft whisper of a name which a week ago he had never read, never heard spoken. Ayrest.

Back at his earlier table, he noticed, Max had joined Pierre and Philippa. All three of them were laughing.

> . . . Zoo zoo zoo zoo
> Zoo zoo zoo zoo zoo zoo, z-o-o-o.
> Kalamazoo.

'I love that song,' said Ayrest absently, as the last note died away. Fluttering her fingers inside her glove, she disengaged herself from Cato's clasp. At the edge of the dance floor one of the purser's men, rosy with port and *bonhomie*, was distributing fruit and raw vegetables to the dancers.

'Ah,' said Ayrest. 'Games.' At her side a passenger was feeding the curling tail of a turnip into the broad bank of his partner's *décolletage*. 'Time, I think, to go.'

Cato nodded. As the bandleader stepped forward on the podium to announce the rules of play, Cato followed Ayrest from the floor. At the edge of his vision, he saw Godfrey Pole-Harcourt tucking a grapefruit beneath his chins.

' . . . and remember, ladies and gentlemen,' boomed the microphone as Ayrest's lips moved soundlessly ahead of him, 'no hands!'

Steeled for the moment of dismissal, Cato was able to

summon a courteous smile. Her expression, however, indicated that she required some sort of answer.

'I'm sorry?'

'I said – my fault, it's quite deafening here – why don't we go and have some dinner.'

'Yes,' said Cato, 'Absolutely.'

He was not in the least hungry, and given a choice would have chosen to continue the evening almost anywhere but in the vast – and surely, by now, all but deserted – dining room, but these reservations were as nothing to the relief that he was not to be abandoned, tonight of all nights, to his own devices.

'Good,' she said simply, slipping a gloved hand through his arm. And once again, as they made their way towards the door, Cato felt himself the object of the room's attention. It was far from an unpleasant sensation, he thought. She walked slowly, at a speed which was comfortable to him after the minor exertion of the dancing, and he felt himself illuminated by her starry phosphorescent beauty.

As they walked past the staircase descending to the dining room – deserted, as he had expected – he realised that they must be going to the Riviera Grill. After proceeding in silence along an endlessly diminishing perspective of carpet, they took one of the few lifts untried by Cato. This, after a brief whirring ascent, debouched in the restaurant itself. As they stepped from the lift, where Cato remembered to tip the bellboy a florin, the *maître d'hôtel* materialised before them. Recognising Ayrest, his ambassadorial features assumed an expression of discreet pleasure.

'You might think that the Captain was the most important person on this ship,' smiled Ayrest to Cato, 'but you would be wrong.' The *maître d'hôtel* inclined his head in grave accedence, and ushered them before him to a table. The restaurant was almost full, but unlike elsewhere in the ship, even in the more privileged quarters, nobody subsided into staring silence at Ayrest's propinquity. Something in the room's atmosphere caught at Cato's consciousness, and then he realised that, alone of all the ship's facilities, the Riviera Grill was unpanelled, and it was the restful absence of warp and creak that had caught at his ear. Instead, the murmur of conversation, the tick of silver and glassware, and the pensive explorations of the piano player found a bed of blessed silence. If, an hour or two ago the ballroom had seemed to represent the most glamorous situation to which Cato might aspire, then the sophisticated intimacy of the Riviera Grill – free as it was of turnips, quackers and false noses – effortlessly doubled, squared even, this quotient. The carpet was black, and the curtains at Cato's side were of red velvet spangled with white stars. On the tiny dance floor, separated from the restaurant by a silver-bronze and etched glass balustrade, a couple clasped each other almost without motion. It was impossible to tell the exact colour of the walls, because these constantly changed. Cato was unsure if this was his imagination, but it seemed that the room's lighting-changes were somehow suggested by the music that was being played. At the moment, apparently to accompany the oblique meanderings of the piano, the walls were washed with blue. Champagne appeared at the table, served from a black, narrow-necked bottle. A waiter bowed at his side. Food seemed an unnecessary addition to the pleasure of simply being there, and in a dream, Cato barely noticed what they ordered. Both of them lit cigarettes.

'So,' she said, soundlessly expelling a plume of smoke. 'Cato.'

'Yes.' He found the self-possession to smile, but silence and the notes of the piano hung between them. The walls, he noticed, were now an undersea green, pierced as if by sunlight. Through the circular bay of curtained windows he could see behind them, faint in the darkness, the pale course of the ship's wake.

'My name's Ayrest,' she said eventually, rising an inch or two from her chair to smooth the faille beneath her. 'You've never actually used it.'

'I'm sorry,' he said. 'You start off formal, and then you have to . . . change horses midstream, so to speak, and get stuck. It's always happening to me. You end up not calling people anything.'

'Well,' she said, 'if I'm going to help myself to your cigarettes, the least you can do is use my name.'

'Ayrest,' he said, wondering at her logic. 'Ayrest. It's a . . . a beautiful name. Does it mean anything?'

'The wind,' she said. 'Or so I'm told.'

For a moment Cato saw her as he had that first morning on the Sports Deck, alone, her face turned seawards.

'Am I wrong,' she asked, 'or wasn't the Roman Cato rather a stern sort of a character?'

'He was a censor,' said Cato, and then, remembering Reginald's words, added: 'a prosecutor.'

'And are you?' she smiled. 'A prosecutor, I mean.'

'I think so,' said Cato seriously. 'My father says so.'

'Well,' said Ayrest. 'He should know.' She extended her gloved fingers over the white linen table-cloth. They shone a dull silver below the parchment-shaded lamp. 'Are you afraid?' she asked. 'Of your operation and everything?'

'Not in general,' answered Cato, unsurprised by the question. 'Not of dying. The details frighten me, when I think of them: the losing of consciousness, the knowing that the blade and the clamps are waiting in the tray, all that. But not so much the dying. I can't die, anyway,' he added wryly. 'My father would never forgive me.'

She laughed. 'He probably wouldn't. I have the impression he is something of a prosecutor, too?'

Cato nodded, wondering whether she knew what his father did for a living. 'Something of one, yes.'

Ayrest suddenly leant forward over her hands. 'Don't be frightened of dying,' she said, almost urgently. 'Dying's nothing, it's easy. It's the living that takes work.'

Cato looked at her, astonished. How could it be that she, so beautiful and authoritative, found it so?

She straightened. 'I'm sorry,' she said, blinking and

waving her hand as smoke from her cigarette found her eyes. 'Perhaps that was hardly appropriate.'

'Do you find it difficult?' he asked quietly, holding his own cigarette away from the table and from her face. 'Living, I mean. Are you . . . unhappy?'

Before she could answer, a hollowed brick of ice filled with Beluga caviare was placed between them. Ayrest removed her gloves and placed them at the edge of the table, where Cato watched their minute, cooling expiry. They sat in silence, waiting for the waiter to leave. The champagne from the black bottle, Cato discovered, was quite wonderful, quite different from any that he had tasted before, which was, of course, not a very great deal. How on earth, he wondered, could she possibly be unhappy? Surely just . . . *being herself* was cause enough for happiness?

A rack of toast was placed at his side.

Ayrest did not acknowledge the waiter's departing bow, but spoke absently, as if continuing a train of thought, as if the interruption had lasted no more than an instant.

'It's as if . . .' she began, 'it's as if before you're born, you're given one of those fairy-tale choices.' She fluttered her fingers like wings. 'You can attract friendship, you're told, or respect, or loyalty – any of those sorts of qualities – or you can attract' – she placed her hand over her left breast – 'love. And, of course, as always in a fairy-tale, you make the wrong choice, and choose love. Now for a long time, when you're young and . . .' she shrugged, ' . . . beautiful and so on and people *do* fall in love with you and everything is bright and fun, you're convinced that you've made the right choice. Some day, you're convinced, some just-round-the-corner moment – Okay, maybe not tonight but *soon*, one of these days – you'll experience what everyone else has been going on about all this time. But it doesn't happen and it doesn't happen and it doesn't happen and the more it doesn't happen, the more you wonder what it can possibly be that makes people – and I'm talking about people who know nothing about you, *nothing* – your friend Pierre, for example – say: "I love you." You begin to wonder what those words can possibly, possibly mean.'

Her eyes were level with his own. He wanted to touch her hair, to reassure her. His hand lifted in his lap, but her sadness and the distance between them was too great, and he let it fall.

'You leave me with nothing to say,' he answered.

'There *would* be nothing to say,' she murmured enigmatically, 'if the story ended there.' Smiling, she held out her small, freckled hand, and this time he reached for it. It felt as he had imagined that it would feel: hard, soft, a little cold. And when he looked up at her again he no longer saw the flawless, unknowable figure who had lifted her chin to the wind of the Boat Deck, but someone quite other: a forty-year-old woman who had grown fearful of the attention which had once been her life-blood. And somewhere – in the fear, in the willow-green of her eyes and the lingering traces of the Highland accent – he saw the child that she had once been.

'Where does the story end?' he asked quietly, but she shook her head, and turned his palm to the lamplight like a fairground clairvoyant.

'Tell me about yourself,' she said. 'Tell me everything.'

With a little prompting, Cato told her. About Newton Priors and Cleeve, his solitary hours in the library, his non-combatant cricket and rugby status, and the half-admiration, half-fear that his condition had inspired in the other boys. About the frequent visits to the silent, over-heated waiting rooms of London specialists that, enabling him to see his parents several times a term – sometimes even midweek – had been the stated envy of the other boys. But not quite their envy, as he had known. For children, too, could be kind. He told her about his father and the river and the water-meadows and the gun that was no longer cleaned and the rod that was no longer taken from its case. And about his mother, dead in circumstances which had allowed of no discussion but only, literally and metaphorically, a burial.

The ice-block which had contained the caviare was removed, and further dishes brought. It was the finest food that Cato had ever tasted, and he tasted not a mouthful of it. He told her all that he could think of – all, that is, that he could possibly have told another – and she listened attentively. The only important thing that he did not tell her was what he intended to do with his life, if life was granted him. For that was between his father and himself, and although the temptation was very great and the champagne quite different from any that he had tasted before (which was, of course, not a very great deal) he kept the faith, the faith of the true believer, and said nothing. He wished to go to Cambridge, he explained. And after that, he shrugged, well, he would see.

When they had finished eating, and with a new confidence – born in part of knowledge shared with her, in part of knowledge withheld – he placed his hand over hers and upturned it, as she had his, to the light.

'And you?' he asked.

'There's so much I could tell you,' she said after a short reflection, 'and so little that would tell you anything. I married my first husband because he loved me, and my second because he didn't. As a model, of course, there was never any question of children . . .' She released her hand from his, and twisted the diamond rings, which gleamed with shallow fire.

'When war was declared, Jack and I were in Bermuda, on someone's yacht. Some other people rowed over and shouted the news through a loud-hailer and we all laughed and had a drink. Jack was my second husband, but at that time I was still married to Johnny Wendover, my first. Johnny hated my working as a model, said now that we were married it was quite unsuitable, it wasn't as if we were short of money, so why couldn't we just . . . Jack, of course,' she smiled, 'loved it, loved dressing me up like a Christmas tree and turning heads in the Orchid Room and the Four Hundred. God knows, though, what possessed him to marry me. Or me him, for that matter. I think I knew even then that I was just . . . loitering, wasting time at the edge of other people's lives.' She fell silent. The walls were a sugared-almond pink.

'And what happened?' prompted Cato.

'Oh, the war ended and I was sort of . . . got out of the wardrobe, given a dusting-down and an airing. But by then, of course, everything had changed, and it was all much, much too late.'

'And where are you going now?' asked Cato.

'Oh,' she smiled softly, 'let's say to . . . Kalamazoo.'

'Really?' said Cato. 'In Michigan? Like in the song?'

'Years have gone by . . .' she half-whispered, half-sang. 'My my how she flew . . . More champagne?'

'Just a little,' said Cato. 'I have to be careful.'

'You'll be all right,' she said. 'I promise. Now and for ever.'

'Now and for ever?'

'Now and for ever. Dance with me.'

He emptied his glass, took her hand, and led her through the gates of the balustrade. Several couples were already edging around the tiny floor, permitting Ayrest and Cato an area of parquet no larger than a gramophone-record on which to manoeuvre. Gradually, as they swayed and turned to the piano's minor-key wanderings, they found themselves drawn inside the circle, their clasped hands locked between them by the press of shoulders. And then, after a brief claustrophobic moment in which it seemed that they would no longer be able to move at all, they found the common heart-beat, and she laid her cheek against his shoulder and closed her eyes. As his senses flooded with detail – the tiny crumbling of her eye-black, the faintly wine-soured breath, the soft press of her breasts – he raised his supporting palm from the cluster of silk flowers to the warm small of her back, and like swimmers on a wave they were held and swayed and gently cannoned by the circling bodies around them.

In the same way that Cato had tasted nothing of the dinner that he had eaten, his eyes registered very little of the 'Balmoral' stateroom. There were several overstuffed-looking chairs around the walls, and once again, the creaking of boiserie, but it did not occur to him to seat himself uninvited. As Ayrest moved around the room touching the light-switches and effecting other arbitrary-seeming rearrangements, he touched his bow-tie, stared unseeing around him, and counted the heart-beats that pulsed at his ears and burst like crimson peonies against his breastbone.

At last, drawing the curtains over the twin portholes, leaving only a small lamp on the dressing table still lit, she stepped out of her shoes and came to him. Without the shoes she was shorter than he had thought her, and her feet were lost in the breaking folds of the ball-dress. As she reached for his tie, the knot falling apart in her fingers, his hands moved uncertainly behind her back, resting on the cluster of silk roses before climbing, a little awkwardly, to smooth at her shoulder blades. Beneath his palms he felt the goose-pimples rise and sensed the shiver of silk. Slowly, she inclined her face towards him, and after a moment's hesitation, he brought his mouth down on hers. He met an impossible softness and a tiny, gasping exhalation and, immediately breathless, buried his mouth and nose in her hair. Closing his eyes, his heart thumping against her breasts, he inhaled the warm freesia and face-powder and cigarette-smoke smell of her.

'You do have to breathe,' she whispered, smiling. 'You're not underwater.'

As he kissed her again, and her lips parted beneath his own, he felt the fluent twist of her fingers as they undid his collar-studs, and, one by one, his shirt-studs. A moment later he felt a narrow hand slip down the front of his thigh inside his trouser pocket, drop the studs, and briefly remain. He lifted his face from hers and his starched shirt-front gaped stiffly open beneath his unbuttoned dinner-jacket.

She took a half-pace backwards. 'You'll have to . . .'

Shrugging off the dinner-jacket, he threw it to one of the chairs, where, as he thumbed the braces clear of his shoulders and the oversized trousers sank an inch or two to his hips, it slid from the quilted chintz to the floor.

She lifted the shirt over his head, and his hands, freed, reached for her again. Running down the curve of her back to her waist, trembling a little, they discovered a parted hook and eye, and a course of others, still secured, beneath the silk sash and the clustered silk petals. He managed to unfasten two of these before, taking his hands and pressing them quickly to the ruched faille at her breasts, she disengaged herself and moved to the other side of the cabin.

'Undress,' she whispered. 'Get into bed.'

His heart leapt with uncertainty at her retreat and then he understood that she needed somewhere to lay the ball-dress. Kneeling, he fumbled at his shoelaces; he had double-knotted them, and while the right-hand lace undid easily enough, the left-hand one tightened to a clinch. As he tugged at the shoe, eventually standing and treading it off with the other foot, he watched as, in silhouette against the lamp, she lifted the tortoiseshell comb and kirby-grips from her hair, placed them on the dressing table, shook out the French roll into which her hair had been pinned and, bowing slightly, reached behind her for the remaining fastenings of the ballgown.

Placing his socks in his shoes as if in a dream, Cato straightened and turned from the light. Unbuttoning the heavy black evening trousers, he lowered them to the floor, along with the Chilprufe underpants which had so shamed him in the swimming pool.

At the dressing table, with the ballgown now unfastened, Ayrest turned and parted the porthole curtains. Grateful for her tact, Cato took three furtively naked steps to the bedside, picking his way as if over glowing coals, and climbed between the cold sheets.

For a moment Ayrest remained at the porthole, and then, turning, she slipped the straps from her shoulders. For a moment, and at several levels still disbelieving, Cato just looked at her, searching her face in the half-dark for the features that he thought he had known. She was the same – her eyes, her nose, her mouth, her hair were all the same – but she had changed, somehow, beyond all recognition. It was as if she had transformed herself into another being, into a child-version of herself, no more in control of events than he. And then she inclined her head, and a finger of lamplight touched her cheeks and forehead and she was once again the starry, unknowable creature that he had seen at Southampton.

Perhaps because of his partial disbelief that any of this was truly happening, he felt no comet-shower flaring before his eyes, no clamping tightness at his chest. Instead, as once on a canopy of snow, he felt a weightless calm, a sense of life suspended, of the moment's endlessness. On the bedside table beyond her stood a white telephone with a frayed and knotted cord; at its side were a glass-stoppered perfume bottle, a cigarette lighter and a lipstick. All had the air of having been there, thus arranged, for ever. She had walked to the bed in silhouette, against the lamp. Already, he could remember nothing of her body. Perhaps he had seen nothing of it. She lay watching him, a yard of banked pillows away, the sheet and the eiderdown tucked almost defensively into the crook of one arm.

'It seems so . . . strange to be here,' he said, surprising himself with the conversational tone of his voice.

'Didn't you know?' she asked.

'Know?'

'Didn't you recognise all that . . .' she smiled, 'all that we shared?' She turned away, became the child-Ayrest, and reached out her arm to him along the pillows. 'We're travelling so much further than the others, you see. So much further.'

Cato had no idea what she meant, but the desolation of her tone overwhelmed him. Gently, he laid his arm along hers, felt the slender unused bicep, the small boss of her shoulder, the razored hollow beneath.

At the touch of her, as his fingers overlaid this fledgling arm, at once old and young, tensioned and loose, he felt desire for her steadily but imperatively unfurl within him, felt the expanding bloom at his breastbone and the needful, insistent crawl at his groin. She turned to him – neither the child-Ayrest or the adult now, but another, third Ayrest, his equal in all things, all wants – and as he moved over the cold sheets towards her, he saw a lamplit tear tremble at the corner of her eye. He hesitated, his face inches from hers, and blinking, she squeezed the tear away.

'I'm sorry,' she said, and wiping her eyes with her fingers, smiled. 'It's nothing. Nothing . . . bad, anyway. Just the way you look at me, so . . .'

'Doesn't everyone look at you?' asked Cato, suddenly remembering her words in the Riviera Grill and that he must never tell her that he loved her. 'Hasn't everyone always looked at you?'

'Not like that,' she said softly, shaking her head. 'Not like that.'

The light touched the tear blurs at her cheekbones. She smiled at him: a grin, deliberately crooked. Extending a finger, he gently touched the fan of shadow at the corner of her mouth. Her mouth twitched, her lips parted, and her expression levelled. Recognising once again the third Ayrest, the equal Ayrest, he reached for the sheet that with unconscious modesty remained lifted to her chin, and drew it down.

For a long moment, a long moment which she deliberately made longer by holding his eyes in hers, by resolutely refusing them permission to leave her own – child-Ayrest again, the little ribbon's-bow smile – he did not look down.

And when he did look down, when his eyes followed his not-quite-steady fingers over the gently ridged prominences of collarbone and sternum to the small pale-nippled breasts which lay a little flattened against her ribcage, her gaze never left his eyes. When they closed, and he laid his hand on her arm and his forehead against her forehead and breathed against her cheek, she waited.

'I'm sorry,' he said. 'I just have to . . .'

'There's no hurry,' she said.

'My doctor once told me – at least I think that's what he was getting at – that . . . I should be very careful. That if I wasn't, something like this could . . .'

'There's no hurry,' she said again, stroking his hair. 'No rush.'

'I get these warning signs.'

'Have you got them now?'

'I did, a moment ago.'

'What happens?'

'It gets hard to breathe. It's like as if . . . Do you know what a Sam Browne belt looks like?'

'An army officer's . . .?'

'Yes. It's as if a Sam Browne or a stable belt was being pulled tighter and tighter round my chest, and at the same time the air was getting thicker and thicker. And then the stars come.'

'Are the stars bad?'

'They're a bit like the stars that you get when you hit your head – a sort of bluish white – but bigger, and slower, like ink blobs on blotting paper but in reverse. And then they drift away like parachute flares.'

'I don't think I know about parachute flares.'

'In the films. For attacking at night. The flare whizzes up and bursts and then it sort of drifts and fizzles and draws those lines in front of your eyes.'

'And that's what you were feeling and seeing a moment ago?'

'A bit. It's gone now. The stars were all around you in a sort of swarm.'

'I think I felt them.'

'Prickling?' he asked.

'Something like that.'

'They're a symptom of anoxia. Insufficient oxygen in the blood. The tips of my fingers go blue, too. It's called cyanosis. Sometimes I imagine that they glow in the dark.'

'Well, they don't seem to be glowing now.' Slowly, she pulled the sheet over their heads. In the near-darkness she was no more than a vague, warm outline of breath and smell and body. He reached out his hand, and tracing the shrouded corrugation of her ribs, enclosed a small sunken-nippled breast in his fingers.

'Perhaps they are, though,' she murmured, as, releasing her breast, he moved his hand hesitantly over the escarpment of her ribs to the floating looseness of her belly. There, her smaller, ringed fingers found his and drew them further downwards over the crupper of bone with its tight, flat-lying curls to the hot liquescent seam between her thighs.

And once again, in amazement and a kind of recognition, he forgot to breathe and lay unmoving, his hands cupping her. When he finally gasped for air against her cheek, his fingers involuntarily parted her and she gave a small cry.

'I'm sorry,' he whispered, half-lifting his hand.

'No,' she murmured, catching his fingers, pressing them back, 'No, that's . . . that's . . .'

As he explored her, the damp curls moved beneath his palm.

He had no idea of the time, no idea of how long they had lain there, only that the lamp still shone at the dressing table and that the sky and the sea were still black at the parting of the porthole curtains. They had arrived at a rhythm of infinite slowness in which, after every wondering foray, every compulsive return to her pale, yielding body, he would rest against her, and allow his heart-beat and his excitement to subside to a manageable level. With instinctive tact, she seemed to understand that she must do very little, that he needed nothing but to know that she was there, that his every short return to her gave her pleasure, that she could wait, that they had time. For his part, the desire that he felt and which pressed more urgently at him with every smell and touch of her was inseparable from a tenderness which was almost pitying. He was inexpressibly moved by her, by the child-mask of her face in the dimness, by the starveling breasts, loose as sparrows in his hand, and by the taut and lucent softness of the skin through which he could feel every web of sinew, every blade and spar of bone. And recognising the physical affinities between them – 'what we shared', in her earlier words – he understood the rest. He understood why she looked to the sea. He understood the unbearability to her of a stranger protesting love for what was no more and no less than the public face of her loneliness. And he understood that the Ayrest he saw in the half-dark was her truest self, an agonised ghost-child who had never been laid to rest in the memories and fondnesses and photograph albums of others, but still waited on forlorn tiptoes, desperate to be called forth, to be loved without condition.

And when the time came, when he knew that he could hold himself back no longer, he whispered quickly to her and she smiled, knowing herself loved, and drew him inside her. Neither of them then moved further, but held to each other, and waited. And when it came there were no hamadryad coils, no comet-storms or parachute flares but just the moment, transcendent and ordinary, and the long rise and fall of the sea.

Cato slept. Once again he was on the train, his mother beside him, and once more the fans slowed to silence as the train came to a stop. This time, though, in place of the empty mudflats and the ranges of waste were fields of silver-streaming grass, through which distant figures could be seen making their way. Unfussily, his mother got to her feet and reached into the netted luggage-rack for her coat. As she opened the heavy door of the train Cato half-rose to follow, but with a quick smile, as if anxious to be gone, she motioned that he remain where he was, that he must continue his journey without her. And this time, understanding that this was her wish, he let her go. She stepped into the field, the grass a river around her ankles, and walked quickly away. At the last moment – the moment before her features became quite indiscernible – she looked back over her shoulder at him and smiled, and then as she turned away again the door swung silently shut and the train shuddered to a start. Through the streaked windows the distant figure became a blur, was lost, and he knew, finally, without regret, that he would never see her again, that she was leaving his dreams for ever. He felt himself shaken forward by the motion of the train and then a hand was at his shoulder and Ayrest was standing at the bedside in a dragon-patterned Chinese dressing gown.

He reached for her sleepily, reached inside her gown, but her hands took his.

'Quick,' she whispered. 'You must go back.'

'Why? What . . .?'

'Sssh. Just get dressed.'

'Can't I stay?'

'Quick.' She kissed his hand. 'Please.'

Unwillingly he climbed to his feet and cast around the cabin for his clothes. His shirt smelt of cigar-smoke. It took a little time to unknot one of his laces, and he pushed his bow-tie into the pocket with the shirt- and collar-studs.

'When will I see you?'

She tilted her face to him. 'Kiss me.'

He kissed her mouth, her eyes, her hair. He parted the Chinese gown and kissed her breasts, but she raised him up, and drew the silk closed.

Frowning, he looked into the willow-green eyes.

'Ayrest, I . . .'

'Sssh. I know. Go now.'

The corridors were deserted. His sheets, when he finally reached his cabin, were cold.

# 5

He woke late and dry-mouthed to Herbert's knock.

'Your father said to call you, Mr Cato.' The cabin steward crossed the cabin and drew the porthole curtains on to a dulled white haze.

Cato groaned, and closing his eyes, tried to draw the night back around him. A bruising pulse beat at his temples and a sour unease lay about his stomach. For a moment he thought he was about to be sick, and then, with the return of the knowledge that everything was different, that his life had changed, that he loved her, a fierce, drug-like happiness flooded his bloodstream, and he buried his face in the warm angle of his elbow as if to recall some touch or trace or sensation of her. It was no good. The day, wakefulness and the light promised too much. And he had so little time.

'What time is it?'

Herbert peered through the porthole. 'Ten, sir. And well and truly fog-bound. Which could, of course,' he examined his fingernails, 'just mess up a schedule or two.'

'What time do you think we'll get in?'

'Hard to say. If the fog lifts and we don't miss the tide . . .' He shrugged. 'Then, of course we could be here all day . . .'

Cato, not listening, lay back and massaged his temples. Every extra hour on board was another hour with her or near her. How would it be between them, he wondered a little apprehensively, in the light of day? How should he present himself? He would telephone, he decided. Perhaps leave it an hour or so until he had finished breakfast with his father.

Cautiously opening his eyes, he saw that Herbert was hovering without obvious purpose between the bed and the opaque light around the porthole. He looked, thought Cato, as if he was about to ask to use the lavatory.

'There's been an accident, sir.'

'What sort of accident?' asked Cato absently, remembering Mrs Klampmayer and the Lalique vase and the lead shot.

'Mrs MacLean, sir. The fashion model.'

'What?' Icy fear drenched him. 'I mean, what's . . .?'

Herbert darted a dramatic glance over each shoulder and peered conspiratorially forward. 'They think she's gone over, sir.'

'Gone over? Gone . . . overboard?'

'Jumped, they think.'

'No,' said Cato definitely, as the Royal Albion monogram on the counterpane swam out of focus. 'No. That's not . . . They can't find her?'

'They found her shoes, sir,' said Herbert, disconcerted by Cato's reaction but compelled by some raconteurial impulse, now that he had begun, to continue. 'With her gloves, and some jewellery. Arranged in a neat pile at the Boat Deck rail. And she's nowhere aboard, of course, they've . . .' His words slowed and fell quieter as he registered Cato's frozen gaze. 'It's the talk of the ship, sir.'

'The talk of the ship,' whispered Cato.

'Yes, sir. Are you all right, sir?'

'Yes, I'm . . . Sorry. Bit of a . . .'

'Can I get you something from the dispensary? Pick-me-up, perhaps?'

'No.' Cato shook his head vaguely. 'No. I'll . . . I should go to my father's cabin. Thank you.'

Soundlessly, Herbert backed from the cabin, and Cato lowered himself, pyjamaed, to the floor.

It was impossible. There had clearly been some mistake. There were several hundred Cabin Class passengers on board, after all, and a pair of shoes or gloves or a necklace could surely belong to any one of them without meaning that their owner had drowned. And on a ship the size of the *Carmelia* there were any number of places that she could be. Weren't there? She was probably at the hairdresser.

Apart from which, of course, there was last night. And for a moment, as he sat bowed and naked on the bed's edge, he felt the feel of her again, smelt the smell of her. But then somewhere behind these physical memories a dark whisper told him that last night was proof of nothing, that no moment of last night presupposed a future of any kind.

Kalamazoo.

'You've heard?' asked Reginald five minutes later. A lint-and-gauze dressing stained with dark yellow antiseptic had replaced the previous day's helmet of bandages, and a fleck of shaving soap lay untowelled beneath one ear. His father looked older and paler than Cato had ever seen him.

'The . . . um . . . No.' Cato shook his head. 'Herbert said something about someone finding shoes and jewellery on the Boat Deck.'

'Look,' said Reginald, wincing as he eased himself into a sitting position against the pillows, 'you don't deserve this, and I understand that she was, um, kind enough to give you dinner last night, but it looks pretty certain that Mrs MacLean took her life early this morning.'

Cato stared.

'The facts, apparently, are these. Shortly after two o'clock she was seen on deck. On the Boat Deck. She was still wearing the grey evening dress that she had worn to the ball and presumably', he raised his eyebrows, 'to dinner afterwards in the Riviera Grill.'

Cato nodded.

'Her bits and pieces – a pair of grey silk gloves and shoes and a diamond bracelet and wristwatch – were found by the rail, close to the place where', he made a small waving motion with his hand, 'we all had our deckchairs. It was possible to establish from the dew on deck that the effects had been there for at least a couple of hours.'

'Did Herbert tell you all this?' asked Cato.

'Herbert certainly appeared keen to discuss the affair,' said Reginald dryly. 'As did Moira and Dr Montmorency and the barber. I'm afraid the whole sad matter's rather common currency by now, because the Captain had it announced that he was taking the ship back on her tracks in the forlorn hope of finding her. But in answer to your question, no. The purser told me. Came along here to the cabin, in fact. And the long and the short of it is that since you were one of the last people to see her alive, talk to her and so on,' he raised his eyebrows and Cato nodded again, 'the Captain wants to have a word with you. I'm to ring the purser, and he'll take you up.'

Dread buffeted Cato's chest, and for a moment he gaped at his father in silence, unable to reply.

'Presumably,' said Reginald, looking studiedly away, 'you returned Mrs MacLean to her cabin after dinner.'

'Yes,' Cato managed, his heart screaming alarm.

'And then proceeded directly to your own.'

'Mm.'

'Do you know what the time was?'

Cato shook his head. Reginald turned to him.

'Sorry,' said Cato, swallowing. 'No. But there were still a fair few people in the Riviera Grill when we . . .'

'When you left?'

'Yes.'

'And that was when you took her back to her cabin?'

'Yes,' said Cato.

'And you . . . what? Said good-night to her, thanked her for dinner, and so on?'

'Yes,' said Cato.

'And went directly back to your own cabin.'

A used emery-board and an orangestick lay on the bed-side table, and there was a broad depression in the pillow at Reginald's side. Had Moira given his father a manicure? wondered Cato. Had she sat on the pillow at his side? Held those rather dry-looking hands? Buffed the greyish, square-cut nails?

'Well?'

'Sorry,' said Cato. 'Yes. That's what happened. I went directly back.'

His father regarded him in silence for several moments and rubbed at his talcumed jowl.

'Well. Tell the Captain that.'

'I will,' said Cato.

'Just routine, I'm sure,' said Reginald. 'Under these circumstances. Rotten thing though. Really rotten. And I have to say that given her . . . she always seemed jolly enough to me, anyway.' He looked away. 'Shows you never ever can tell with people.'

Learn from this, his father seemed to be saying. Use everything. Every failure. Every pain. Just learn. And although it was unsayable, although it would never be mentioned, could never be discussed, he was suddenly sure that his father knew what had happened between himself and Ayrest MacLean, knew precisely what he was suffering at that moment. Deal with it, the half-closed eyes seemed to be saying. Do and say what is necessary. Not what is true, but what is necessary.

I am my father's son, thought Cato. I am fed by pain. Pain will not destroy me. I am my father's son.

He reached for the telephone.

Around them, almost tangible, sat the fog. Cato could no longer see or hear the sea: instead, the hull descended into a damp and muffling whiteness through which, it seemed, the ship barely progressed at all. In silence, and very slightly exaggerating his infirmity, pausing for breath rather more often than was strictly necessary, Cato followed the purser upwards through the decks. There, everything had changed. The long perspectives of promenade were now interrupted by mounds of baggage and rickety tenements of strapped and labelled trunks from the hold. Relays of harried-looking stewards, avoiding as best they could the querulously raised hands and voices of the passengers, carted further luggage forward to the Well Deck in preparation for its transfer to the tender. In consequence of the reduced deck space, both Cabin Class decks seemed suddenly overcrowded, and a general air of preoccupation and bored impatience prevailed. As Cato and the purser edged past them, however, several passengers looked up with sudden interest, nudging each other, nodding, and whispering. They must all know, thought Cato, with sudden panic. Dozens of people must have seen me with her, after all.

'This way, Mr Parkes. Mind your backs, please, gentlemen.'

The purser, grimly courteous, was unrecognisable as the jocose distributor of quackers and false noses of the night before. He displayed no outward sign of impatience at their slowness, but Cato could sense exasperation in the set of his braided shoulders. They wound their way between the hand-carts of the overworked stewards, past the slow-moving queues at the postcard and souvenir counters and the bureau de change, and finally proceeded via a roped-off double flight of steps to the uppermost-level of the bridge superstructure – normally forbidden to passengers – known as the Tops of Houses. This last ascent – for Cato was genuinely exhausted now – took the best part of ten minutes.

With brusque courtesy the purser pulled open a steel door marked 'Officers' Chartroom', and ushered Cato before him into a low-walled office containing a single fixed table and two chairs. At the table, with his back to them, a ship's officer was performing a navigational task involving dividers, charts and a ruler, while beyond the further chair, his cap clutched in his hand, stood Tudor. The bellboy, Cato saw, looked nervous; his spots and his buttons shone.

'Just take a seat, Mr Parkes,' suggested the purser, and Cato, glancing briefly at the erect and staring figure of Tudor, did so. He sat in silence for several minutes, his mind a blank, until a second officer stepped half-way through the door and gestured that Tudor follow him. The colour draining from his acne, Tudor did so. The purser, glancing at Cato, appeared to consider conversation, but remained silent. The officer at the table pursued his navigational mysteries. Cato stared through the thick glass windows at the white nothingness beyond.

Eventually, and without Tudor, the officer reappeared. Cato followed him to the end of one of the narrow wings of the bridge superstructure where, seated in a swivel chair in a small look-out box high above the invisible sea, the bearded figure of the Captain watched and waited.

'Mr Parkes, is it?' he said without taking his eyes from the blankness before him. 'How d'you do. You'll forgive me if I don't stand up. Busy, y'see.' He placed a small unlit pipe between his teeth and flickered Cato an interrogative sideways glance. 'Cold North Labrador Current meets warm Gulf Stream. Result?'

'Fog?' hazarded Cato, realising just in time that he was being asked a question.

'Good lad. Scrambles sound, y'see.' He chewed at the thick pipe-stem. 'All the Albion ships carry radar now but there are still things only a Master hears. Mothers wi' babbies and Masters, y'see. Sixth sense. Saved more ships than ye'll ever read about.' Cato nodded, held to the steel rail, and wished that he had worn a coat.

'Sad business,' continued the Captain, his tone unchanged. 'Always know the deepest places, of course.'

'I'm sorry?'

'Suicides,' said the Captain. 'They always know the deepest places to jump. Look at the charts, I suppose. Know her well?'

'No,' said Cato. 'We'd never met before.'

'Had dinner wi' her last night, though.'

'My father was laid up. She had a deckchair next to us on deck.'

The Captain lowered the pipe to his pocket where, single-handed, he began to fill it from an oilskin pouch.

'How did she seem?'

'She seemed . . . normal, I suppose. Quiet, perhaps.'

The Captain nodded, and returning the pipe to his teeth, beat at his pockets for matches. 'Didn't say anything that might lead you to believe she was thinking of doing away with herself, then?'

'No. I really didn't know her very well.'

'After dinner you escorted her back to her cabin?'

'Yes.' As the Captain tamped at the glowing bowl with a fireproof fingertip, the look-out box filled – not unpleasantly – with pungent brown smoke.

'What time might that have been?'

'I'm not sure,' said Cato, inhaling smoke. 'Before the restaurant closed, though.'

'And then?'

'And then I went back to my own cabin.'

The Captain nodded. 'Pass anyone you know on the way?'

'Um, yes,' Cato improvised, 'there was a clergyman. Drunk, I think. Maybe just limping. And one or two people I'd seen earlier with Major Farrell who I don't think noticed me.'

'Still, there were people about.'

'Oh, yes,' said Cato. 'Quite a few.'

'Well,' said the Captain, 'I doubt we'll ever know exactly what happened. Her bed certainly wasn't slept in.' He shook his head, clamped at his pipe, and peered into the fog. 'Apologies for the third degree, but I have to make a report, d'you see. Ye'll be asked the same questions by the police in port, but I suspect that will be the end of it.'

'What time do you think we'll . . .?'

'Late this afternoon. We've lost several hours on the

search.' Hand outstretched, he swivelled to face Cato. 'My thanks to you, Mr Parkes.'

The interview was at an end. From the chartroom Cato was accompanied back down to the Boat Deck, and inside. Once there he excused himself, and attracting considerably less attention alone than he had with the purser, made his way to the lifts. These were crowded around with passengers laden with coats, flowers and hand-luggage, but as he had hoped, he discovered Tudor back on duty there. The bellboy looked no less anxious than he had half an hour earlier. Bundling Cato into an empty lift, and ignoring the other passengers milling at the gates, he pressed the 'Down' button and, half-way between 'A' and 'B' decks, deliberately brought the gilt cage to a shuddering halt.

'So,' said Tudor, jumbling amongst the change in his trouser pockets. ''Bine?'

Cato shook his head. Tudor struck a match on the sole of his shoe and drew hungrily at the pinched-out cigarette end.

'It was you, then?' said Cato, eventually. 'You were the last to see her?'

The bellboy nodded.

'Yeah, just my luck.'

'But what were you doing up there?'

'With a blood, wasn't I.'

'A passenger?' asked Cato.

Tudor exhaled and rolled his eyes. 'Gentleman from Tourist.'

'What were you doing?'

'Can't you guess?'

'And you saw her.'

'Hard to miss her, chum,' said Tudor, bitterly. 'There weren't many on the Boat Deck at three in the morning in party frocks 'n diamonds.'

'Three o'clock?'

'Something like that.'

'What was she doing?'

'Just . . . going past. Didn't take much notice at the time.' He laughed sourly. 'Had my hands full.'

'So why did you tell anyone you'd seen her?'

'Caught coming off deck, wasn't I. Senior first officer. Didn't say what I was doing, 'course – though he knew – but when the other came on top he asked if I'd seen her. I was bubbled by then, nothing to lose, so I said yes. I had.'

'What'll happen?'

Tudor shrugged. 'Dunno. I was going to sell some blood down the donor place and go out on the beer at the Harbour Diner. Don't look like it now, though. Still,' – he traced the ruvid topography of his chin with a bitten finger – 'the news boys'll come on at Quarantine, and with any luck I can make a bob or two for the story.'

'Well,' said Cato. 'I hope you can.'

'Tell me something, mate,' said Tudor. 'Was you . . .? I mean, did you know she was going to do herself in?'

'I hardly knew her,' said Cato.

Tudor stared at him for a long moment. 'Oh well,' he shrugged, treading out the cigarette end and sliding it beneath the square of carpet. 'Hey-ho.' He stabbed at the 'Up' button and the lift gulped upwards again.

'Good luck,' said Cato, sliding open the 'A'-deck gates.

'And to you, mate. And to you.'

He supposed that he ought to pack. Slowly, crushed by the loss of her, by the fog, by the whole ragged end of things, he trailed through the deserted public rooms and along the galleries where desultory groups of passengers sat tense and over-organised around their luggage. The ship seemed smaller in scale than when they had first embarked, more comprehensible. He had scoured its mysteries, gorged himself on the privilege of his situation, but without Ayrest – who, he now understood, had embodied all privilege, all desirability – it was suddenly intolerable that they had to remain aboard. Everything that he saw and everywhere that he went was dulled almost to invisibility by her absence.

One thing moved him above all other. That at the moment when it must have been least bearable to do so, she had made the bed – made it so competently that it looked as if a stewardess had performed the task – and redressed herself exactly as people had seen her earlier in her jewellery and ballgown. For a moment, Cato saw her undressing by the light of the dressing-table lamp, saw the care with which she had lain out the ball-dress. She had known, even then, that she would be refastening its hooks and eyes before the night was done. And all of this, he knew, was so that no suspicion of involvement in her death should attach itself to him.

And, he finally admitted it, everything of the previous night, of their conversation, their dancing and their love-making, had about it a gentle finality, an air of sad farewell. She had marked herself for death and for the cold Atlantic long before he had ever met her. No future had been imaginable. Only Kalamazoo, the sea-become-land.

And that, he realised steadily and without fear, was what she had recognised in him. She had seen that he, too, was marked for death, and had chosen to give him all the heart and all the life that remained to her. The silver-grey figure that the ocean had taken had been dead already.

His cabin was empty, bright, and smelt faintly and impersonally of furniture-polish. Nothing remained in the wardrobe except coat hangers and fresh lining paper, and of his clothes and luggage there remained no trace. It was no longer his cabin, but that of the passenger who, in twenty-four hours' time, would begin his journey eastwards, and Cato felt himself a trespasser.

He discovered his father suited, still bandaged, and seated in a wheelchair. The cabin had been made up around him, and Herbert – whose politeness now that he had been fully and finally tipped had a detectibly impatient edge to it – was removing to the corridor the coats and overnight bags that would serve as their hand-luggage.

'I thought that we might go up on deck,' said Reginald.

'How are you feeling, Dad?' asked Cato, concerned by the wheelchair.

'Right as rain. Corcoran's been a persistent caller, though. Keen on a last game, as you said he'd be. I told him I was in no state for bridge, slight memory loss and so on, and persuaded Montmorency to lend me this contraption. In which connection,' he lowered his voice, 'where's the . . .?'

'In the lining.' Cato nodded at the overnight bag.

Reginald nodded approvingly. 'Good. I'll thicken up my wallet with paper. I'd guess that a spot of pickpocketing's going to be their final gambit. Meanwhile you keep a weather eye on the bag.'

'Okay, Dad.'

'Boat Deck, please, Herbert.'

They set off in convoy.

Habit led them to their accustomed place. The fog finally appeared to be thinning, and visibility had improved. Cato moved casually to the rail and looked down to the sea. This, he thought, was where she . . . She would have slipped overboard with barely a splash, the cold turbulence and the grey ball-dress bearing her down fast. You didn't suffer when you drowned, he had read, but how could anyone know? And then there was the other thought, the unthinkable thought of flesh and silk and the vast churning blades of the propellers.

He looked up to find his father eyeing him, thinking his thoughts, and he turned away from the rail. The rugs, they discovered, had been removed from the deckchairs, and Reginald signalled to Dusty who was maintaining a cursory patrol.

'Souvenir hunters, I'm afraid, sir. Wouldn't credit it,

would you, but there it is. So we lock them up on the last day.'

'Get the colonel a rug, Dusty, there's a good fellow,' said Farrell, sauntering up behind them and pressing a note into the steward's hand.

'Very good, sir.'

Cato felt disinclined towards a conversation with Farrell, was untempted by his rugless chair, and discovered to his surprise that he was hungry. Excusing himself, he took the overnight bag and made his way along the promenade. A thought occurred before he left the rail, and he unstrapped the bag and reached inside it. The money, his fingers told him, was still there. Carefully, he drew out the Lilliput girls – Sonia, Heather, Annamite Astrid, evil little Trixie – and with a small farewell smile released them to the wind and, after a long disappearing flutter, the sea.

At the dining-room table under the balcony he discovered Docherty, Pierre and – to his surprise – Philippa. Docherty looked up and winked, a smile cracked the black stubble at Pierre's cheeks, and Philippa waved a fork-impaled oyster at him. The room was as full as it had been on the first night.

'Extraordinary, isn't it?' said Pierre, as Cato looked around him at the bustling tables. 'It's as if they've all suddenly realised how much they paid for their berths, and how little they ate when they were seasick. How . . . are you?'

'I'm all right,' said Cato, realising that, in the light of his departure from Pierre and Philippa the night before, this was something of a many-layered question. 'I'm fine.'

Uncharacteristically, it seemed to him, Philippa asked him nothing. Seeing her sitting there at the table in her limp cotton dress and cardigan he had dreaded an onslaught of enquiry, but instead she sat there in silence. From time to time, with grimaces at Pierre that were both complicit and culpatory, she lifted slivers of oyster-shell from her tongue. What kind of an evening had they had? he wondered.

'We'll never get to New York, you know,' she announced eventually.

'What do you mean?' asked Cato, simultaneously irritated and relieved by this return to form.

'What I say,' she said, drawing a squeezed-out lemon segment away from its peel with her long front teeth. 'My Dad was explaining it to me. We'll get half the distance there, then half the distance that's left, then half the distance that's left after that, and so on to infinity. We'll never get there. We'll be on the ship for ever.'

To his side, as the Irishman expertly pared the pink flesh of his trout from the bone, Cato caught Docherty's smirk. On the staircase Max Amber, accompanied by a neat, pale Loelia, was in conversation with a pair of the ship's officers. It seemed to Cato that he was pointing at their table.

'So we'll starve?' Pierre asked her.

'No, silly. We'll eat half the food in the kitchens, then half of what's left after that, then half of what's left after that, and so on. The journey will last for ever and so will the food. For ever and ever.'

'Sounds all right by me,' said Cato, his eyes returning to the menu. 'What do you think, Pierre?'

But Pierre wasn't listening. He was looking up at the two officers who were purposefully, if a little awkwardly, approaching the table.

'Mr Watson, is it, sir?' asked the older and stouter of the pair, consulting a passenger list. 'Mr Pierre Watson?'

Cato lowered the menu. Docherty continued his patient surgery on the trout.

'Ah,' said Pierre, shooting grime-shined cuffs and pressing nervously at his hair. 'Yes. I've . . . um, rather been expecting you gentlemen.'

'Perhaps it would be as well if you were to accompany us, Mr Watson.'

'Yes,' said Pierre, quietly. 'Perhaps it might.'

Cato, not understanding, froze. Philippa, understanding everything, looked from officer to officer. 'You . . . buggers,' she breathed. 'Can't you even let him . . . finish his lunch?'

'I didn't order any fish,' murmured Pierre vaguely, straightening his knives and forks. 'It's quite all right.'

Philippa shook her head in disbelief. Docherty's move-ments had slowed almost to stillness. The officers stepped backwards a pace as Pierre folded his table-napkin with deliberation and, standing, drained his wine glass.

'All the best, chum.' He extended his hand to Cato who, dazed, shook it. 'Philippa. Docherty.'

He led the officers briskly towards the staircase. Still incomprehending, Cato stared after them.

'It didn't occur to you?' asked Philippa. 'State of him and that?'

'No,' said Cato. 'Not ever. He was a poet. They dress like that.'

'Not just his clothes,' said Philippa. 'The way he was. I knew straight away. I told him last night. I said, you've no more right to be here than I have. Less, in fact.'

'And what did he say to that?'

'Oh, he laughed. Told me the whole thing. That he hadn't fully decided to go through with it till the ship blew at Southampton, and then it was such a lovely windy day he just . . . couldn't resist. I thought that was lovely.'

'But how did he get aboard?'

'Visitor's pass. Threw his case on the trolley with Mrs . . .' she inclined her head towards Cato, ' . . . your friend. With all her bits and pieces. Collected it on board. And then just didn't get off.'

'But where did he sleep?'

'Pinched a couple of blankets from deck and kipped down snug as a bug behind the cinema screen. Easy. It was washing, he said, that was the problem.'

Cato caught Docherty's smirk, and shook his head. 'I still can't believe it. I thought he was going to Hollywood.'

'Oh, he is. Or he was, I should say. But I'm not so sure they're expecting him there.' She speared a slice of salmon from Cato's plate. 'Here, give us a try of that.'

'So it was all untrue, then. All those films. All those people he said he'd met.'

'Oh he met them, all right . . . Anyone can go to a pub, after all. But the other stuff, the posh dad and that, I told him, I said, "That's not true and you know it." ' She smiled ruefully. 'Charmer he was, though, right enough. No,' she said, 'all he had to sell was these.' She reached into the pocket of her dress. 'Here.'

She handed Cato a metal disc the size of a small saucer. Cato peered at it. Several paper-thin and concentrically riveted circles of tin, each covered in tiny print, overlaid each other like a target. Into each of these discs windows had been cut, through which some of the minute words printed on the disc below were visible.

'Cronshaw's Key Words to All Speech,' read Cato, with difficulty. 'Abstractive, Modal, Discrete, Pulverulent, and . . . Moral/Canonical. What on earth . . .?'

'He bought a thousand of them,' said Philippa. 'They're to help find the right word at a glance. Ideas at your fingertips, he said. You turn the dials. The King uses one. And Mr Cyril Connolly.'

'I'm sure,' said Cato, blinking at the tiny letters. 'Life,' he read, 'Death, Killing, Corpse, Cerement . . .'

'He's got a suitcaseful,' said Philippa. 'I told him, you should have brought more clean shirts.'

'Wait a minute,' said Cato, patting the breast pocket of his jacket for his wallet. 'I'm sure he gave me something last night, too. Yes.' He drew a fold of ship's writing paper from his wallet.

'What is it?' she asked.

'His latest poem,' said Cato, smoothing out the paper on the table cloth. 'DYING, EGYPT,' he read aloud, but then his words trailed into silence.

233

The nights were very bad,
and patches of night, dressings,
applied to the pale day.

Something of a look, a well used smile, a nod,
confirm me. Happy? We knew it.
Take your time and the things you need.

The trodden dust of a path to a hopeless plain of
    papers,
uneasy movement, the tired edges of an old wind
plucking at an edge (all this will never burn).

So this is what I really have to do, I should have known;
I've always known. Happy? We knew it.
Take your time and the things you need.

It's all there, that's the joke, to fly,
to strike invisible. Back? Don't make me laugh;
a rushing cold, all grey, Yes. The light is very bad.

One thing at a time. Hold tight. We're here, still
It's hard and then it's easy, but yes,
the nights are very bad.

'What does it mean?' Philippa asked, as Cato sadly refolded
and pocketed the paper.

'It's not what it means,' said Cato. 'It's who wrote it. This
poem was written five years ago by a Bomber Command
navigator called Colin Jones who was shot down and killed
over Essen. His brother taught senior English at our
school.'

'Ah,' said Philippa, thoughtfully helping herself to
another forkful of salmon. 'I see, yes. Poor old Pierre.'

'The major had him to rights,' said Docherty, pushing
away his pudding plate and reaching amused and heavy-

fingered for his brandy glass. 'Ruddy shyster, he called
him.'

'Why don't we go on deck?' asked Philippa, ignoring
Docherty. 'We should be able to see the skyscrapers soon.'

'I've ordered a main course,' said Cato. 'Lamb cutlets.
And then trifle.'

'Do you really want all that?' asked Philippa.

'I can't just . . .'

'You can just,' said Philippa. 'That's the whole point
about all this.'

It was the same as with the desks at school. The horizontal
cuts were easy, running as they did with the grain of the
wood, but the verticals were harder work. You had to cut
in at an angle, flicking out the little triangular wedges as
you went. The curves – and the letters C and O were all
curve – were harder still. If you weren't careful, or you
had blunted your knife on the uprights, you got a series of
little steps.

'C-A-T-O,' she read the scratched outlines of the letters.

'That's me,' he said. Here it comes, he thought.

'Why do you think that . . . she did it?'

His penknife, which he used for balsa modelling, had
been whetted to a razor-sharp concave against one of the
stone steps of the school kitchens. Carefully, he thumbed
its edge.

'I think . . .' he began, 'I think that when we left, when
we set out from Southampton, she really hoped – meant –
to reach the other end. She had all this luggage, in matching
suitcases, pigskin, all numbered. What I'm saying is that
one part of her always behaved as if everything was all
right, just fine, like things always had been, while at the
same time the other – the other half of her – was finding
it harder and harder to carry on. To the point, I suppose,
where it finally became impossible to imagine finishing the
journey.' He blew wood-scrapings from the incised rail.

'But why? Why did she do it? She had everything.'

Cato looked at her. 'She wouldn't have said so. I think she simply . . . I think she saw her future, in the way that rich people can, and just couldn't face . . . living it.'

She tilted her face. 'You went to bed with her, didn't you? And don't look at me like that, I won't tell anybody, but you did, didn't you?'

'What did you do last night?' Cato asked after a moment's silence, lowering his head to the rail again. 'You and Pierre.'

'We talked. I told him he wasn't on the passenger list, I'd checked when I went to the Ladies. He laughed and said he wouldn't be, would he, and to be a good sport and keep my mouth shut. He was watching you and her, mostly.'

'Mrs MacLean.'

'Who else? I said to him you'll not see her again – not tonight. I knew as soon as she came over like that. Plain as the nose on your face, I said, but he wasn't having any.' She shook her head, pulled a grubby handkerchief from the sleeve of her cardigan and blew noisily into it. 'That snake's dead too, I heard?'

'Yes. The owner's wife shot it with a Webley service revolver. The doctor said she was unhappy.'

'Busy old ship, eh?' said Philippa, tucking the hankie back into her sleeve.

'Where are you going?' asked Cato, stepping back to admire his work. 'Where in America?' He snapped closed the penknife's main blade, and drew out the smaller one to carve the serifs.

'California. Ventura.'

'For a holiday?' he asked, wincing with concentration as he cut.

'For ever.'

He nodded. She tilted her head, admiring the pale inscription. Taking his fountain-pen from his top pocket, he droppered blue-black ink on to the letters and rubbed it in with a finger.

'Mess-pot!' she admonished. 'Now you'll have to go into hospital with inky fingers.'

'I expect I will.'

'Are you frightened?'

'No.'

'I knew you went to bed with her,' she said.

As they walked to the forward part of the Boat Deck, Cato felt the wind on the back of his neck, saw it lift Philippa's flat, fine hair to her cheeks before, strand by strand, releasing it. From his wheelchair, Reginald watched them come. On the deckchair beside him Farrell whistled in furious sleep, while at the rail Docherty had reassumed his unmoving custodial slouch. A little self-consciously, Cato introduced Philippa. Frowning, she wiped the palms of her hands on the back of her skirt, and Reginald touched his cap.

'Will you be doing any tours?' she asked. 'Sightseeing and that? Or straight to the hospital.'

Cato looked at Reginald.

'Straight to the hospital,' said Reginald. 'Tonight. Plenty of time afterwards for the sightseeing.'

This is how he must be with his agents, supposed Cato. Not saying much. Letting them know that he knew the odds, but knew, too, that they'd do their best.

'Look,' said the girl. 'America.'

At the horizon, very clearly defined, Cato saw a deep bank of cloud. Beyond it – perhaps – lay a city, but if so it was made invisible by the endless ranges of white, by the fantastical crags and plains and anvil mountains of the sky-become-land.

'You're right,' said Cato. 'America.'

'Ready for it?' asked his father, lifting an uncertain hand from the wheelchair arm, as if to shield his eyes.

'Ready,' said Cato, taking the hand.

Approaching the group for no particular reason except that he had not yet collected all his tips, Dusty Hay was struck with its absolute stillness. Like statues, he thought. Like a painting. For a moment he considered leaving them be, cutting straight across to the starboard deck, and then common sense reasserted itself.